EXISTENCE

THE ELEMENTAL TRILOGY BOOK THREE

DEBBIE KUMP

This is a work of fiction. Names, characters, places, and incidents are products of the author's imagination or are used fictitiously and are not to be construed as real. Any resemblance to actual events, locations, organizations, or persons, living or dead, is entirely coincidental.

World Castle Publishing, LLC
Pensacola, Florida
Copyright © Debbie Kump 2017
Paperback ISBN: 9781629898216
eBook ISBN: 9781629898223
First Edition World Castle Publishing, LLC, November 20, 2017
http://www.worldcastlepublishing.com
Licensing Notes
Cover: Karen Fuller
Editor: Maxine Bringenberg

DEDICATION

In memory of my father-in-law Richard, who encouraged me to keep writing.

CHAPTER ONE

I expected Liam to explain the reason he needed me to join forces with the other Elementals, or at least to mention why they had run out of time to find someone to replace me as the Fire Elemental on their team. Instead, he grabbed my hand and dragged me to my feet. A sudden, massive rogue wave washed up the shore and swept around our waists, yanking us off solid ground. I struggled against its powerful current, but Liam gripped my hand tighter.

"Just relax," he insisted.

Easy for him to say. I glared at Liam, still bitter because he had never disclosed his identity as the new Water Elemental after I destroyed his twin sister, Hydros. It wasn't like I expected him to blurt it out the first time we met. Still, he could've mentioned *some*thing aside from his random "clues" to let me know the truth before I started to like him. Now I didn't know what to think, with my conflicted heart and mind at war.

"What are you doing, trying to drown me?" I asked, alarmed when the waters reached my neck. My feet beat at the water, unsteady without land beneath me. "I thought you told me to trust you!"

He nodded and squeezed my hand tighter. "I need to show

you what's coming."

My eyes grew wide as the water swelled higher. I gulped a big breath of air seconds before the water rushed over my head. Horrific memories invaded my thoughts of my near drowning in Atlantis when Hydros, enraged by Gaia's pressure to join her team, flooded the opulent city. I thrashed at the water in an attempt to reach the surface, but Liam tugged me down and enveloped my head in a bubble of air. I gasped with relief inside the protective sanctuary, and fought to remain patient. He must have a good reason to bring me into his realm.

He smiled in reassurance, wrapping both arms securely around me. Before I could open my mouth to protest, a flurry of bubbles encircled us, spinning at an incredible rate. Liam gripped me tighter to prevent the water from penetrating my necessary air bubble. The current swirled faster, impossible to escape, then dragged us feet-first, spiraling into the inky depths below. For long minutes the tremendous speed increased steadily, silencing my scream. I closed my eyes and cleared my mind to focus on Liam's purpose. Whatever his reason, I hoped it would unlock some answers to the myriad questions bouncing about in my mind.

Suddenly, without explanation, our rapid motion ceased. Liam let his arms drop from my body.

Startled, I opened my eyes. I anticipated a view of the black recesses from the ocean bottom. Instead, a brightly lit city basked in the faint rays of sunlight filtering through the water column. Encased in a shielding dome like a forcefield against the cold surrounding sea, activity bustled and hummed inside. I turned to Liam, a thousand questions competing for priority, yet none of them voiced. I stood frustratingly mute, the unexpected scene shocking me.

Liam wore an amused smile. "What'd you think? Better than

Pele's white fire?"

I blinked. So he hadn't intended to drag me downward to my death; that was his method of traveling through time and space within his Element. I wistfully recalled Pele training me to use white fire, or *ke ahi kea* in her native Hawaiian tongue, to travel through mine.

"Not a chance," I replied, quelling my unsettled stomach. Never mind the fact I had no idea how he could transport me outside of my Element. Rather than asking him to explain, I opted for the foremost question in my mind. "Why are we here?"

"To show you what happened the last time he arrived."

I was about to say, *When who arrived?* But Liam had already begun to swim toward the dome with confident pulls of his arms and a swift whip of his feet. He turned a few strokes away, beckoning for me to follow. Curiosity getting the best of me, I swam awkwardly, unsure I would ever grow comfortable in his watery domain.

Schools of sleek, silvery fish darted past as we approached the domed, underwater city. From the surface far overhead, a shimmering light danced upon the sandy seafloor. More noticeably, a brilliant yellow beam radiated from the city's center, casting a bright glow against the marble structures. Liam stopped in front of a pair of city guards blocking the entrance. "Welcome back, Lir," one of the guards addressed him and stepped sideways, allowing us to enter. I suppressed a shudder at the sound of Liam's Water Elemental name. I was having a hard time getting used to people calling him Lir.

The dome's force field dissolved around our forms with a suctioning effect that instantly dried our clothes and dissolved Liam's bubble of air around my head. Within seconds the dome sealed behind us, enclosing us inside. I wanted to reach out and touch the dome again, to see if its wall felt solid beneath my palm,

7

but Liam slipped his hand in mine and led me forward.

A small troop of men walked past, wearing bronze chest plates and helmets with an aqua plume stuck in the top. Each bore a sharpened trident, gripped upright, by his side, and a short blade strapped to his calf muscle.

"Who are they?" I asked, too low for the men to hear.

"Those are the city's Protectors," Liam explained.

"Protectors? What are they worried about? There's no one else down here."

"And they'd like to keep it that way. This ancient civilization has survived unnoticed for a few thousand years. They only permitted me to bring you here so you could understand the tragedy they endured to ally against the future attack. They survived, and want to make sure they will make it again."

Liam led me through the crowd of citizens, all dressed in togas of shimmering silk draped over their shoulders and fastened about their waists. Each individual also wore a peculiar pale blue triangle-shaped tattoo adorning the middle of their forehead.

I wanted to ask Liam about the significance of the tattoos, but he pressed onward. "It's not much further," he announced.

Liam stopped in front of a gate armed by two of the city's Protectors. They wore their helmets low over their brows, so I couldn't tell if they bore the same triangle tattooed forehead as the rest of the citizens. Liam addressed the men with a simple, "He's expecting us." Surprisingly, they stepped sideways to let us pass.

Once inside the gate, a servant greeted us and directed us toward a wide sweeping patio lined with marble busts of ancient gods carved with omniscient eyes. Every statue made me uneasy, seeming to scrutinize my unwelcome presence in their resplendent city.

A booming voice broke the unsettling silence. "Welcome,

Lir." The man wore a golden laurel wreath atop his head and a longer toga than the others, embroidered in decadent gold thread. He strode toward us with a regal step. From the reverent bows of his servants and Protectors, I guessed he was the ruler of this underwater city.

"How does everyone know you?" I whispered to Liam. "Are you a minor celebrity down here or what?"

Liam let an amused grin slip across his face. "Actually, their allegiance lies primarily with Hydros. But they treat me almost the same. One of the benefits of being her twin." Liam turned to address the man. "King Rio, I'd like you to meet my friend, Jordan."

I gave the king a deferential bow, partially surprised Liam still considered me his friend after our battle on the beach. "I am honored to meet you, sir."

"The pleasure is all mine," he said to me before continuing. "It's good to see you again, Lir. Though not under these circumstances, I'm afraid." As he spoke, I noticed a magnificent chambered nautilus shell around his neck, similar to the necklace Gaia had gifted to Hydros.

"We have heard the time draws near before Aether's return. After his last visit led to our city's demise at the surface, we have vowed to aid you in guaranteeing his defeat."

"What happened?" I wondered aloud, eager for more details about their encounter with the Fifth Elemental, about whom I knew so little.

The ruler swept his arm over his entire underwater kingdom. "On the eve of war, he sent forth a monstrous wave that obliterated our society. Again and again the wave surged across our land, until our entire city sank beneath the sea."

I tilted my head sideways, his words striking a familiar chord.

He continued, "Our scientists had perfected the process

of removing salt from the ocean to secure potable fresh water, and had harnessed an abundant oxygen supply to sustain our population lest danger befall us. We needed a backup plan in the event our war with Athens destroyed our city and forced us to seek refuge underwater. The city's scientists safeguarded their desalinization equipment in a hollowed chamber inside the mountain, so when the city flooded, we were able to begin anew down here in relative safety. Our advanced technology enabled us to survive a disaster that would have proved catastrophic for any other civilization," he concluded proudly.

The ruler led us toward the light source at the center of the city, explaining as he walked. "We are conveniently situated over a hydrothermal vent that supplies our city with an endless source of energy and heat, using chemicals released from inside the earth. Daily, men leave the dome to collect fish and kelp for our residents. So you see, we are quite self-sufficient here, and safe from the dangers that lurk above."

I nodded in silent understanding, impressed with the efficiency and sustainability of a world I previously deemed impossible to exist so deep below the surface. When we neared the radiant shaft of light, I detected a strangely familiar sight situated behind the beam. Tall marble pillars supported a roof of glittering gold, muted from its former brilliance beneath the water overhead, but recognizable nonetheless. I remembered seeking shelter at the highest ground when Hydros's tsunami swamped the city, lashing my wrist to the top of this temple to prevent the current from dragging me out to sea. And I remembered what I expected would be my last view of the setting sun, dipping below the mountain peaks and painting the sky in shades of bronze as the waters surged above my head.

"The Temple of Poseidon," I breathed, astounded to see it intact.

10

The ruler replied, "Fortunately, Aether did not destroy our most sacred part of the city. We thank the gods for sparing our temple from destruction."

I turned to him. "So you're telling me that *you* are the lost civilization? That this is the city of *Atlantis*?"

He nodded slowly. "You are correct."

My mouth fell open. "But I don't understand. Why do you keep saying Aether destroyed your city, when Hydros was the one who unleashed a tsunami against your shores? I was there; I saw her. She called the sea to attack your land."

King Rio narrowed his eyes at my accusation. "That's impossible. Hydros and Gaia are the city's sworn allies. They constructed this sheltered spot for us here beneath the waves. Hydros herself erected this dome to protect us inside her Element."

"You mean Gaia, the Earth Elemental? How could you believe *her*?" I countered. "She manipulated the truth to deceive you."

"Perhaps you were the one she deceived," King Rio corrected me. "The wave merely cleansed the city of filth, and those who were unworthy to exist in our magnificent city beneath the sea. Only the pure of heart were permitted to stay."

I remembered the poor slave girl, Monifa, ripped from my grasp by the receding current, and the pain I'd felt watching her drown in the rushing water. "Filth? How can you say that about Monifa? She was just an innocent little child!"

I heard footsteps behind me.

"You called?" a high-pitched voice asked.

I turned around, my jaw hitting the floor. Before me stood the same heart-shaped face trimmed in a pronounced widow's peak that haunted me in my dreams...with one minor change. Like the ruler, she wore a triangle shaped tattoo in the middle of

11

her forehead. "Monifa?" I dared. "But how can this be? I saw you carried away! I thought you had died."

"Still lucky," she beamed, "just like my name says. The city's Protectors saved me and brought me here. The widow Vallejo is gone, so now I serve King Rio instead."

I smiled with relief at the miraculous sight of her alive. "I still don't understand. Atlantis sank thousands of years ago, but you look the same age as the day I last saw you."

In response to my questions, Monifa pointed to her tattooed forehead, and then turned to the ruler, waiting for him to explain. King Rio placed a gentle hand on the little girl's shoulder. "It's all in the water," he said simply.

"The water?" I glanced at Liam to gauge his reaction. He shot me a knowing smile while the ruler elaborated.

"You've heard of the Fountain of Youth, I'm sure." He pointed to a magnificent marble fountain near the hydrothermal vent in the center of the city. Two tiers spilled over, creating a melodious background noise of falling water. "So many have sought the secret to everlasting life. At the surface, we guarded this secret closely, defending ourselves from invading armies like the troops of Athens. The secret is far easier to protect here in the shelter of our underwater dome.

"And our tattoos," King Rio continued, lifting his golden laurel wreath to reveal the full ornate triangle upon his forehead, "bear the symbol of Atlantis, and permit only those who are worthy to drink of these sacred waters."

"Amazing," I gasped, still unable to believe Monifa stood before me, alive and well. Maybe I'd misinterpreted Gaia's actions all along. Pele and Liam obviously trusted her. So did the Atlantean citizens, even though I'd seen Gaia drive Hydros to fury, causing her to flood the city.

Still, why would Gaia intentionally blame this destruction on

12

Aether, who wasn't even around at the time? What did she hope to accomplish through her accusation? Before I could ask Liam to explain, a wizened woman approached. Her long, shiny black hair wrapped her head in an elaborate loop of braids. Similar to King Rio, she wore a golden laurel wreath and an ornately embroidered toga that swept her ankles with every step.

The ruler introduced her. "And this is my wife, Rayna, our queen and soothsayer."

I extended my hand in greeting. "It's a pleasure to meet you, Queen."

She reached out her hand to take mine then paused, viewing me with sudden alarm. Her hand started to tremble, and then her eyes rolled back into her head.

"What did I do?" I whispered to Liam, afraid I'd broken some ancient rule by attempting to make physical contact with their royalty.

He shrugged. "No clue."

The old soothsayer aimed a spindly finger directly at my chest and announced in a clear, crisp voice, "She killed Hydros."

A murmur spread amongst the concerned citizens, who pointed at me and stepped away in fear.

"You said she was your friend. Why did you bring her here?" King Rio turned on Liam.

"No, you don't understand," Liam stated in my defense. "Jordan didn't mean to hurt my sister. She was only defending herself."

Before Liam could explain further, a trio of Protectors lunged in front of the ruler to distance him from harm, and aimed their tridents at my back, neck, and heart.

I swallowed hard, the sharpened point of one trident lightly grazing my jugular. Panic gripped my throat. *I need to get of here... now!*

Desperate for space from the weapons surrounding me, immense heat fanned outward through my feet, turning the sandy sea floor into a soup of hot, liquid glass. The barefoot Protectors yelped in alarm and jumped a step backward. I only needed that single second of distraction. I stretched one hand straight above my head and an explosion of molten material showered over me, like an umbrella of fiery rain operating in reverse. People shrieked in fear, though I posed no immediate threat; I only meant for my action to deter the other Protectors from capturing me.

I sprinted across the sand, the heat of every step transforming the ocean bottom into a path of melted glass. *If Gaia fixed it once, she can do it again*, I rationalized my actions, and headed toward the hydrothermal vent. With an index finger directed at its center, I split open the vent, allowing the lava to seep outward. Hot gases burst upward, making the light grow blinding in intensity.

"No, Jordan," I heard Liam call, a step or two behind me.

But I ignored him, my mind fixed exclusively on escape. A couple of paces further I leapt high into the air, planning to ride the thermal of rising gases to freedom, when a pair of hands clasped my ankle. I looked down, shocked to see Liam dangling below. Still, the added weight provided little resistance against the opened vent. The billowing gases caught our bodies and jettisoned us upward, away from the clutches of the city's Protectors.

"Look out, Jordan!" Liam warned, his eyes wide with fear. I followed his gaze, realizing we were rocketing toward the top of the dome at an alarming speed. I didn't know what would happen if we struck Atlantis's protective force field. Would it allow us to pass through? Or would we collide with a stunning blow? Deciding I'd rather not take the chance, I shouted, "Ke ahi kea!" to summon white fire and transport myself from this place just before my head would have struck the dome. I caught a short glimpse of Liam covered in a liquid layer of water a second before my view of the underwater city went black. We traveled through time and space, and landed on the fine-grained black sand, my heart racing from the narrow escape.

Liam coughed and sputtered next to me, hunched over on the beach.

"What were you trying to do back there when you grabbed my ankle? Did you want them to kill me?" I gasped, while my heart raced up my throat.

"I had to stay with you," he explained, wrapping his hand around mine. "I couldn't risk the chance of losing you. Not now, with Aether so close."

"That's all I am to you, isn't it? A way to stop Aether. Nothing more." I pulled away from his grip and scrambled to my feet.

"You said it, Pyr. Not me."

I cringed at the sound of my Elemental name, still not prepared to fully accept the identity as he had done. Frustrated with myself for trusting him, I turned and backed away.

Before I could take another step, Liam wrapped his arms around me and jumped into the water, where he wielded the upper hand.

"Why are you doing this?" I shouted, choking on seawater. "Why did you bring me down there? To die?"

"You can't possibly think that's true. Jordan, I had no idea they would turn on you. I only needed you to understand."

"Understand what?" I said.

"That Gaia and Hydros aren't bad people. They helped rebuild the city, giving the Atlanteans a chance to live long beyond their time."

I stopped struggling for a moment, letting his words sink in. True, they had spared Monifa and granted her a happier life. But I also remembered the anger in the queen's eyes when she declared me a murderer…and the graze of a Protector's trident against my throat.

"C'mon, Jordan. We don't have time for this right now. The Fifth Elemental's coming, and we need your help."

"Why should I believe you? Gaia and Hydros lied to the Atlanteans. They probably lied to you, too." Without waiting for his response, I channeled my powers from my core and expelled a fiery ball under my feet that launched me out of the water and high into the air. I hung, suspended for a long moment, reveling in my newfound freedom. I could breathe easier now, far away from the water. My head cleared, reminding me of the reasons I couldn't afford to trust any of them. Not anymore. Not after what happened.

Why would Gaia erroneously pin Atlantis's destruction on some unseen threat? It didn't make any sense. I wanted to ponder my question further, but I began to fall straight down.

Darn gravity.

I frowned, wishing I'd had the foresight to rocket myself back onto land. Unable to manipulate the rising thermals below me in time to slow my descent, I tried to spin myself, hoping to hit the water feet first. Unfortunately, I over-rotated and landed flat in a huge belly flop. A sharp, stinging sensation spread across my face, belly, and thighs. I didn't care that I'd ended up back underwater. I only wanted to curl up in a fetal position and nurse my hurt.

Liam took advantage of my weakened condition. He grabbed my wrist in a seemingly inescapable hold and began to swim to shore with me in tow. Up ahead, I spotted three figures peering down at us from the edge of the sea. One had a head of curly russet hair, while another had long flowing hair of almost pure white. The last figure appeared a hazy Essence of his former vibrant self, muting even the fiery nature of his flaming red hair.

And I could tell none of them looked happy.

The Earth Elemental stood with crossed arms, a scowl fixed upon her face framed in russet curls. "What happened? You said you could handle this," Gaia fumed. The Air Elemental, Skye, set her hands on her hips and narrowed her white eyebrows at me, mirroring Gaia's mood.

"I thought bringing her to Atlantis would help, but it only made things worse," Liam sputtered, treading water beside me.

"I don't get it," I told Gaia, spitting seawater from my mouth. "Why did you lie to those people? What were you trying to prove?"

"I planned to rally forces in support to prepare for Aether's next attack. With their advanced technology, the Atlanteans could prove valuable allies against the Fifth Elemental," Gaia explained, justifying her actions. "It was only a slight manipulation of the truth. You saw the power they wielded. The Atlanteans could help us stop Aether when he returns. The Fifth Elemental threatens their civilization — he threatens *every* civilization — unless we can find a way to stop him. I only did it to aid our cause."

"And theirs," I proposed. "Right?"

"Of course," she added unconvincingly.

"Well, I don't buy it," I said, kicking at the water to keep my head afloat. "And as for your team, you can count me out."

A displeased frown settled across Gaia's face. Her right eye twitched with irritation. "I know someone who can change your mind." She glanced to her side and gave Brandr a nod.

Before I could protest, Brandr's Essence of the former Fire Elemental leapt off the side of the rock, completed a double flip that would have likely impressed any official at a high school swimming and diving meet, and plunged into the water headfirst, aiming straight for my body.

In that flash of a second I knew I should sprint away, but it was too late. I coughed on the stale smell of air filling my nostrils. I started to scream, "Brandr! How could you?"

Only when I opened my mouth, his voice escaped my lips instead. "I've got it from here," he told Liam.

Liam nodded and released his grip. A saddened look filled his eyes before he shook the seawater from his hair and climbed onto shore. I had let him down. It only seemed fair after he had lied about his identity, leading me on to the point I had started to fall for him.

Though furious with Liam's deception, I possessed zero control over my limbs. I couldn't fight back; the fusion of Brandr's Essence with my Elemental body was complete. I knew Brandr would hold me a prisoner in my own body until I chose to comply with their demands.

Unless I could find a good reason to make him leave first.

CHAPTER TWO

Meteor Crater, Arizona, Present Day

There's nothing like seeing the end of the world and feeling powerless to stop the destruction. A prisoner in my own body, I wielded no control, following my former enemies across a barren Southwestern desert, unsure of our eventual destination.

"What's the point of coming out here, anyway?" I muttered, disgruntled about Brandr's fusion.

"You'll see," Brandr replied in an irritatingly cheerful tone, enjoying his new abilities far more than he should. Funny to think that the last time he'd fused with me on our journey inside the earth, I had found his bold, brash actions somewhat amusing. Now I felt the complete opposite as his every action involved me, regardless of my desires.

I held partial blame for my predicament, but that didn't make me feel any better. My heart barely had a chance to heal after Liam Innis Reilly disclosed his identity as the new Water Elemental, Lir. After our intense battle of fire versus water on the beach, he'd managed to catch me and explain the importance of our next — and potentially final — mission.

Up ahead, the Air and Earth Elementals, Skye and Gaia, spoke in urgent, hushed voices. Cursing Brandr for his sluggish pace, I strained my ears, unable to catch a single bit of their conversation, though I suspected it had something to do with me. Especially since Liam walked in the middle of them and me to bridge the gap between disagreeing factions. Gaia had convinced Liam to join the team after his twin sister, Hydros, perished. Gaia had needed him to win my allegiance, at the expense of my heart.

A white dog led our whole brigade, her tail curled high in the air with delight. She pranced on the tips of her toes across the hot desert sand, aiming for a cluster of buildings adjacent to a large parking lot. The dog had been my trusted friend, Kea, a stray I'd met by the beach in Hawaii. Little had I realized there was more to her than I'd first perceived.

"People are starting to stare," Brandr said, moving my own mouth to voice his thoughts. "I think we're supposed to leash our pets."

The dog turned, her eyes flickering a fiery orange. A stripe of fur bristled along the length of her back. She crouched low on her forelimbs and bared her teeth.

At me.

Brandr! I screamed inside my head, wondering why he intentionally wished to infuriate Kea...especially when the Essence of the tempestuous Hawaiian goddess of fire, Pele, resided inside her.

"Hey," Brandr chuckled through my own lips, taking a purposeful step backward. "I'm just saying it looks a little suspicious having a dog leading our party."

Brandr moved my head to follow the dog, watching her trot behind a brick building. Just before she slipped out of sight, I saw the dog dissolve into a swirl of white vaporous mist. Seconds later, Kea transformed from her four-legged self, and emerged as a striking young maiden with long black tresses that stretched to her ankles. A tight-fitting dress accentuated her swaying hips. As she stepped toward us, her every motion seemed like a step from a beautiful dance. I felt Brandr let my mouth drop open with amazement. Pele's deep brown eyes focused on him intently. "How's this?" she asked. Not bothering to wait for his response, she continued to lead us toward the entrance by the parking lot.

We passed three couples on our way up the path. Each girlfriend shot their significant other an admonishing look when his eyes glued to Pele's stunning form.

"Um…I'm not really sure that's any better," Brandr cautioned. "People are still staring at you."

"Or maybe they're staring at you," Liam said under his breath. "With your deep voice coming out of Jordan's mouth every five seconds, it looks like she's possessed."

"I feel like I'm possessed," I protested, struggling against Brandr's control with little results.

With a deliberate roll of her eyes, the young goddess veered off the path and slipped behind the building once more, changing into the aged form of Auntie Lulu, who had kindly taken me into her Hawaiian home. In all the time I'd lived with her, I had never suspected the goddess Pele used the guises of Auntie Lulu and Kea to watch over me while I trained to better understand and manipulate my fire powers.

At that moment, I decided I'd relinquish my training and fire powers in an instant to have the gift of reading Liam's mind. Since we'd escaped from Atlantis, he'd been acting differently… more quiet and aloof. Not that I should care how he felt after everything he'd hidden from me. What did he expect? That I'd be overjoyed to discover the guy I liked had been chosen as the new Water Elemental? Especially after I'd destroyed his twin sister, Hydros?

Well, I wasn't.

21

And I think he'd realized that now, too, after our violent clash of water and fire powers on the beach in Hawaii.

My mind and heart warred. A part of me couldn't ignore the attraction I'd felt toward him just a few days before, while anger consumed the other part of me. I'd suspected Gaia had a crush on Liam when she tried to kiss him on the beach.

I couldn't believe it. *Gaia!* The one who'd killed my family and friends, robbing me of a normal life as she pursued me through different times.

Besides, even if I wanted a chance to be alone with Liam to sort through my feelings, it'd never happen. Not when I couldn't get away from our so-called "team" of Elemental powers with Pele at the lead. And definitely not with Brandr occupying my body and controlling my every move.

"Your every move?" Brandr replied, reading my thoughts.

"Ugh," I grumbled aloud. "Will you get out of my head already? Why can't you give me a little privacy? I feel so violated."

"Will you two just cool it?" Gaia hissed, wheeling around. Her long auburn curls gave a delayed bounce, staticky and unruly in the dry, desert air. When Gaia turned back around, her eyes lingered on Liam for a little too long, confirming my suspicions. I could tell she liked him, and wouldn't easily let him go.

Get over it, Brandr advised me alone.

It's not that easy, I snipped back at him.

Brandr brooded in silence the entire way, past displays of meteorite fragments and paintings depicting scenes of mass extinctions, before following the others into the auditorium. Brandr plopped my body down in the seat next to Liam before the lights went out. While the video trailers began, he leaned my head against Liam's shoulder, despite my objections.

What are you thinking? You are so dead. I directed my thoughts at Brandr.

22

Thanks for the reminder, he said in a wounded tone that made me remember to choose my words carefully. If our places were reversed, I probably wouldn't like him reminding me that I had died and returned to this planet as an Essence of my former self, either.

Oh, you know what I mean. What are you trying to do? Make things worse between me and Gaia? I moaned.

She's a big girl. Let her deal with it, he replied.

I couldn't see past Liam to determine what Gaia thought, but I figured I should at least explain my behavior to him. The last thing I needed was to mess things up before we even began.

"This isn't me," I whispered in Liam's ear. Liam shot me a puzzled look, but didn't pull away, making me question my feelings all over again. Our entire relationship had been contrived. I couldn't believe I'd begun to fall for Liam...before he spilled his secret. I'd known from experience that fire and water didn't belong together.

I soon realized a resolution must wait when the movie opened with a collision of two massive rocks in the asteroid belt beyond the orbit of the planet Mars. Within seconds Brandr drifted away, the sound of his snoring ringing in my ears while he used Liam's shoulder as an impromptu pillow. Even in his slumbering state, I couldn't muscle him from my body. So I watched. My eyes froze with fear when one of the cratered rocks tumbled through space...toward planet Earth.

The scene cut to the point when the rock entered Earth's atmosphere, irresistibly drawn to the planet's tug. Its surface glowed of molten magma as it plummeted. The layers of our atmosphere stripped fragments from the rock's exterior like a perimeter guard protecting the castle. Still the rock persisted, dwindling in size and speeding closer to the ground. The background music increased in tempo, making my heart pound

23

furiously inside my chest with anticipation. *How could Brandr actually sleep through this?* I wondered. I held my breath, bracing for the impact, when a new image unexpectedly entered my head, overriding the movie before me.

I looked back out to space where the Fifth Elemental, Aether, loomed. He readied another rock of much grander proportions, aimed at the earth.

"*No!*" I screamed, focusing my powers toward the object of greatest fire potential in our solar system...the sun. Closing my eyes, I forced all my efforts outward, making my entire body radiate an intense, superheated blast toward Aether and his next meteor. Only my power unleashed a weapon I never expected. Using the sun's gases to fuel my powers, I quickly depleted the stellar resources. And before I could reverse its course, the sun swelled at an enormous rate, engulfing the rocky planet, Mercury.

What have I done? I shut down my powers, seeking escape. But the sun continued to swell, transforming from a yellowish color into a bright red, a giant reaching toward Venus next.

Oh, my God. I quickly used white fire to transport myself back to the earth. Only the planet no longer resembled its former, hospitable self. The atmosphere had burned off, leaving nothing for protection from the ferocity of the encroaching solar winds. The oceans boiled away into giant pits of roiling mud. I gasped in horror, wondering how I'd let this happen. But before I could answer my own question, a piercing shriek escaped my lips. I watched the sun suffocate the earth in its deadly embrace.

CHAPTER THREE

Liam's cupped hand stifled my scream and jolted Brandr awake inside my body. In an instant, the frightening images of Earth's destruction fled my mind.

"What are you doing?" Liam whispered firmly in my ear, forcing me low in the seat. "And to think you were the one worried about drawing attention before."

"It wasn't me. It was Brandr," I protested, but my words came out garbled beneath Liam's palm.

Gaia leaned across Liam's vacant spot, her emerald eyes narrowing to thin slits. "I thought you said you could keep her under control," she snapped at Brandr in an acidic tone, while Skye gave a deliberate roll of her eyes.

"Well, excuuuuuse me," Brandr retorted. "Geez. Can't a guy get a little shut-eye for a change? Like she has a clue how tiring it is keeping you under constant surveillance."

"It's time to go. You must see it for real," Auntie Lulu said. With a disparaging look, she motioned for Gaia and Skye to follow her from the theater.

I hadn't intended to disappoint Auntie Lulu, but inside I couldn't slow my racing heart. "Instead of the movie, I saw a terrible scene in my head," I admitted to Liam. "I tried to stop

Aether. Instead, I unwittingly caused the complete destruction of the earth."

For a split second, worry filled Liam's face. "Don't let it happen again, Brandr," he warned.

"You got it," Brandr replied.

"Let what happen?" I asked, curious as to what I'd missed.

"Never mind," Liam said, quickly changing the subject while the credits rolled. "Your powers aren't that great. You couldn't make that happen, even if you tried." Without another word, he rose from his seat and walked outside.

I blinked, watching him leave. I knew he only meant to make me feel better, but something about the way he said that came off more like an insult than a reassurance.

Let what happen? I asked again, this time to Brandr alone.

I'll tell you later. For now, don't let it get to you. Liam didn't mean it that way, Brandr told me, and stood up.

What if I'm not ready? What if I don't want to go? I asked him. *Don't I get a say in this?*

Not really, he replied, and marched out of the auditorium despite my protest. *You need to see why you are here.*

Outside, I squinted into the bright desert sun. An unnatural quiet filled the air, disrupted only by the hot breeze that stirred my hair. Brandr headed toward the others perched by an overlook. He walked right up to the railing that lined the edge and peered over the side.

"This is what Auntie Lulu wanted you to see," Brandr explained, his voice exiting my lips.

"Oh, my God. Imagine the devastation," I said with a low whistle. I gazed out upon a vast crater, more than five-hundred feet deep and almost one mile across. Suddenly, the video I had just watched replayed uncontrollably in my mind. I relived the scene of the iron-nickel meteoroid entering the earth's atmosphere like a fiery ball. It streaked across the sky and slammed into the desolate landscape where we now stood. I envisioned the shock wave that radiated outward from the impact, sending rocks and dirt airborne in a matter of seconds.

The blood drained from my face. It had happened before... and would happen again. How could *I* possibly help to prevent this? The answer seemed completely outside my grasp.

Auntie Lulu had angered me after sending me on so many dangerous missions and setting me up to like Liam. I didn't entirely trust her, but I also didn't know who else to trust. Brandr had essentially taken me captive. Gaia and Skye had hunted me down in an effort to trap me. And Liam had toyed with my heart. The only one I could trust was Sully...but his life seemed a world apart from mine.

I glanced at Liam, unable to hide the nervousness that prevailed. Finally, I understood Gaia's urgency...a blast of that magnitude could alter the climate, potentially resulting in mass extinctions, decimate everything in its path, even cause the end of humanity. I couldn't imagine anything more dreadful.

Liam's hand sought mine, giving it a small squeeze. I relaxed, realizing Liam hadn't changed as much as I'd thought. He still cared about me, despite the trials our relationship had recently endured. A sense of calm filled my heart, reminding me somehow everything would be fine, until I noticed Gaia's mouth turn into a disdainful frown. I quickly tried to pull my hand away, but Brandr overrode my actions, leaving it securely in Liam's grasp.

Brandr, what're you doing? I questioned inside my head, anxious to be rid of Gaia's scorn.

Loving every minute of this, he replied in a smug tone.

I thought you said we had other issues to think about right now, like preventing Aether's return.

He chuckled. *Yeah...but did you see the look on Gaia's face?*

27

Arrrgh, I groaned, and forced myself to focus on something besides my frustration with Brandr and my conflicted emotions for Liam.

Auntie Lulu continued. "Other meteors have been the size of a city — or the state of Ohio." I realized she had chosen this excursion for a reason, one I feared I would understand all too soon.

"So you're saying this gaping hole in the ground is only a precursor of what's in store for us?" I asked her.

"This was only a fragment of rock," Auntie Lulu stated simply, letting the gravity of each word linger in my mind.

"Only a fragment," I repeated. The resulting devastation from such a relatively small piece stunned me. I tried to imagine the size of the crater formed by a rock two times the size of this fragment. Or ten times the size. A gasp escaped my lips, pondering her implications. I imagined Skye and Liam felt the same while they stared silently at the crater, but Gaia placed her hands on her hips in a haughty sort of way. This was the message she'd been trying to tell me all along.

"He's grown greater and more powerful since his creation," Auntie Lulu warned. "Long ago, the other Elementals cast Aether into the heavenly realm. He resented their neglect, and periodically returns through various periods of time to retaliate against those he believes have wronged him."

"So what you're basically saying is, the only original Elemental is Gaia, and this is all her fault. Now that anger and resentment is directed toward us?" I wagered.

Gaia narrowed her eyes, making me doubt my summation pleased her.

"You got it," Auntie Lulu replied. "Now Aether threatens our very existence."

A defiant look filled Liam's eyes. "We'll stop him. We

28

promise."

"Things could be worse than this the next time he comes," Skye said softly.

I gazed across the gaping hole in the ground, letting Skye's words sink in. After a long moment, I raised my head and turned toward Auntie Lulu.

A grim expression clouded Auntie Lulu's brown, aged face. She gave a small nod before she spoke in a low, sad voice, "Much, *much* worse."

CHAPTER FOUR

"There's one thing I don't understand," I said after we headed away from the crater's rim.

"Go on," Auntie Lulu replied.

"Why is Aether a threat?" I wondered. "I mean, why does he want to hurt us? What kind of power does he even have if he's out in space? I remember Brandr telling me that fire existed in other parts of the universe. Is that why you need me? Do I have the same powers as Aether?"

Gaia blew her frizzy curls from her face. "We don't have time for this. She should already know."

I glowered back at her. "When do you expect I would've found out? Maybe if you'd taken the time to tell me instead of always hunting down my family and friends, then I'd —"

"Seriously. I say one thing and she's down my throat," Gaia said with an unnecessarily dramatic eye roll. "In case you didn't remember, I am the first and only original Elemental."

Now you understand why she's so bossy, Brandr said to me alone. Luckily, he stifled my chuckle so she couldn't hear.

"Prior to becoming an Elemental, another Elemental must have died, just like you saw with Liam replacing Hydros or you replacing Brandr. Only one Elemental can exist at a time for any

30

particular Element. Should the Elemental die, their spirit can persist as an Essence."

Why'd you choose me? I asked Brandr.

For your empathy toward others. And to balance Gaia's strong personality.

Strong? I chortled. *Don't you mean "wicked"?*

Gaia was originally selected for her strength and determination, but she grew edgy over time, lacking patience. Now she feels like it's her responsibility to lead the other, less experienced Elementals.

"So there are other Essences besides Hydros and Brandr?" I said aloud.

Skye nodded. She looked at Gaia with admiration when she spoke. "Yes. Except for Earth. No Earth Essence exists. Only the Earth Elemental."

Gaia's face lit proudly. She combed her fingers through her hair.

"Then how is the new Elemental chosen?" I wondered aloud.

Gaia released an exasperated sigh. "This is going to take all night," she moaned. "How about we meet you back at camp, Auntie? We've got lots to prepare while you catch Pyr up on what she's missed," she said in her arrogant way.

Auntie Lulu nodded.

"My name's not Pyr," I muttered under my breath when Gaia, Liam, and Skye were out of earshot.

Not yet it's not. But just wait, Brandr chuckled inside my head.

Oh, great. Now she's turned you against me as well.

Nope. I'm still on your side. Brandr reminded me. *I just want to win.*

I didn't really know what he meant by his comment, but decided to ask him later. Auntie Lulu continued her explanation of the history of the Elementals, and I needed to catch every word.

"On Earth, the four Elements have existed since the beginning of time. Across the planet, winds blew, currents carried water, forest fires raged, and earthquakes trembled the ground," Auntie Lulu related her story. "The gods fused the Elements with humans to make individuals immortal inside the realm of their element. These individuals learned to control their powers and slow their aging process as they became more in touch with the Elemental side of their soul. Over time, they adopted a greater connection with the forces of nature that shaped the earth."

"But Aether could wipe out all four Elementals simultaneously," I said. The thought made my stomach churn.

"You are correct," Auntie Lulu replied. "In this event, there would be little chance the new embodiments would be able to protect the earth in time, even if the Essences and those of the past could quickly locate and train the new selections. But there's more."

"More?" I inquired.

Auntie Lulu waved her hand, making herself disappear into a misty white vapor. It swirled in a circle for a moment, and then reformed in the shape of the beautiful Hawaiian goddess, Pele. "Aether can truly kill an Elemental's Essence, thereby destroying the soul and preventing their return in any form." Her solemn expression conveyed the power of her words.

"That doesn't sound good," I stated.

"Not good at all," Brandr agreed.

Pele continued, "You have to trust Gaia. She may not act very patient at the moment. You must understand that she's eager to get the team to learn to work together before Aether returns. She had known him personally from when the Elementals were first created, and she had expelled him from Earth. She has much at stake in her next encounter with the Fifth Elemental. And time is running out."

In other words, she's stressed, Brandr explained.

Plus, she's not the type to politely ask for a favor, I reminded him, thinking of all her vicious encounters in the past.

"What is Aether's power, anyway?" I asked Pele.

"It's not as easily defined as yours, I'm afraid. I guess the closest way to describe it is gravity."

I snorted. "Gravity? But that doesn't make any sense." I remembered Mr. Tabor's American History class in Pacifica. The textbook picture of the Apollo 11 astronauts showed them floating weightlessly inside the spacecraft. "I thought there wasn't any gravity in space."

"But there is. Gravity depends on the masses of the objects and the distances between them. When Aether gains in mass...."

"His gravity increases," I finished for her.

"Exactly. Gravity is a powerful force, not just here on Earth but in space as well. Long ago, the Maya of Mexico and Central America used science to prevent mere mortals from questioning the complexities involved in the magic of the Elementals."

"Similar to the Atlanteans?" I suggested, remembering the height of their civilization before Hydros unleashed her tsunami and destroyed it all.

"In a way, yes, but their civilization did not disappear overnight. The Maya understood the inherent risk to the Elementals if the general populace became cognizant of the powers the Elementals wield, and the immense threat that exists from above."

"Kind of like a conspiracy to minimize fear and guarantee the safety of the Elementals," Brandr explained.

"But how did that work? Didn't some people still find out?" I asked, thinking about Sully and Micah and Cam. I had showed them my powers and explained the truth to them. Had I unwittingly placed them at risk because of my folly?

"Hypotheses grew into theories and theories into laws,

providing ample evidence to support these ideas, explaining everything humans observe with logic and data. Soon people became blind to the magic around them and provided explanations for every occurrence in nature. Legends to explain early man's observations of the sky were soon replaced with scientific theories. Science described Earth's rotation and revolution to justify the rising and setting of the sun and the change of the seasons. Science attributed the mystical auroras — which you call the Northern Lights — to the sun's solar wind deflecting off the magnetic field surrounding the earth's poles. And according to science, in a parallel universe, the impossibilities of events that contradict our known laws of physics could actually happen — even something that sounds as absurd as walking through a wall."

"But no one can walk through a wall," I protested.

"And no one can control fire and travel through time, either," Pele reminded me with a touch of sarcasm.

I chuckled. "Touché. So if you can do all those things, then you must be an Elemental too, right?"

Pele laughed deeply, her eyes twinkling in the starry night. "My dear child, I am no Elemental. I am a *goddess*."

"Goddesses have much greater powers than us Elementals," Brandr spoke through my lips.

"In that, you are correct. However, like I mentioned before, few people still believe in us. The ancients meant well in protecting your magic from others. But it's like a double-edged sword. Remove the mystique around you, and you no longer need to believe."

"So that's why everyone I asked in the Hilo airport in Hawaii told me I'd never find you?" I surmised.

"Those individuals assumed they were correct. Though I do make brief appearances to forewarn my people of an eruption, few believe. They would rather look to the scientists for answers, hanging on the predictions of volcanologists who measure the swelling of the volcano, gas emissions, and focus depth of earthquakes. It doesn't matter that these predictions are often inaccurate and volcanoes still erupt without warning; in these technologically-savvy times, numbers and scientific evidence trumps the power of faith."

In an unguarded moment, Pele sighed, her face forlorn. "Sometimes I miss the old days, when I captivated the hearts and minds of my followers. But that doesn't matter now. Everything will be lost if you don't triumph over Aether."

Her face grew rigid again. She spoke in a commanding voice, "Stop fighting against your destiny. You must embrace your Elemental name and the powers bestowed upon you. You must ask yourself, do you believe?"

"I do," I said softly, frightened by the power represented in Pele's face.

"Say it with conviction."

Brandr made me stand straighter, squaring my shoulders, when I declared, "I do."

Pele's face softened and the flickering light from within began to fade. "Good," she said, satisfied. "Because without your true belief, we cannot progress."

My mouth grew dry. I dared to ask the question that burned foremost in my mind. "So when is he coming?"

Pele turned her head slowly to gaze directly into my eyes. Her deep, dark eyes echoed the sincerity of her short response. "Soon."

"How soon?" I begged, wondering how much time remained to prepare for this rising threat.

"Like you, Aether's timeline is incongruous, meaning that he returns to Earth at different time periods throughout history."

35

"Then how do we know he's coming now?" I wondered.

"Good question. By studying the ancients, we have learned to understand the apocalyptic predictions to prepare for future attacks."

"And these predictions say he's on his way?" I guessed.

Pele said, "We think so. But we need you to determine that for sure. You must return to the past to find the exact date."

"You keep saying 'you.' Does that mean you're not coming with us?"

She reached out to touch my shoulder in a comforting way. "My job was to get you all together. The rest is something you have to work out on your own."

My eyes grew wide. "We have to figure everything else out by ourselves?"

"Yes...and no. Gaia knows how to contact me if needed. But for now, she and I have to travel to England together."

"Without us?" I asked, relieved to have some time away from the Earth Elemental.

Pele dropped her hand and smiled, making me think she'd read my mind. "You remember Hina, the Hawaiian goddess of the moon?"

I nodded. Not only had she healed me from a potentially lethal wound in my original battle against the other three Elementals, she'd slipped down a moonbeam one starry night to first introduce me to Brandr.

"Hina has arranged for you to meet a priest from the Yucatán Peninsula in ancient Mexico to learn more about the apocalypse the Maya astronomers predicted."

"You mean the apocalypse that has Aether written all over it?" Brandr wagered.

She nodded. "Precisely."

"Well, then...let's get this party started!" Brandr sang with enthusiasm, and threw my body into some hip-hop dance moves that I never could've pulled off on my own.

That's it, I decided. *He is loving this occupation thing way too much.*

CHAPTER FIVE

Northwest Wyoming, Present Day

My brain chewed on Pele's comments the entire way to the location where she'd set up camp in a forest. A ring of plain canvas tents erected on wooden platforms stood around an old campfire. Pele told me she had chosen this remote location for our team to train out of sight of civilians. Compared to the noisy, bustling San Francisco Bay Area, I had to admit the woods seemed eerily devoid of manmade sounds.

While Pele, Gaia, and Skye made final preparations for our trips, Brandr selected a free tent and climbed inside to check out the accommodations. Feeling overwhelmed, I hadn't spoken to him since we'd arrived. He'd taken my silence to mean he had complete control. Not that I cared; I had too many concerns burdening my mind.

I heard a rap on the canvas of the tent flap. "Come in," Brandr called, and turned my head toward the tent entrance. Much to my surprise, Liam entered.

Brandr couldn't hide the conflicted emotions that registered across my face…bitterness for being imprisoned in my own body, fear of the threat that lay ahead, and confusion regarding my relationship with Liam...if you could even call it that anymore. Liam looked at me with a mixture of sadness and concern... and perhaps a little pity that I hadn't heard the truth about my background until now.

Finally he spoke. "Now I guess you understand why it's so important for you to support this cause. Everything depends on it."

His words offered little hope. No matter how hard I tried, I couldn't figure out a way to rekindle our friendship without jeopardizing the tenuous team of Elementals.

Let it go, Jordan, Brandr said to me alone. *Maybe it wasn't meant to be. I bet you'll eventually meet someone else who'll make you happy. Actually, I know you will. But that can't happen until we get through this next obstacle. Remember that big, brawny dude, Aether, that's headed our way?*

I remember, I told him. *It's not that. Well, not just that.*

Cheer up, Brandr replied, his thoughts resounding inside my head. *This is the most alive I've felt in a millennium!*

His words left a hollow ache in my gut. Brandr had nailed it. That was precisely the reason I resented his fusion and subsequent occupation of my body. He felt alive, while I felt virtually nothing. What did it matter where we went when I held no power to make even the slightest decision about my life?

Liam placed a hand on my arm. "What is it, Jordan? What's wrong?"

"I don't get why you don't trust me. Why do I have to stay under Brandr's constant surveillance?"

Liam gave me a sideways look. "Is that what this is about? The fusion?"

I tried to nod, but Brandr shook my head forcefully, negating my thoughts.

"No, it's great!" Brandr answered in a falsetto—a very poor

impression of my voice if you asked me. "Everything's peachy here!"

Liam frowned. "I'm sorry, Jordan. I had no idea how difficult this was for you."

A lone tear slid down my cheek, something even Brandr couldn't contain.

"We couldn't afford to have you run off again," Liam said, his voice sincere. "There isn't enough time."

"But what if I promised to stay?" I suggested

"It's too risky. Can't you see? We need you."

"We?" I asked, wishing he'd chosen a different, more personal word instead.

"Yes, we do."

My eyes sank, crestfallen.

Liam's hand left my arm. "I need you," he clarified, letting his palm brush the side of my head to soothe my worries.

I allowed myself a moment to grasp onto his words and lock them away deep inside. Gazing into his brilliantly blue eyes, I forgot everything but him. I forgot about Gaia's interest in Liam and using him to win my support. I forgot about Brandr dictating my every move, trapping me inside my own body. And I forgot about the dread of Aether's arrival raining destruction upon the land.

For the first time in what seemed like forever, I wielded complete control over my actions, my emotions, my fate. In the quiet of the tent, nothing existed but Liam and me, exchanging unspoken thoughts of the memories we shared.

Liam slowly leaned toward me. This time, I didn't move away. My previous anger dissolved in an instant, replaced with a sudden desire to touch him again. His nose briefly slid past mine, and then his mouth parted. He stood so close I could smell the sweetness of his breath. I inhaled deeply, my heart fluttering

40

with anticipation. I remembered how he'd held me tight, erasing my fear of the water, and kissed me sweetly. His lips hovered over mine, ready to reunite, when Brandr blurted through my mouth, "That's it. I'm outta here."

A loud squishy suctioning noise followed as Brandr extracted himself from my body with a swift, sudden lurch. He cringed and shuddered before giving Liam a vaporous clap on the back. "I, for one, believe her, and am willing to take the chance." He drifted out of the tent, muttering something that sounded a whole lot like, "That was *way* too close."

I looked back at Liam, hoping I could rid my mind of Brandr's interruption enough to finish what we had started, but the moment was lost. Liam opened the tent flap and watched Brandr float into the distance.

"Liam," I began, taking his hand in mine. "It's just me."

"Good," Liam said with a wink. A small smile lit his face. He pulled his hand from my grip to slap me a high five. "Then I guess it worked. Besides, I agree with Brandr that you'll keep your promise, right?" he added, almost as a threat.

My jaw fell open. Had he actually wanted to kiss me? Or was it all a show to oust Brandr from my body?

"So that's all that was bothering you?" Liam asked.

Here was my chance to vent everything: how much I couldn't stand Gaia ruining our relationship, and how I wished things between us could be like they were before. I opened my mouth to tell him, and then shut it without a sound. What if Liam's confession on the beach was only a part of his plan to keep my trust? Wouldn't he have actually kissed me right now if he truly liked me?

"Yeah, that's all," I lied. At that moment, I realized I had a choice: either accept Liam's friendship or willingly relinquish him to Gaia's growing interest. Still, I couldn't stop my heart from wanting more.

CHAPTER SIX

"This really sucks," Liam grumbled. "Big time. I feel like I've got a major wedgie." Liam's face turned a fast shade of pink.

"It's called a loincloth," Pele explained. "Girls wore dresses woven from cotton, and guys wore…well, those instead."

Brandr laughed while Liam adjusted his garment, trying to find a more comfortable arrangement while keeping his back conveniently pressed against the side of his tent.

"Shut up," Liam joked. "You're just happy that you're supposed to be invisible. Otherwise, you'd be wearing the same thing and you know it."

"One of the few benefits of being an Essence," Brandr gloated.

"Your job is to collect information," Pele reminded us. She looked straight at me when she reiterated, "Don't interfere with the course of history."

"You got it, Pele," Brandr said, pretending to stand at attention.

"And you," she said, pointing a finger at Brandr's translucent chest, "make sure you aren't seen."

Brandr saluted her. "Aye, aye, Cap'n."

Pele rolled her eyes and walked away with Gaia.

"Guess that means it's time for us to go," Liam said.

Though I wasn't quite sure how all of us would travel together and ensure we'd end up in the same destination at the same time, the others didn't look a bit worried.

"Ready?" Liam asked, and extended his hands, one for me to take, the other for Skye. He glanced up, causing a sudden, localized shower to drench his spot.

Skye spun her free arm over her head. A swirling vortex of whirling winds surrounded her, obscuring her form except for her hand clutching Liam's.

"We're waiting for you," Liam reminded me. His dripping wet hair plastered his face.

"Oh. Right," I said sheepishly. "Ke ahi kea," I whispered, and snapped my fingers to produce a ball of white fire. I tossed the fireball over my head and let it spread until raging white flames engulfed my entire body.

"We're outta here!" Brandr exclaimed, and doused himself in a spontaneous burst of flame, then grabbed my free hand.

I felt a quick jerk, pulling my body upward into the black void to travel between different times and space. Our speed increased at a dizzying rate, darkness enveloping everything around me in a tight cocoon. I turned my head, looking for Skye, Liam, and Brandr, but could see nothing aside from the depths of space. Afraid of separation, I squeezed Liam's hand tighter and closed my eyes, praying we would soon arrive at our destination. Just when I couldn't stand the speed of our transit any longer, we made an abrupt stop.

Chichén Itzá, Yucatán Peninsula, Mexico, 900 A.D.

On impact, Brandr and Liam released my hands and I stumbled forward, catching myself on my elbows and knees. While Skye and Liam brushed the grass from their knees, I scrambled to my feet, noting our surroundings. High overhead, the sun burned intensely. We stood in the middle of an open field, surrounded by dense scrub brush and sweet-smelling trees. Up ahead, the dark silhouette of a figure with a huge head of hair approached. When he neared, I could better make out his features.

A bare-chested man dressed in an embroidered loincloth greeted us upon our arrival—the priest Pele had mentioned, I assumed. The priest had a round face and broad nose, and dark skin to withstand the intense tropical sun. He wore bands of jade and shells around his upper arms, large earrings, and an intricate necklace with carvings resembling the faces of gods. But he didn't have a huge head of hair like I'd originally thought. Instead, he wore an elaborate headdress of iridescent tail feathers of brilliant turquoise, unlike any bird I'd ever seen before.

"Welcome." The priest studied us, deliberately scanning each person from head to toe. Even dressed as Pele had recommended, he recognized us as foreigners. "I can see you have traveled a long way to see me."

Liam nodded. "We heard you could predict the future…an apocalypse, for example."

"Our calendar does reset after the long count is completed," the priest confirmed.

"Long count?" I asked. "What do you mean?"

"The long count is an astronomical calendar used to track lengthy periods of time in the Maya civilization. Each universal cycle lasts 7,885 cycles around the sun."

"You mean 7,885 years for one calendar?" Skye asked, sounding as amazed as I was that they would keep track that far into the future.

"We believe the universe is destroyed, then created anew at the start. Some interpret this as the end of the world, like your apocalypse for example. Others think of it as a new beginning.

"The moon goddess, Ix Chel, told me you would be coming here with questions. I never expected so many, however." The priest chuckled to himself. "Nevertheless, it's probably best if I show you. Follow me, if you will." He turned and led us to the open path through town.

We started after him. "Ix Chel?" I whispered to Brandr. "Doesn't he mean Hina?"

"Sometimes gods can have different names in different religions, but still represent the same earthly or celestial power," Brandr explained in a low voice. "Just like your name is Jordan and your Elemental name is Pyr...once you truly accept this identity, of course."

"Haven't I already done that?"

Brandr shook his head. "Not quite, I'm afraid."

My brow crinkled. "I don't get it. I've trained with Pele and accepted my destiny as part of our team of Elementals. What must I do?"

"You'll see in time," Brandr said.

I mulled over his response, wishing I had something more tangible than a vague reply to grasp Brandr's meaning.

The priest led us through the bustling Maya marketplace. Women in long cotton dresses and men in little more than loincloths moved freely from one stand to another. Some stands sold corn tortillas, beans and squash, fish, or spotted jaguar pelts. Other vendors crafted jewelry from green jade and colorful seashells. Merchants used sticks, stones, and shells in an ancient way of making change for the customer.

The vibrant colors attracted my attention like a honeybee in a field of wildflowers, making me forget my plaguing thoughts and focusing on our task instead. With my head on a swivel, I soaked in everything, hoping to find purpose in our visit. Pele wanted us to come here for a reason, even if that reason eluded me.

"Our counting system is based on the number twenty," the priest explained while we walked. "Using the concept of a zero and simple shapes like lines, dots, and shells, we are able to make change on traded goods in the marketplace—"

"Or predict the end of the world," Liam finished for him.

"Exactly." A twinkle lit the priest's eyes. "It is also my job to use numbers to predict good or bad luck. And right now, you might say we are having a bit of bad luck." He pointed up at the sun burning brightly against a cloudless sky of deep blue. "Unfortunately, this drought has no end in sight. We pray this will change with our celebration later today."

I knew I should concentrate on the priest's every word about the upcoming festivities, but I had the attention span of a gerbil. Passing by a group of children, I quickly grew intrigued with their game. It resembled an ancient version of "Rock, Paper, Scissors," that Micah's little brother, Cameron, used to play with me to determine who would go first in our impromptu soccer games in his backyard. Cam and I usually played best two out of three, but these kids continued for several rounds, giving me enough time to decipher which hand position won over another.

Each time, the dueling pair would pound their fist three times against the palm of their open hand, and then reveal their selection to see if they won. They might choose to keep all five fingers together like the "piece of paper," or make a fist with the thumb tucked neatly beneath their four fingers, much like the "rock" from our game. Or they might extend a single index finger outward, similar to our "scissors," but with only one blade. When the five fingers covered the fist, like the paper hiding the rock, the winner would seal the fist in a victorious grip. But when the index finger stood alone against the flattened five, the winning child made a slicing motion against the "paper" hand to represent the blade of a sword cleaving the opponent apart.

I sensed a deeper meaning that impacted our team underlay the premise of this game, but didn't have time to ponder it further. When I looked up, I realized I'd lagged far behind. I scrambled to catch up to the priest and the other Elementals.

We only walked a short way further before the priest stopped in front of a cylindrical building capped in a dome, situated on a high platform above the surrounding vegetation. It looked nearly identical to a modern observatory, where astronomers could peer into space through a telescope.

"We have built this building, our pyramids, and ball courts, where we compete to honor the gods to correspond with our studies of astronomy," the priest explained, leading us up a spiral staircase in the tower. "Venus is very important in our culture, so this observatory was constructed to match the position of different objects in the sky at specific times in our calendar."

"That's amazing," I said with a low whistle, remembering how Sully and Micah used the calendar app on their cell phones to track nearly every aspect of their lives. Who knew that back in ancient Mexico, they had their own way to record the passage of time through their architecture?

"Just wait," the priest declared. "I have much more to show you." And with a wave of his hand, he led us up a grand staircase toward the observatory. The structure sat upon a wide platform, elevated above the trees and dense scrub brush, perfect for viewing the night sky.

We followed the priest up the long, steep staircase of stones laid entirely by hand. By the time we reached the top, my heart thudded inside my throat. Liam, Skye, and I doubled over from the exertion of the climb, but the priest and Brandr showed no strain.

"One of the other benefits of being an Essence," Brandr whispered with a light laugh.

Desperate for air, Skye, Liam, and I couldn't offer a response.

The priest motioned for us to continue inside. Still trying to catch our breath, we slowly followed. The priest plucked a torch off the wall to illuminate a winding staircase, spiraling up to the top of tower. An altar stood alone in the center of the structure's floor.

He pointed around the room. "We have determined the location of the stars and planets with specific times of the year, aligning their precise locations with these holes in the walls."

I followed his gaze, wondering how this information applied to us determining when Aether would arrive.

"We can use these same calendars to help answer your question," the priest stated. "But first, we must call upon the gods." He laid three square-shaped stones across the altar. I noticed a design carved into the surface of each stone. One had rounded ears and a feline face baring its sharpened teeth. The second possessed the wizened eyes, sharp beak, talons, and broad wings of an eagle. And the third bore the shape of a slithering serpent, with a back of feathers resembling the bright turquoise plumes of the priest's headdress.

Next, the priest reached for a sharpened piece of obsidian — the same type of black volcanic glass Pele had used in the amulet that helped me to travel through time. He brandished the rock high into the air and recited a prayer in his ancient tongue, then dragged the rock across the palm of his hand, letting a single fat drop of blood splatter across the face of each stone, as black as ink in the dim candlelight.

Skye and I winced, but the priest showed no reaction, immune to the pain.

"A prolonged drought has stricken our region, so I offer my

blood as a sacrifice to the rain god, Chac, hoping he will bless us with gifts from above. Let the stones awaken," the priest announced. Within seconds, a green mist swirled around the stones and coalesced into the shapes of three animals, waiting for his command: the fierce jaguar, the swift eagle, and the half-snake, half-bird Maya plumed serpent.

"I have assigned these spirits as your personal protectors," he said, passing each of us one of the stones. "Call upon them in your time of need and they will rise to your aid."

The animals' eyes fixed on us, each holding a residence in our outstretched palms. They gave a deferential bow, recognizing the transfer of loyalty to us, their new owners.

"Call upon them?" I asked. "How do we do that?" I cringed at the thought of splitting my own skin in an act of bloodletting to activate the stones.

A knowing grin spread across the priest's round face. "I have bestowed each stone with a special magic that you alone can unlock. Simply press your palm to the stone's face. A rush of wind will release the eagle's majestic wings. The heat from your fire will trigger the vessel to open and let loose the mighty jaguar spirit. Or a splash of water will unleash the plumed serpent. They consider the three of you their new masters. And they will fight to protect you from harm."

"That's amazing," Skye said, admiring the eagle beside her.

"Thank you," I said, tracing my index finger over the whiskers of the jaguar's face in stone. The spirit jaguar playfully batted his nose, making me comprehend the connection the spirit animal shared with its likeness in the priceless priest's gift.

"The final part we need to determine is when Aether, the Fifth Elemental, will arrive."

Eager, Liam leaned closer. The jaguar spirit floated to my side, placing his head beneath my hand while we waited for the priest's revelation.

The priest let a final drop of blood splash onto a piece of bark paper. He placed the blood stained paper in a bowl on the small altar. Using a piece of flint, he created a spark and ignited the paper. It writhed and shriveled in the small flames, sending a spire of smoke up through the air. "This rising smoke is an avenue for me to communicate with the Sky World," the priest explained as the flames lit his face. "I pray Chac is listening this time," he concluded in a defeated voice. Soon, the fire exhausted itself, leaving nothing but a small pile of ashes.

The priest spread a book of paper made from a type of bark across the table. He consulted the astronomical tables before drawing two horizontal lines in the sand. It looked just like an equal sign from my Algebra II class back in Pacifica. "I estimate that is the amount of time you have before the end," the priest announced.

"Before the apocalypse? Before Aether arrives?" Liam guessed.

The priest nodded slowly. "Yes."

I swallowed hard. "So what does that mean?"

The priest explained in a factual tone, "In our system of mathematics, one short horizontal bar represents the number five, so two bars are equivalent to your value of ten."

"That's all very interesting," Skye spoke up, her voice impatient. "But can you elaborate a little for us? Exactly how much time are we looking at? Ten years? Ten weeks?"

The priest shook his head. "Ten sunrises," he stated.

"Ten sunrises? Do you mean ten *days*?" I gasped. My brow creased with worry. "Oh, my God. We'll never be ready in time."

My eyes scanned the observatory walls, searching for an answer or a loophole, something the priest might have missed to misjudge the date. Instead, I saw only depictions of the gods carved in stone similar to ours that contained the animals' spirits. Some showed good times, while others represented bad fortune, similar to the future we inevitably faced with Aether's imminent arrival. The carvings of the gods appeared to move in ghostly ways in the flickering candlelight, making them appear ominous and cruel with little regard to their worshippers. I hoped the priest was right and Chac would be pleased. After studying these images of the gods, I decided I wouldn't like to see what happened when they grew angry.

"We can't thank you enough for the gifts and information," Liam began, storing his stone securely inside his pocket, "but I think it's time for us to go." He took a step forward, but the priest placed his hand on Liam's chest, halting his progress.

"Not so fast," the priest ordered in a chilling voice.

Liam shot me a quizzical look. I shrugged a response, wondering what made the priest's demeanor change so quickly.

The priest's eyes narrowed. "The gods demand payment in exchange for their generosity."

A shiver ran down my spine, fearful of what he had in mind.

CHAPTER SEVEN

The priest led us out to the ball court to prepare for the game, past vibrantly painted murals that covered the walls. He looked straight at Liam. "You have been chosen by the rain god, Chac, to be captain of the team."

"That's great!" Skye congratulated him and patted his back. I agreed with Skye. Maybe I had misread the priest's apparent change in attitude. This payment to the gods didn't sound so bad compared to what I'd imagined.

We walked past the high priest's temple in silence, then past the great pyramid in the center of the area. Steep, vacant staircases of nearly a hundred steps led up each side of the massive limestone pyramid. The priest pointed out how the afternoon shadow on the side of the staircase created the impression of a giant serpent slithering down the pyramid. I hoped the presence of the serpent was a sign of good luck.

"So the rules are similar to soccer?" I asked when we entered the great ball court, remembering the times I'd kicked the ball around with Cameron to prepare for his first game.

"Except the goal is up there." Brandr craned his neck to look at a small stone ring perched high on the side of the rock wall, far above our heads. Carved images of feathered serpents adorned

53

the ring, like guards protecting the ball from passing through. "And you can only use your elbows or hips."

I gulped. Maybe the serpent's shadow wasn't a sign of good luck after all. "Oh, no. That's impossible."

"Thanks for the vote of confidence," Liam muttered. Servants fastened leather hip guards around his loincloth before the priest directed him to take his place with the team.

While Liam joined his team on the far end of the court, the priest led us to a temple overlooking the center of the playing field, a plain rubber ball lying in the middle. From our high perch we watched the game begin. Players from both sides charged toward the ball, fighting to gain possession. Liam won the footrace to the ball and kicked it to a teammate. A second later, he took an elbow to the face.

"Ouch," I cringed, watching an opponent drop his shoulder and lunge into Liam, knocking him flat. Liam popped right up, ready for more, even though raspberry abrasions from the rough ground covered his entire thigh.

Still, Liam's teammate managed to keep control of the ball and passed it to another player, who jutted out his hip and sent the ball sailing into the air. The ball drifted toward the ring mounted high on the side of the wall and slipped through. The crowd erupted into riotous cheers.

I glanced at Brandr in surprise.

"Maybe we didn't have to worry about Liam after all," he whispered back to me.

On their next attempt, Liam's team won the ball again, using their elbows, hips, and feet to pass it amongst themselves. When the ball came near Liam, he stuck out his elbow, knocking it to a teammate who tipped it up toward the goal. The shot hit the bottom of the stone ring before falling back into play. The crowd released a collective groan of disappointment.

When Liam tried to rebound the ball, the opposition shoved him to the ground, skinning his knees and palms. He hopped back into play and regained control, passing the ball to another player, who shot a goal through the high ring.

"They're pretty good," I commented to the priest, surprised when Liam's team took an early 2-0 lead, despite the rough nature of the sport.

The priest nodded. "It is a great honor to win for the gods and offer one's blood to the fertility of the earth."

He'd told us before that we didn't need to spill our blood on the stones to activate them, but could use our Elemental powers instead. Confused by his statement, I turned to the priest. "What do you mean, 'offer one's blood'?"

"Why, the captain of the winning team is prepared as a human sacrifice to honor the gods. In today's game, we play to serve the rain god, Chac, hoping he will grant our land with much-needed rain."

As he spoke, Liam's team won the ball off the ground and passed it up the field to an open man to take another shot. For a moment, my eyes left the game and focused on the walls lining the great ball court. The stone carvings along the base of the walls depicted scenes of sacrifice to honor the gods.

I felt the blood drain from my face. "Oh, my God. He doesn't know." I leaned toward Skye, clutching her hand discreetly. "Skye, you have to do something. Please. Liam doesn't know."

Brandr reminded me, "Pele said we're not supposed to interfere."

"But we can't let Liam die! We need him," I implored. "Please, Skye. Who knew the price the winners would pay? Plus, no one suspected he actually had a chance of winning this game. We all thought it was nearly impossible to make even a single goal."

Skye looked at me and then turned back toward the field to

watch the game.

I had to tell her something I probably should've said ages ago. It was the only way I could get her to change her mind. "Skye, I'm sorry."

She tilted her head to peek at me, waiting for me to continue.

The words came fast, bottled inside for too long. "I never meant to hurt you with those comments I said back in Bora Bora. I didn't know how else to get you to use your powers. I was wrong to make you mad, especially when none of it was true. You have to believe me. I loved you like a sister, and I wanted to keep you safe. But I failed and I'm sorry. Really, I am." I stared into her smoky eyes, hoping she believed me.

She blinked once. Her face relaxed while a hint of a smile wound across her lips.

She forgives me. That knowledge pulsed through my veins, alleviating the burden I'd born since that ill-fated day when Gaia and Hydros had stripped her from my life. I threw my arms around her, my heart swimming with relief.

"Okay, I'll help," she consented in the softest of voices, and pulled away from my embrace to train her eyes on the ball court. The next time Liam's team shot, Skye twirled her finger. The ball drifted too high at the very last second, apparently caught on a sudden cross-breeze. The crowd moaned its displeasure, but inside I celebrated.

"Thank you," I quietly exclaimed to Skye, giving her a wide grin.

Skye returned my smile, but kept her attention focused on the game. Every time Liam's team shot, the ball magically ended up in the opponent's possession, then passed through the ring scoring a point for the other team. A deep frown began to set onto the priest's face. Maybe the unexpected turn of events disappointed him. After all, Liam's team had dominated the game at the start. I agreed it seemed appropriate we repay the gods for their gifts of the animal spirits and the predicted date of the apocalypse, only not with Liam's blood.

Thanks to Skye, Liam's team lost by three goals at the conclusion of the game. While the players shook hands on the field, the priest led us down the steep temple steps to rejoin Liam after the game. Bruises and scrapes covered his body; otherwise he seemed fine. A part of me wanted to toss my arms around him in relief. But I restrained myself, fearful the priest might suspect our involvement in the outcome of the game.

I left the ball court with a big smile smeared across my face until I saw the priest in front of the altar, preparing the captain of the winning team for sacrifice to the rain god, Chac. The man climbed upon an altar, where the priest anointed him with blue dye. The priest prayed to the god to accept this sacrifice and grace the land, thereby ending the drought.

Four elder men walked up to the corners of the altar to hold the man's arms and legs immobilized. The captain lay bravely, stoically, accepting his fate.

"Can't you do something to save him?" I whispered to Liam.

"The priest told us they believe it's an honor to die for the gods."

"But, Liam," I pleaded. "That easily could've been you in his place. Can't you help these people?" I asked. "Their game, their rituals, their calendar...all sought the promise of a better life through pleasing the gods."

"I don't think it's our place to interfere," Liam replied. "We came here for information, nothing else."

"Liam, Skye helped spare your life. How can you just walk away?"

"Jordan, Pele said—"

"I know. I know. But these people are *dying*. And you're the

Water Elemental. If anyone could help, it'd be you. Besides how would *they* know you were the one who returned the rain to their land instead of their god, Chac? It could be our little secret."

"Let it go, Jordan," Brandr interjected. "You already asked Skye to influence the game. Enough is enough. Like Pele said, we're not supposed to interfere."

"I know," I replied in a saddened voice. "She told me the same thing before I went on my other missions, too. But that didn't stop me from trying to save a few people I met along the way."

The priest raised his ceremonial knife, carved from obsidian, high into the air. The bright sun glinted off its black volcanic glass blade, sending a chill of remorse down my spine. The sacrifice could've been Liam. And we'd done nothing to save this innocent man.

I leaned toward Liam and whispered a single word in his ear, "*Please.*"

The priest spoke a few words in preparation of offering the captain's heart to Chac. So little time remained for this unfortunate soul.

Next to me, Liam closed his eyes, whether from fatigue after his brutal match on the ball court or irritation with my prodding, I couldn't say. He swayed, unsteady on his feet. I was about to ask if he was feeling okay when gray clouds suddenly obscured the blistering sun.

The priest paused, his hand in midair, considering the sudden change in weather an auspicious omen. A light drizzle began to fall.

I looked at Liam and grinned.

Liam opened his eyes. "What?" he said, feigning innocence.

My grin widened. "You're the best," I told him, planting a quick kiss on his cheek.

The rain rapidly transformed into heavy drops that slipped off the slave's bare chest. The priest tilted his head toward the heavens, puzzled by this unexpected turn of events. Raindrops slid off the sharpened blade of the raised knife in a steady stream.

The people raised their hands to the heavens. Some sang jubilant choruses. Others wept tears of delight.

More drops pelted the priest's face and landed inside his open mouth. He let his hands fall to his side. "Release him!" he commanded the four elder men. Then in a crisp, clear voice, he announced to the crowd, "Today, I grant this man his freedom."

The captain sat up. His confused expression dissolved into a broad smile that lit his face. He rubbed the blue dye with the palms of his hands, smearing the priest's painted lines into wide streaks that would fade with time. He proudly climbed off the altar and down the steps.

"Well, I'd say our work here is done," Brandr said, fixing his gaze on me. He turned and walked with Skye away from the multitudes celebrating in the street.

When Brandr wasn't looking, I slipped my hand inside Liam's and gave him a small squeeze, unable to wipe the grin off my face. "Thank you, Liam," I whispered. "Like I said before, you're the best." I pulled my hand away before anyone noticed.

Liam rolled his eyes and followed Brandr and Skye. For a split second, I saw Liam glance over his shoulder at his former opponent. His mouth turned up at the corners, pleased with his decision.

CHAPTER EIGHT

Ten days until Aether's predicted arrival

Ten days. That's all the time we had left in the world.

What do you even do with that kind of knowledge? I know some people might choose to live life to the fullest and travel to exotic locations so they could go out with a huge bang. Others might choose to spend those few days with family and close friends.

Me? I ended up stuck in the middle of an argument between Gaia and Brandr.

Lucky me.

"So what did you learn?" Gaia questioned when we returned from our visit with the Maya priest.

I replied, "He said we've got ten days."

"Ten *days*? Are you sure you heard him correctly?" she asked, alarmed.

"Yes. In fact, I did. Like you, I found that news quite difficult to digest, so I asked him to clarify. 'Ten sunrises,' he said, to be exact, meaning Aether could arrive on the evening of the tenth day."

Gaia moaned, "Oh, God. This isn't good."

"You're telling me," Brandr muttered.

Without provocation, Gaia wheeled on Brandr. "It all comes back to the last line again, doesn't it?" she accused him. "'There is one' or 'they are one.' It's still a mystery, isn't it? If only you hadn't burned that section of the parchment, then we'd know the answer for certain."

"Oh, so it's all *my* fault now?" Brandr retorted, growing suddenly defensive. "You know, that section of the prophecy would've never been destroyed if you hadn't cornered me."

Parchment? Prophecy? Cornering Brandr? I suspected this wasn't the first time they'd had this argument, bickering over the semantics of something I didn't comprehend.

"What's she talking about?" I asked.

"You haven't told her about the prophecy?" Gaia wagered. She set her hands on her hips and tapped her foot impatiently.

I paused for a brief moment, wondering how many other important facts still lay hidden from me. "Prophecy?"

"Ugh!" Gaia groaned, her mouth turning down into a scowl. "We're running out of time. I thought someone already filled you in on these details so we didn't have to take time out of training to teach you things you should've known by now."

My throat tightened when her vicious tone shifted so quickly from Brandr to me. "Well, maybe I would if you just took a moment to explain things to me," I countered. "Why didn't *you* simply tell me yourself instead of chasing me throughout time?" I retorted.

"Oh, I tried. Believe me, I tried. You simply refused to listen."

My eyes glazed with tears of fury. "Maybe that's because I was trying so hard to defend others from your violent attacks."

"Easy, Jordan," Brandr warned in a low voice. "This isn't helping you right now."

But I couldn't say another word. Not to him, and definitely

61

not to her. How dare she accuse me of slowing the progress of the group when there were countless other ways she could've gained my support besides using violence, lies, and treachery? My entire body shook with uncontrollable rage and a prevailing sadness mixed into one.

Gaia pressed her fingers to her temples and closed her eyes in a dramatic show of trying to maintain her patience. "Just do something and figure it out by tomorrow morning. We have lots of work to do," she said, turning on her heels and marching away.

"What's gotten into her?" I sobbed, my voice choked with emotion. "Why is Gaia so crabby? And why does she hate me so much?"

"Crabby?" Brandr scoffed. "Personally, I would've used a different, not so kind adjective to describe her, but we can go with 'crabby' if you'd like." Distracted by his comment, my mind ran through a list of other words he might have chosen when Brandr continued. "In case you hadn't noticed, Gaia feels challenged by you."

"By me? Why?"

"You present a threat unlike that of the other Elementals."

"Because I can move the earth using the heated currents that lie under the crust?" I hypothesized, remembering our trip into the mantle beneath Earth's surface.

"That's part of it."

I hesitated, trying to think of other reasons I might pose a threat.

"C'mon, Jordan. Don't tell me I have to spell this out for you," he said, frustrated.

"What?"

"Seriously?" Brandr let out a noise that verged on a guffaw. "What about Liam?"

I scrunched up my nose. "What about him?"

"Oh, puh-lease. Don't be so naïve." He shook his head in a condescending way. "You know she never expected him to be so successful in accomplishing a feat that she could not."

"That doesn't matter. Things aren't the same anymore," I explained. "Besides, I don't think he ever really liked me in the first place. It was all an act."

Brandr sounded unconvinced. "Whatever."

"It was. Why else would he totally ignore me now? I mean, really, he's hardly spoken to me since I conceded to work with the team."

He shrugged. "I'm sure he has his reasons."

"If you say so." I sighed, uncertain of what reasons could completely drive Liam away. I guess I didn't know him nearly as well as I'd thought. "So…what do you recommend I do?"

"Keep your distance," he suggested.

My eyebrows perched high on my forehead. "From Gaia? Or Liam?"

Brandr thought for a moment, and then looked me straight in the eye, the firelight dulling in his irises. In a cautioning voice, he replied, "Both."

Chapter Nine

"I don't get it," I told Brandr later that evening after everyone else had gone to bed. "Why does Gaia particularly hate us? She's best of friends with Air and Water, but she really has it out for us, doesn't she?"

Brandr ran his fingers through his flyaway red hair. "It goes back a long ways."

"What do you mean?" I asked.

Brandr shrugged. "It didn't start with you, or even me for that matter. A long, long time ago, the first Fire Elemental, Ignis, confronted Gaia. It didn't end well."

"Tell me," I prompted.

"I wouldn't get the details right," he said, dismissing my request.

"Then I have to meet Ignis. You can introduce us," I suggested.

He shook his head of wispy red hair. "I don't think this is a good idea. We have so many other things we need to focus on right now. Besides, it's not like I had someone to help me."

I scrunched up my brow. "What do you mean?"

"Ignis isn't exactly like me. Let's just say he's kind of wrapped up in his own issues."

"Oh." I recalled the times Brandr had spent with me, the one

64

person I could count on for support when everyone else seemed against me. "Then why do *you* do it?"

"Do what?"

"Help me. Why bother?"

"Isn't it obvious? Aether's coming sooner than we thought, and we're a little short on time to prepare."

"But, Brandr, don't you see? I'm so tired of not knowing about my past and the past of the other Elementals," I implored. "I have to meet him and learn everything that happened in the past, so I won't...." My voice trailed off, unable to verbalize that final thought.

"So you won't *what*?"

I shook my head. I just couldn't say it. Not to Brandr. Not to anyone, in case admitting that fear would make it come true.

I wished I had a better poker face, because Brandr understood my implications anyway. "So you won't *die*," he guessed.

"Brandr, I'm sorry. I didn't mean...."

"No. It's fine. I get it," he said in a saddened tone. "And you know something? If it were me, I'd want to guarantee I didn't make the same mistakes as those who possessed this power before me, either. I admit it...I'm just a little jealous, okay? If I could go back and change the past, I would. But I can't, so I'm stuck here as an Essence, watching you have all the fun, watching you enjoy *life*."

"Brandr, I —"

"Forget it. We'll do this your way."

Before I could say another word, Brandr leapt into my body and bucked me from the controls, letting a sudden burst of flames consume my body and rocket me off my feet. We spiraled at super speeds through the continuum of time and space, until we stopped with a lurch. Brandr leapt out of my body faster than a pilot could eject from a downed jet fighter. A wave of nausea overcame me and I hunched forward on all fours, trying to keep my food down.

"Oh, my God, you've gotta stop doing that," I whimpered. My queasy stomach twisted into a whorled knot from the speed of our trip. I took a deep breath of the cool breeze spilling off the water to calm myself, then gazed upward at this land of remarkable beauty, where snow capped mountains sloped toward the sea, and wide bands of green and pink light danced across the midnight blue sky.

"Where are we?" I asked once my stomach settled, somewhat at least.

"Iceland."

"*Ice*land. This is a joke, right? You're telling me the *Fire* Essence chose to live in a world of ice?"

"He's not really living," Brandr stated in a deadpan voice.

I rolled my eyes. "You know what I mean."

"You might be surprised, but Iceland is actually the perfect location for Ignis to reside," Brandr explained, seeming to forget his initial irritation with me. "The island is situated above a mantle plume like the hot spot that created the Hawaiian Islands, or the supervolcano in Yellowstone National Park. Also, Iceland's located right on the ridge of sea floor spreading. It sits on a divergent plate boundary that drives the North American and Eurasian coastlines farther apart, so you can actually see these forces working above the surface of the Atlantic. With more than one hundred volcanoes, it's one of the most volcanically active places on Earth. It even has volcanoes that can erupt beneath a glacier and create huge floods of meltwater. Pretty sweet, huh?"

I stared at him, dumbfounded. He'd recited a similar scientific explanation when he'd first fused with my body on our journey inside the mantle of the earth. He'd almost killed me, staying in one place for so long that we nearly created a plume to generate new volcanoes under the island of Hawaii, but that was besides the point.

"Seriously, Brandr. How do you know all this stuff?" I asked.

Brandr shrugged. "I've had a lot of time on my hands. Plus, I think it's wicked cool that we can control some of these forces." His eyes glowed red with excitement. "I can use knowledge for my personal gain, making me nearly invincible within the realm of Fire."

I raised one eyebrow high on my forehead. "I dunno. That sounds a little dark for you."

Brandr chuckled and his eyes simmered to their normal color. "I didn't say I planned to become invincible. I just said I could. You know, if I ever needed to."

"Uh huh." I rolled my eyes. "Like we ever need *you* to go on a power trip."

Before I had a chance to razz him further, I detected the wispy orange glow of a figure not far ahead. *An Essence.* I watched the figure throw his arms about in exaggerated motions. He had a full face, a thick but undefined chest, and an even wider waist that spilled over the front of his jeans and jiggled when he moved quickly. He had strong sausage-thick fingers that he clenched in furious fists. Even from this distance, the expression of pent up rage was clear. His breathing came out in short, rapid bursts. His dark eyebrows narrowed when he focused his energy and released it with a loud groan.

The ground heaved and bulged, buckling under the tremendous force of something rising from below. Suddenly, a spurt of glowing molten rock spewed into the sky, disturbing the peaceful landscape. I jumped backward with surprise when great globs of lava shot upward, hung in midair, and fell back to Earth with a loud splat.

Next, Ignis aimed his hand at a sleeping volcano, awakening

it with a sudden, violent eruption. A thick black cloud of fine particles of ash billowed outward from the crater, choking the air. Huge drops of molten lava flew into the black cloud, creating a few sparks. The sparks quickly transformed into bright bolts of electricity, illuminating the dark cloud from the inside.

"Is that what I think it is?" I asked Brandr, awestruck at the sight.

"The separation of positively charged ash and negatively charged molten rocks resembles the conditions needed to create a storm cloud," Brandr told me matter-of-factly.

I stared at him, befuddled once again as to how he recollected such detailed explanations. "Are you telling me he made *lightning*?"

Brandr nodded. "Volcanic lightning. Like I said before, *wicked cool.*"

"That's amazing! We definitely need him on our team."

"It's not that easy, I'm afraid," Brandr admitted. "But we'll give it our best shot."

Strained from exertion, the Essence wiped a thick sheen of perspiration from his brow. He collapsed onto the ground, doubled over from exhaustion, and let his temper sizzle until his energy stores replenished.

"You're telling me that's Ignis?" I wagered.

"Yes."

He looked nothing like I'd expected. If I hadn't witnessed him splitting the earth into a tempestuous volcano, I never would have imagined that he was the Fire Essence. He seemed quick to anger, like any minor catalyst would send him over the edge. "So he's got some unresolved issues, huh?"

"You think? Let's just say he needs some closure. He hasn't quite come to grips with his death yet."

"What happened to him?"

"He and Gaia had an epic showdown in prehistoric Earth that ended with...." Brandr's voice trailed off, like he'd revealed too much.

"Ended with what?" I prodded.

"I'll save it for Ignis to share," Brandr said. "I think he tells the story better himself." Brandr took a few steps forward and then yelled, "*Ignis!*" Brandr waved animatedly.

The original Fire Essence turned and gave Brandr a disinterested nod before continuing with his work.

"Come on," Brandr told me, and walked right up to Ignis, tapping him on the shoulder.

Ignis gave a weighted sigh and faced him. "Yes?" he asked, twiddling his stubby thumbs impatiently.

"I'd like you to meet Jordan."

"I know who you are," Ignis snipped. "Now if you don't mind, I have a few things to take care of."

I peeked at Brandr, surprised at Ignis's reaction.

Brandr spoke up. "You've probably already heard the Fifth Elemental approaches as we speak. Jordan just wants to know more about what happened to you so she can prepare for the upcoming fight. Surely that's not too much to ask a powerful Essence like yourself," he said, laying on his charm pretty thick.

"And this affects me how?" Ignis replied with an exaggerated roll of his eyes.

Brandr ignored his question and pressed on. "We were just wondering if you could at least tell Jordan your story so she's prepared. After all, you tell it best."

The faintest of smiles flickered across Ignis's lips. He turned away from us and started for an ice cave by the sea.

I leaned toward Brandr. "Did he have a change of heart?" I asked in a voice too low for Ignis to hear.

"He likes the flattery," Brandr whispered back, waving me to

69

follow the original Fire Essence.

I smiled and hurried to catch up. "You know him well."

A short distance away, we entered a cave constructed entirely of surrealistic sculptures of wavy ice suspended over our heads. Ignis pointed his finger at the ground and produced a small flame. The fire ebbed and flowed, its colors changing from red to orange to blue and green. I sat, transfixed by the flickering light. Satisfied with his work, he turned to face us and launched into his story.

"Unlike you, Gaia had no Essence to train her. She could only teach herself by attempting new challenges and perfecting her abilities over long periods of time." Ignis paused to wipe the sheen from his brow. "In her youth, she grew arrogant of her superior powers. Traveling back in time two hundred million years, Gaia joined all the landmasses together into a single supercontinent, later called 'Pangaea.' The prefix *Pan* means 'all,' and...." He paused, waiting for me to make the connection myself.

"Gaea...it's almost like Gaia, isn't it?" I mused.

Ignis nodded. "You guessed it.... 'Gaea' is the Greek word meaning 'Earth.'"

"All Earth," I repeated.

"Exactly. And as you can imagine, I wasn't quite pleased with Gaia's conceited overuse of her powers, so I decided to play a little game with her, just to show her who was boss. I followed her back in time and watched her pull all the continents into a single giant landmass. I laughed at her boastful show, then decided to offer her a bit of a challenge by splitting apart the land." Ignis's face lit with pride at his clever attempt to foil her grandiose plan.

"Pangaea was the result of Gaia's arrogance. I merely ripped her supercontinent apart using forces inside the earth. I stirred things up a bit, creating massive currents that cleaved it in two, then further into the continents we know today, hoping to divide her strength into more controllable entities."

He waved a hand over his head and I looked up, noticing the colors of his firelight had taken on the shapes of the characters and scenes from his tale, illuminating the sculpted ice of the cave's ceiling. I saw the green light form the shapes of the continents, breaking apart when Ignis warred against Gaia's growing powers.

"I dove deep into the middle of the mantle to create currents of molten material that rose and sunk in a cyclical motion," Ignis continued, "similar to the convection cells in an oven. Soon, these cells began to move the crust above, until chunks of the land and seafloor flowed like giant plates on the molten material of the mantle. The motion never ceased, so Gaia couldn't create a single mass of land again, and would never be able to wield total control over all the earth's power, even to this day. I wanted to teach her a lesson about the dangers of exercising too much power for her own good. But it didn't go exactly as I planned."

I held my breath, waiting for him to continue. His explanation might prove to be exactly what I needed to hear to spare me from Aether's imminent attack.

"Furious with my countermeasures, Gaia forced me underground, holding me prisoner inside her rock walls."

Ignis's light show reflected this scene. I saw the orange firelight of Ignis's character driven deep underground.

He continued. "I knew I couldn't stay there for long with the rock pressing against me tighter and tighter. So I drew power from the intense heat inside and unleashed a violent volcanic eruption. She capped off my explosion with a dome of impenetrable rock, sealing me inside the rocky earth. Though my body perished, my Essence remained, wandering through the heated layer of mantle underlying the crust for many years until I found a place

71

that suited my needs. Here in Iceland, I can release my anger in whatever method I choose. For the most part, people leave me alone."

"So now that you've had all this time to perfect your skills, you will be ready to help us defeat Aether," I said.

"Maybe, but that depends on one thing," Ignis replied.

"Name it," Brandr offered.

Ignis paused for a moment before asking, "Is Gaia still with you?"

I looked at Brandr, nervous to respond.

"She is," he conceded.

"Then my answer is *no*." He snapped his fingers and the colorful firelight diminished, reflecting his soured mood.

"I don't understand. You're a valuable asset. You have so many skills that would greatly benefit our team," I said, hoping my attempt at flattery might change his mind. "Can't you forget your grudge for just a little while and help us against Aether's attack?"

Ignis shook his head resolutely. "No."

"Are you sure there's nothing we can say to get you to change your mind?" Brandr asked.

"Nothing at all," he said in a cold, unwavering voice. He kicked dirt over the leftovers of the fire, until only a thin trail of rising smoke remained. With an angry snort he floated away, leaving Brandr and me in a warring world of fire and ice.

CHAPTER TEN

Questions flooded my mind on our return trip. Questions I couldn't wait for Brandr to answer. He exited my body, turned, and stepped in the direction of his tent. "Brandr? There's something I don't understand."

He sighed, obviously tired from our journey and my endless stream of inquiries.

"If Ignis had contacted you before, then why hadn't you done the same for me?" I wondered aloud.

"I wanted to...and I would've...but Pele held me back. She had another plan in mind, one that required my patience. So I watched you from afar, hoping she'd made the right choice in keeping you isolated from other magical powers. Everything seemed to be going in your favor when you located Skye on your own."

I remembered the island of Bora Bora where Skye and I had lived like sisters, cooking our fish until Gaia and Hydros found us. I shivered, recalling the torture they'd inflicted upon us until Skye finally broke. Then I remembered my role in turning Skye away. In an attempt to anger her into using her powers against them, I'd lost her trust.

I kicked myself, thinking of how different my life could've

been if only someone had told me about the background of my life, rather than my piecing small bits together whenever Gaia confronted me with her evil, wicked attacks to break my spirit.

"I wish you hadn't listened to Pele. I wish you'd told me all of this before. Then maybe I would've joined sooner if I'd known what was at stake."

"It ended up working out after all, thanks to Liam," Brandr said. "Pele thinks he's just what we need to bond this team together."

"Or to break us apart," I countered.

"Only if you let it. Do you know what I think?" Brandr said with a pointed look, as if slightly hurt I hadn't bothered to ask his opinion.

"Go on," I replied, trying to keep my mind from drifting toward confusing thoughts about Liam.

"I think none of this matters unless you truly believe."

He said it in such a succinct manner that it seemed logical. Still, his statement pinned all the blame on my shoulders. "What's left to believe in when I've been fed a bunch of lies?" I snipped, angered by his accusation. After all, Pele had saved Cam to gain my debt, and had driven Sully away with her magical firelight. She had withheld vital information about my past and future. She had approved of Liam as both the stray Kea and the elderly Auntie Lulu. Plus she had sent me on those dangerous missions to gain sympathy for Gaia and Hydros. In my eyes, she had manipulated my every action. Now Brandr had the audacity to suggest my life would've been different if only I'd accepted my Elemental name of Pyr and the powers I'd been granted?

"Yourself," Brandr answered in a soft, heartfelt voice, one I'd never heard him use in all the time I'd known him. He sounded tired of my petulant, arrogant youth, and wished the world of heartache and loss I'd already endured would bring clarity to my thoughts and actions. "Believe in yourself. The rest will come with time."

"I don't understand. Isn't that what I've already been doing?" I had resolved to trust no one but myself. If everyone else had deceived me, where else did I have to turn but inside my own heart?

I opened my mouth to protest a few seconds too late. Brandr's Essence had already trailed off into the distance, leaving me alone with my thoughts…and a decision that could dictate the fate of this world.

CHAPTER ELEVEN

Lately my perspective had grown skewed, and I needed to remember what I was fighting for. I had to go back and see my old friends.

I summoned a palm full of white fire, prepared to unleash its full effects when Liam stopped me. "What're you doing?" he exclaimed, his bright blue eyes wide with surprise. "Where's Brandr?" Liam said, surprised to see me alone.

"He left," I stated, still stunned by the unexpected turn of events. Brandr had been my steadfast companion through this whole ordeal. The only one I fully trusted. Guess I'd been wrong about him, too.

Liam scratched the top of his head. "He *left*? What do you mean he left?"

I shrugged. What was I, Brandr's personal assistant? "I dunno," I replied. "He told me some stuff I didn't really want to hear and he took off." I let the flame grow larger in my hand, ready to end this uncomfortable conversation.

Disappointment registered in Liam's frown. "Well, are you going after him?"

I responded with a simple, "No." My voice sounded strangely dull and void of emotion.

"Jordan, how can you say that? In case you hadn't noticed, things are getting pretty serious, and we can use all the help we can get."

"Ooooh. You sound like an anchorman on the six-o'clock news. Thanks for the update," I said with a bundle of sarcasm.

Liam blinked, puzzled by my reaction. "You know, you've been acting so differently in the last few days."

"You think? Why don't you try having your body taken over by someone else, and see how much you like it!" I snapped, my pulse rising with a fresh wave of anger surging through my veins.

Liam cupped his hands over mine, extinguishing my flames with a quick douse of water. "This isn't like you," he said in a soft voice.

I looked from his face to his hands and back, trying to decipher his intentions. Why did he mind what I did, anyway? Since when did he care about me at all?

He wouldn't release his grip, even after the flames died. Funny enough, my anger began to simmer the longer he kept my hands in his grasp. I soon lost myself in his radiant blue eyes, forgetting all the emotion of our battle on the beach.

"I've missed this," I admitted, unable to release my gaze.

I expected Liam to agree. Instead, he gave an exasperated sigh. "C'mon, Jordan. Don't do this right now. You know what we're up against. You saw what could happen when only a fragment of space hits our planet. What do you think will happen when Aether drops his full force upon us?"

I frowned, confused by Liam's intentions. Why had I believed he wished a moment alone to rekindle our past? His focus lay purely with the good of the team. He didn't care for me any more than the wicked, evil Gaia herself. Luckily, I'd never disclosed my true feelings for him. It would only have given him more leverage in supporting his cause.

"I need a fresh perspective," I explained. "Gaia told me to figure things out by tomorrow morning. I decided I need to talk to someone on the outside. To remember why we're risking our lives, our futures, to fight this new threat."

Liam's brow pinched together as he released his hands from mine. His face held steady, trying to mask the underlying hurt embedded in my words. "Don't you think it would be better if you stayed here with me?"

I couldn't reply. To say yes meant I'd probably never see Sully or Micah or Cam again. And to say no meant others weighed above Liam in my heart.

Liam stared intently into my eyes, waiting for a response.

"It's complicated," I finally muttered, for lack of a clear answer. I recalled how much Cam reminded me of my little sister, Sarah, before she died. Gaia had collapsed the roof of my house upon my family, and then redirected my defensive fire to the structure, sealing my family inside. And I remembered how Sully's first kiss dredged up memories of the last time William Mills embraced me in Salem Village, before Hydros held him captive and spilled his blood. Why should I feel guilty about wishing to cling to those memories of my past when I'd already experienced so many losses?

Things were different for Liam, I decided. He had accepted his role from the start. Plus, he hadn't lived as many distinct, painful lives as I had. I shouldn't have to apologize for wanting to see Sully…even if Pele had used her magical firelight to make him fall for the bubbly Bethany Donovan.

Others had chosen so many aspects of my life for me. Losing my family. Watching Lucius and William die in front of me. Driving away Sully and Micah. And falling for the new Water Elemental, Liam. Why couldn't I do one little thing for myself for a change? Why should I deprive myself of a single choice of my own free will?

"So you're going to go after him, aren't you?" Liam prodded.

I sighed stubbornly. "No, I'm not."

"Then where are you going?"

"It's nothing personal. I only need some closure. And to remember why I'm here," I said, unwilling to verbalize further details. My life in Pacifica seemed so completely different from my life now. But I wasn't ready to forget my past...nor did I want to share that past with Liam. Not yet, at least.

"I don't get it. I thought I already told you all the reasons why we need you," Liam pressed.

I noticed he selected the phrase, "why *we* need you" rather than "why *I* need you." Though he probably didn't intend it, his choice of words now served as another reason why I must go.

I shook my head sadly. "It's not enough."

The expression on his face looked like I'd just slapped him across the cheek with the reality that he no longer ranked foremost in my life. Because there was a point in the not so distant past when I would've given up everything for him. But those times were over...and I doubted they'd ever return.

"Fine," Liam acquiesced. "If that's how it has to be, I guess I can understand. Just promise me one thing, Jordan," he said in a low voice, staring at me intently. His hand bridged the gap between us to softly trace the contours of my face. His touch seemed so gentle and caring, I couldn't help but think he still possessed feelings for me beyond the need to complete our team of Elementals.

My heart skipped a beat. I gazed into his rich blue eyes, longing to hear his next words. Three little words, to be precise. Three words that would make me never want to leave. "Go on," I prompted, hoping he didn't notice my thudding heartbeat.

"Promise me you'll come back. To me." His hand drifted to

the nape of my neck. He pulled me closer to him and let the full effect of his words register in my mind.

I had to admit, those weren't the words I'd longed to hear. But they were close. Very, very close.

"I promise," I said, knowing I meant every word.

We stood together, unmoving, the warmth of his hand pressed against my flesh. I waited, wondering if he might attempt to kiss me once more like he had on the beach after our fight. Had I sacrificed everything we'd built between us by refusing that last kiss? At the time it hadn't mattered, since his lies and deception clouded my thoughts.

But before I could ponder if my action held lasting repercussions for us, Liam released his hand. Without another word, he turned and left me with a choice that I alone could make, but one that impacted the success of our whole team.

CHAPTER TWELVE

Pacifica, California, Present Day

Using white fire for transport, I entered Pacifica through a bonfire on the beach we'd narrowly escaped from when Hydros's tsunami hit the coast. A romantic couple by the fire seemed oblivious to my entry, their tongues so far down each other's throat that they failed to see a person emerge from the flames. Even so, I still couldn't contain the nervous energy inside of me, like I was on a clandestine mission to regain my focus. I shouldn't be here; I'd already forged a new life. Still, the life I'd known in California with Sully, Micah, and Cam drew me back with ties too powerful to ignore.

I took a deep breath and soaked in the details of my surroundings, guarding them like a precious memory within the safety of my heart. I recognized the scent of brine that hung in the air, and the familiar contours of the hills silhouetted against the darkening sky. The warm, cozy glow of oceanfront homes dotted the hillsides. The light of the crescent moon danced upon the tumbling waves that rolled up on shore in a rhythmic fashion, producing a calming white noise. I felt like I was home, even though I knew I could never stay.

Nearby, black scaffolding lined several seashore buildings, evidence of undergoing repairs in the aftermath of Hydros's tsunami. I remembered the rush of water covering the streets when I raced away from the coastline with Micah, Sully, and Cam. The superstorm seemed insignificant compared to what lay ahead.

I gazed overhead, where cool pinpoints of starlight flickered. The midnight blue sky seemed so peaceful and serene, oblivious to the imminent threat that bore the potential to eradicate life on this planet.

I took another breath, reminding myself of the importance of my visit. I wasn't here to linger in past memories, only to resolve the issues that clouded my mind and to refuel my desire to persevere, regardless of the cost. An inexplicable tug inside my heart pulled me to Sully for answers.

I scanned the faces of the crowd of local teenagers, recognizing a few people from my short time at high school: Isa, Justin, Karli, Mark, and Bethany...with Sully. The sight of them together flooded my head with a pang of jealousy and made my stomach twist in a knot, even though I knew Pele had bewitched Sully into liking Bethany Donovan with her magical firelight. Pele had her reasons; she needed him to break up with me so that I could get close to Liam. I had trusted Pele and Liam, and look where it got me: hurt and alone.

Seeing Sully and Bethany together suddenly made me question my motives. I remembered my last phone conversation; Sully said I had ignored him despite his aid in locating the fire goddess in Hawaii. In reality, Pele had sent me on all those missions, purposefully delaying me so Sully would find someone to replace me. Someone normal like him. I wished it didn't hurt so much to see him. I wanted him to be happy, but a part of me wished he could've found that happiness with me.

82

Reminding myself I didn't have much time, I took a step toward them before reconsidering. How would he react to seeing me again? Maybe I'd made a huge mistake in coming here, making Liam second-guess my intentions when now I doubted them myself.

Just get it over with. I forced my feet in his direction. Luckily, Bethany stood up and left just when I approached. I took advantage of my break and walked right up to him.

"Hey, Sully," I said hesitantly.

His jaw fell open. "Jordan? Ohmigod! What are *you* doing here?" He threw his arms around me in a spontaneous, quick hug that allayed my fears in an instant.

"I had to see you," I admitted, slipping my arms around his waist in return. I'd forgotten how much I'd missed the warmth and comfort of his embrace.

"Me?" He took a surprised step backward, so I reluctantly released my grip. "Why's that?"

"I need you to convince me."

"Convince you?" He tilted his head sideways. "Of what?"

"That this — that everything — is worth fighting for."

He flashed me a wide smile. "Jordan, you don't need me for that. You've always believed that deep within your heart. I know this because otherwise I wouldn't be here now. You got us out in time, before that wave hit."

"Yeah," I agreed, grateful for the boost to my confidence.

"I'm sorry I didn't wait for you to come back," he said wistfully. "I mean, I wanted to, but...."

"It's not your fault. It's mine." I took a deep breath, trying to ignore the ache that plucked at my heart. "It's okay. I found someone else." No need to tell him I had new, unresolved issues with that someone else.

"That's great," Sully said in a tone of false enthusiasm.

83

Did I sense a tinge of jealousy? Suddenly, his reaction made me feel a whole lot better.

"And he understands?" Sully asked. "You know, about *you*?" He snapped the fingers of one hand together and mimicked a ball of flame resting in his palm.

I nodded. He didn't need to remind me that I was different from everyone else. "He understands more than I ever expected."

"So I guess you need to ask yourself if *he's* worth it."

I pinched my brow together. "Worth what?"

"Fighting for."

"You mean 'dying' for?" I corrected him.

Sully chortled. "I sincerely doubt you'll die. Not you. Not if you're prepared."

I closed my eyes, thinking of my memories of Liam: our fight when I first discovered Liam was Hydros's replacement as an Elemental, plus the pain and bitterness that consumed me from his betrayal. I remembered the warm memories we'd shared: washing the car, swimming underwater at the reef, and our kiss on the moonlit beach. "Yeah, he is," I admitted, a renewed confidence surging through my veins.

"That's great. I'm happy for you, Jordan. Really, I am. You deserve it." An awkward silence fell between us. Sully jammed his hands deep inside his pockets and shifted uncomfortably on his heels. His eyes shifted, focusing elsewhere in a distracted way. Maybe he checked to see if Bethany noticed my return, or maybe he'd run out of things to say. I couldn't be sure.

I used the awkward silence to scan the crowd, looking for Micah, though I didn't exactly know why. Tears filled my eyes. I'd never see either of them again, would I? Which meant this would be my last goodbye.

Sully followed my gaze. "Would you like me to get Micah?" he asked.

84

I shook my head. "He doesn't want to see me again." Besides, this was where they belonged. At home and safe...provided I completed my task with success.

Sully shot me a quick, pitying look, quickly changing the subject. "I didn't mean for this to happen," he apologized. "You didn't call. Didn't text me. Honestly, I didn't think I'd ever see you again."

I frowned. "I know. I understand." Peeking at Bethany over my shoulder, I noticed her face wrapped in an irritated expression.

"But it doesn't have to end like this," he continued hopefully. "I mean, you'll be coming back again this summer, won't you? We're going to be seniors this fall. It'll be awesome."

"Sully," I began, at a loss for how to tell him this would be the last time I would ever see him. My eyes found my feet. "I don't think so," I finished in a weak voice.

"You don't think what?"

I raised my eyes to give Sully a pleading look, wishing I could voice all the fears that swam inside my head. "I can't. I'd like to come back, but I'm afraid I can't."

"Just once," he asked, and reached for my hand. "We're here every Friday night. You're always welcome."

I wanted to pull away, but I couldn't. I knew I should let him go, but my hand stayed stubbornly in his. I looked at Sully and knew I'd miss everything about him if I didn't agree: his lopsided smile, the sparkle in his pale blue eyes, the way he wore his baseball cap backward so his hair spiked out the sides, the smell of his warm jacket warding off the cold rain, and most of all how he was always there for me when I needed him. Even now.

"Just once," I agreed softly, praying I hadn't made a promise I couldn't keep.

His mouth turned up in a wide, satisfied grin. "Then I guess this isn't goodbye. Not yet, at least."

"Not yet," I said, wishing my mind wasn't so wrapped up with sentimental longings that I could come up with something more creative to say instead of repeating his words verbatim.

I glanced over his shoulder, spotting Bethany on her way back with two soft drinks. She wore a puzzled, somewhat disturbed look on her face.

"I guess I should be going," I said, nodding my head in her direction.

"Right. So I'll see you soon," he said with an amiable wave.

"Soon," I replied lamely and turned on my heels, putting a good distance between us before Bethany returned.

I glanced over my shoulder, hoping for one last glimpse of him. But he didn't look up, already engrossed in conversation with Bethany.

It's okay to let him go. It's better this way. You got what you needed…a reason to fight. I just wished it wasn't so hard to convince my heart. I wiped a stray tear from my cheek, focusing once more on my upcoming task. Creating a handful of white fire, I let the white flames consume me and transport me back to the reality I must face.

CHAPTER THIRTEEN

Nine days until Aether's predicted arrival

Early the next morning I found the other Elementals in the clearing. I was relieved to see Brandr had returned on his own, despite my absence. I also noticed another bluish Essence next to him. And it didn't look at all like Hydros.

Skye, Liam, and Gaia stood together, discussing their plans. Putting my differences with Brandr aside, I approached him, curious of the identity of this new Essence.

Brandr nodded a stiff greeting, but I couldn't take my eyes off the other Essence. Unlike Ignis, he was tall and lean, with a long, fair ponytail pulled behind his neck.

"I'm Jordan," I said, without waiting for Brandr to introduce me. I stuck out my hand.

"I know," the Essence replied with a jovial smile, and took my hand in his vaporous grip. He didn't act anything like Ignis, either.

"So is this the one you hang out with?" I asked Brandr, immediately preferring his personality to that of the irritable, introverted Ignis.

"You got it,' Brandr said, clamping his arm over the Essence's shoulder. "Jordan, I'd like you to meet my best friend, Aquous."

"Aquous?" I repeated. "Then you must be...."

"Yep. The original Water Essence. But don't worry. I'm not afraid of you. Gaia asked me to come and help her today."

I took a shameful step back. Even though I'd never seen him before this moment, I could tell my history with the Water Elementals had tarnished his image of me.

"So what's the plan?" I asked Brandr, eager to change the subject.

"Gaia's planning to create a replica of Stonehenge using massive boulders. It worked to expel Aether the last time he returned to Earth."

I scrunched my nose, confused. "If Gaia said his powers had grown, why does she think this method will work? Why doesn't she try something entirely different?"

Before Brandr could reply, Gaia turned and noticed my presence. "Well, now that we're all finally here," she said, giving me a pointed look for my tardiness, "I guess we can begin. Since we only have a short time to prepare, we will start with a method that proved effective in the past. We need to refine our skills and communication before we can tackle something of this magnitude.

"As you know, while you were enjoying your little visit to the ancient Maya in Mexico," Gaia continued, "Pele and I traveled to the structure of Stonehenge in the Salisbury plains of southern England. The original Elementals had arranged large rocks at Stonehenge to vanquish Aether to his heavenly realm. Unfortunately, Pele and I could not unlock the power of the stones on our visit, so we will attempt to rebuild it here today."

"I thought no one knew how Stonehenge was actually built," I interjected, remembering bits and pieces of the history book I'd read in Mr. Tabor's class back in Pacifica.

"Oh, there are plenty of theories, that's for sure," Gaia replied. "But you're looking at the real cause." She puffed out her chest.

"You?" I guessed, which wasn't much of a leap when she strutted around like she was the Queen of England.

"Me," she said proudly. "That's the reason no one knows exactly what Stonehenge was used for. Some say a temple to the sun, others claim it was designed to worship the moon, still others believe it served as a calendar for the early people in the area."

"It's not?" I wagered.

"Since I had constructed it, other people indeed used it for those purposes. But originally, no. It had an entirely different function. One the ancients kept hidden by shrouding the truth in secrecy." Gaia explained, "I created Stonehenge to expel Aether into the heavens. His power had grown so strong that it threatened the safety of those here on Earth."

"What do you mean?" I asked. "How could one Elemental be that powerful?"

"Unlike us, who have tangible connections with our Elements, Aether's Element is best described as the force of gravity. As his powers grew, he began to create dangerous anomalies in the gravitational field here on Earth."

I cocked one eyebrow. "Such as?"

"Variations in the tides."

I remembered the high and low tides by Auntie Lulu's house on the Big Island of Hawaii. The tide only changed a few feet at most on any given day. "So? That doesn't sound so bad."

"It is when you're talking about fifty feet or more in a period of a few hours," Gaia explained.

I nodded. She had a point. I imagined what would happen on the beaches in Pacifica with tidal swings of that magnitude. It would make Hydros's tsunami seem like a regular occurrence.

89

"Plus, he could draw the moon and other objects in the sky closer to the surface of the planet. Objects like comets and meteors could collide with the earth, resulting in the mass extinctions of millions of species. He could alter the speed of Earth's rotation, changing the length of a day on our planet. He could reverse the magnetic polarity of Earth."

"What do you mean?"

"The magnetic north would point down and the south would point up, disrupting the orientation of many migratory birds and marine mammals."

"Okay. I get it. So having him stay would've made things a bit more complicated around here. So instead, you booted him from the planet," I said, summarizing her lengthy explanation.

"We had no other choice. It was the only way we could save our planet from Aether's intense gravitational field. Aquous and Airis and I used this arrangement of rocks to banish Aether into the heavens. The circular arrangement of stones provided a platform to intensify Airis's winds. Then Aquous infused his cyclone with water and cooled it into ice, trapping him inside for his journey into space."

"What about Ignis?" I asked.

She looked uncomfortable. "He…um…wasn't around then," she said.

"Well, then shouldn't we be able to accomplish the same feat, especially with all four Elementals present?"

"Not necessarily, especially if his powers have grown far stronger. This happened very long ago."

"And…?"

"It's hard to say. Remember, he'll be back with a vengeance."

"We'll stop him," I assured her.

"I wish I had your confidence." With a heavy sigh, she announced, "It's time to begin."

90

While Aquous helped Liam understand his prior role in the construction of Stonehenge, Gaia and Skye labored alone.

"Why isn't Airis helping Skye today?" I asked Brandr as we walked off to the side. Well, I walked and Brandr kind of floated.

"Airis?" Brandr chortled. "Like that would ever happen."

I waited for him to elaborate, but he refused to say another word. Impatient, I crossed my arms over my chest.

"I noticed she conveniently omitted the part about Ignis," I muttered to Brandr.

"Which part was that?"

"The reason he wasn't around to help...because she'd *killed* him," I replied.

"And didn't bother to invite his Essence to this fiesta," Brandr added.

I sighed. "Which explains why we're doing nothing right now."

"Bingo," Brandr replied, watching idly while Gaia carved massive rectangular slabs of rock from the side of the mountain.

To expedite the process, Skye encircled the rocks with a rising current of air and helped arrange the heavy boulders into a large circle in the meadow. Next, Liam and Aquous saturated the ground to cement the rocks in place.

"No, no, no," Gaia corrected them. "I want three on that side, not two. Wait a sec, Aquous and Liam. Don't start with the water yet." Gaia's commentary seemed endless. "Ohmigod, Skye. That was brilliant, but a little too soon."

Brandr and I watched from the sidelines like benchwarmers at a varsity game. "She's a bit of a control freak," I observed.

"I'll say," Brandr agreed with a nod. "She's taken her Type-A personality to a whole new extreme this time."

I soon noticed that every time Skye paused to wait for Gaia to orient another rock, she glanced over at Brandr sheepishly, laughing lightly at his comments. At a loss for anything productive to do, I looked from Skye to Brandr and back.

"I think Skye likes you," I commented, never expecting my observation would drive Brandr to anger.

He dismissed my opinion with a simple explanation. "I can't get involved with an *Air* Elemental, okay?"

"Why not? What's wrong with Skye?"

Brandr dragged his fingers through his flaming red hair. "Forget it. You wouldn't understand."

I shrugged. "Well, maybe I would if you'd tell me."

"Just give me some time, okay?" he said, turning away.

"Time?" I laughed. "You've had plenty of time. In fact, you've had nothing but time."

Brandr stormed off without another word.

"What did I say?" I called after him, but he refused to answer.

I was tired of having them withhold information, purposefully choosing what they disclosed at precisely the right time and not a moment earlier. Why were they so compelled to shelter me from the whole truth? Did they think I couldn't handle it?

Maybe Brandr's right. What's the point of all of this after all?

The sun traveled high across the sky while I sat there alone, watching them work. By the time the sky turned a rosy red in the evening glow, Gaia looked devastated. Her replica of Stonehenge hadn't worked out as she had planned. "We've wasted an entire day and we've run out of time to start over. Now we're down to just eight remaining days."

Aquous threw one arm over Gaia's shoulders for comfort. "We did it before," he reminded her. "And we'll do it again."

She sniffled in an uncharacteristic show of defeat. "But will we be ready in time?"

CHAPTER FOURTEEN

Eight days until Aether's predicted arrival

My trip to California was supposed to help me focus on the purpose of my training. Instead, it drove my mind wild with a longing for a lifestyle I knew I couldn't have.

Trudging behind the others, I kicked a round pinecone down the path, reminding me of the times Micah's little brother, Cam, and I practiced passing the soccer ball to prepare for his upcoming game. Funny how much I wanted to return to my friends in California, but couldn't. And even though I'd mastered traveling anywhere I desired via *ke ahi kea*, or white fire, I wouldn't leave. My promise to Brandr and Liam held me back. It all seemed so pointless, really, especially after Gaia had gone out of her way to exclude me from their training exercise today. What was the point of us working together when she purposefully chose a task that didn't involve fire? Just to prove to me she was still in charge?

Questions burdening my mind, I failed to notice Liam also lagged behind Gaia and Skye until he stood right by my side. Without a word, he grabbed my hand and ducked behind the massive trunk of a towering Ponderosa pine, whose sweeping branches began dozens of feet above our heads.

My brow knitted with confusion. I opened my mouth to ask, "What is it?" But before the words could escape my lips, Liam kissed me.

My eyes grew wide with surprise. A part of me felt I should push him away, angered by his actions. Yet the other part longed to hold him, reliving the memories of our time together, before he had disclosed his identity as the new Water Elemental.

Only his lips left mine before I could react in either a positive or negative way.

Liam grinned at me, a grin I hadn't seen since before our violent clash on the beach in Hawaii. His smile widened, parting his lips and revealing all of his teeth. The twinkle that illuminated his brilliantly blue eyes quickly erased all my former hostility toward him, making me curse my impressionable heart that wielded such control over my emotions.

Speechless, one eyebrow crept up my forehead. Was the kiss a *thanks* for trusting him and joining this team of Elementals? Or a simple *thanks* for keeping my promise and coming back to him?

I didn't have a chance to ask. With a quick squeeze of my hand he scurried away, quietly trotting up the path to catch the unsuspecting Gaia and Skye.

I knew I should follow, but my legs refused to move, seeming fixed to their spot with permanence like that of the knobby tree roots beneath my feet.

Why so clandestine? Did he think he might jeopardize the dynamics of our team by getting involved with me?

Still, I couldn't help but wonder about the way Gaia intentionally positioned herself near him, or let her hand accidentally brush his when she passed. How she whispered in his ear, her lips practically grazing his cheek as she spoke in hushed tones. And how she made his face light in an endearing smile…a smile I'd previously thought he reserved for me alone.

94

The way he acted around her left me uncertain of his true intentions. Did he like me or Gaia? Sometimes I wished I could sever my ties to him completely, if only that thought didn't widen the ache in my heart.

I leaned against the rough bark of the pine, more confused than ever.

****

I expected Liam's behavior toward me to change after his surprising short kiss behind the tree, but it didn't. Around Gaia, he paid me little notice throughout dinner, barely acknowledging me or catching my eye. I decided I had to do something else... and solving the mystery hidden in the prophecy ranked first on my list.

"Maybe I should go back to Delphi," I told Brandr on the way to my tent after I'd barely touched my meal. "Maybe the Oracle can give us the information we need to stop Aether."

"Don't bother," Brandr said with a flat voice.

"But why not? Gaia already spoke of a prophecy. Maybe there's more we can learn from the Oracle to unravel this mystery."

He shook his ghostly head, giving his red flyaway hair the appearance of a muted crackling fire. "There isn't."

"I don't get it. Why are you so stubborn? Why won't you even try?"

"Because I already went to the Oracle," he said with a hint of regret. "I had the prophecy."

"*You* did? Well, that's great! So what did it say?" I exclaimed, ignoring the dismal tone in his voice. I was thrilled to make progress for a change.

"That's the problem."

My face fell. "What do you mean?" I dared. "Does this have something to do with the reason you can't like Skye?"

He didn't respond. A distant look clouded his eyes.

"Oh, Brandr. I'm sorry," I replied, realizing his intent. "Is this when you...?" I couldn't verbalize the single word that carried great despair.

"Yes." His voice was a whisper above the cool evening breeze.

"I know I asked you before, but you don't have to tell me, you know. It's too much."

"No. Gaia's right," he said. "I need to tell you more about my past." He took a deep breath before beginning his tale. "I'd bought passage aboard an old fishing boat to return to Norway."

I scrunched up my nose. Since when did an Elemental need help traveling across time or space? "Why didn't you simply use your powers to travel back home? You could've summoned fire for your transit."

He shook his head. "It wouldn't work. I don't know why. Maybe I was depressed. Maybe I was scared. It's kinda hard to realize you know nothing more about yourself than you had when you set off on a journey."

During my first visits to Pele, I'd understood so little about my powers and the history of the Elementals. If it weren't for Liam straight out telling me that he was the new Water Elemental, I probably still wouldn't have a clue.

"I had expected the Oracle's message to enlighten me about the purpose of my life," Brandr continued. "Instead, her message confused me more than ever."

"I think I know what you mean," I replied.

"Not yet you don't. But you will," he said, his tone growing dismal. "Buckle up. You're in for a wild ride." Without another word, Brandr took a step forward and fused his Essence with my body. At that precise moment, I realized he had no intention of telling me his story. Instead, he planned to have me live the experience firsthand.

CHAPTER FIFTEEN

Norway, 120 B.C.

When I opened my eyes, I stood upon an old fishing boat, rocking back and forth amidst the choppy seas, sending an icy spray over the sides. Men with oars battled the rough waves, making slow progress until we reached a break in the mountains. The stiff ocean breeze died the instant we entered the inlet. Under calmer conditions, we proceeded at a faster rate down the narrow channel, where steep forested slopes surrounded a stunning fjord. Thin caps of snow clung to the peaks, melting into trickling waterfalls that spilled down the mountainsides like tulle sewn into bridal veils. I gazed outward, finding comfort after a long journey in the familiar sights of home.

I leaned over the side of the boat, recognizing the mop of red flyaway hair framing a steep nose and square jaw in the water's reflection. I cocked my head sideways. Gazing back at me from the same sideways tilt, I saw a pair of deep brown eyes outlined in black and flecked with bright tints of burnt orange, vibrant and full of life. In that moment, I realized our fusion had reversed. Rather than having Brandr's Essence occupy my body, I now resided in his.

I had become Brandr.

How clever of him to reverse our roles in order for me to relive his experience. Only I couldn't tell him that. In fact, I couldn't tell him anything at all. I had no way to communicate with him whatsoever since he had immersed me in his memory.

A mild chop distorted my image of Brandr's youthful self. I glanced down the inlet, where a dense fog off the cold ocean waters mingled with the warmer air over the land, creating an opaque wall that sealed off the fjord's mouth behind us. It hovered inches above the inky water, obscuring my view of everything that lay behind us. *That was surprisingly fast, but not entirely unusual.*

Ignoring the foreboding chill that ran up my spine from the sudden change in weather, I reached inside the pocket of my cloak and pulled out a piece of parchment, spreading it flat along the wooden railing of the boat. A message written in ancient Greek letters lay before me. *Of course! The Oracle from Delphi lived in Greece.* This must be the prophecy Brandr had told me about.

Brandr's voice exited my mouth as he recited the words aloud in a low measured tone, committing the sequence to memory. "The ends must become the middle, or all will be lost."

I shook my head, puzzled by the first line. It made no sense, especially in this potentially dire situation. Why couldn't she be a little more clear and say exactly what she meant? "How can the ends become the middle?" I hoped the question would seem more obvious when spoken aloud. "The ends of what?"

I stopped abruptly as a bolt of lightning split the gray sky and struck the water with a tremendous clap.

"Thor almighty!" I heard Brandr's voice swear from my lips. My heart pounded inside my chest with fear. A surprised burst of flame accidentally erupted from my fingertips as I prepared to defend myself if necessary. My eyes scanned the coast, searching for the threat. A strange smell of burning paper filled my nostrils. I glanced downward, alarmed to see one corner of the parchment aflame.

The prophecy. My eyes widened, furious with my carelessness. Using the corner of my cloak, I smacked the paper to muffle the flames. Luckily, the message stood intact, except for one side of the parchment that remained blackened and illegible.

The wind heightened. Pea green clouds swirled ominously above the boat. Thick, impenetrable clouds bathed the mountain peaks, essentially boxing us into this small section of the fjord and obscuring the sun in a low ceiling of uniform gray. I pulled my fur lined traveling cloak tighter around me to ward off the bite of the wind, and hoped we could make it to shelter of the fishing village nestled inland before the storm. Little did I realize a bigger threat lay just ahead.

From the corner of my eye I spotted a disturbance on the water, unnaturally smooth, like a glassy footprint upon the windswept surface. The flat patch grew in size, suggesting a massive object lurked beneath its surface. I slowly turned my head, squinting through the fog for a better view.

A rounded form rose from the dark waters, as if I witnessed the birth of an island in the middle of this deep fjord. But unlike any rocky island I had seen, water spilled off the black surface, giving it a shiny, slippery appearance in the dim light.

"What is that?" I asked the seaman beside me, and pointed a finger at the growing mass.

His face froze with fear. "Hafgufa!" he declared in his native tongue, loud enough for the entire boat to hear over the roiling water of the newborn island. Others took up his frantic cry, "Monster of the sea mist!" They echoed and rowed madly away from the creature.

I recalled the tales of fishermen from my village. At the time,

I had found their stories unbelievable fables…but perhaps a hint of truth lay in them after all.

"Isn't that the…?" I began. The words caught in my tight throat. I watched in disbelief, my mouth agape.

A golden eye the size of a water well protruded from the water, its iridescent black center fixated on our vessel.

"Yes," the man exclaimed, panic rising in his voice. "It's the Kraken!"

The name conjured up Brandr's memories of fishermen's tales about a legendary monster of the deep more than fifty feet in length. It was said to crush vessels with its massive tentacles, plus swallow entire ships and all their crew inside its gaping mouth.

Goosebumps spread up my arms and the back of my neck, making my hairs stand on end. Stuffing the burnt parchment back into my cloak, I leapt onto a bench nearby and grabbed a hold of the end of one man's oar. "Let me help," I offered, hoping to put some distance between us and the behemoth rising from the inky depths.

My eyes trained on the great monster. The portion of its head visible above the surface spanned nearly half the width of the fjord. I couldn't imagine what terrors lay unseen. Bubbles frothed around its head, remnants of an underwater belch from its last meal. Then three separate waves sliced through the surface, each revealing a suction cupped arm that extended from the beast's body to our boat like a trio of thick-bodied snakes racing across the water. The tips of the three arms broke free of the wave in succession, dripping buckets of water upon us when they reached far overhead. Each wrapped around the vessel in a tight embrace.

Men screamed, dropping their oars in exchange for weapons. Brandishing swords, axes, cleavers, and anything they could find, they slashed furiously at the arms but could not penetrate the monster's tough skin. Unimpeded, the Kraken's arms lifted our boat clear out of the water, splintering floorboards in its tight grip. Loose fishing gear, supplies, and backup oars spilled over the sides. Men clung to the railings, desperate to avoid a plunge into the unforgiving, cold waters below.

"Look," one of the men cried and pointed. When I glanced over my shoulder, my eyes met the most amazing sight.

Far below, I spotted a tall, thin young man, with long blond hair pulled back in a ponytail, wearing a plain shirt, jacket, and pants cut off around his calves. Something about him looked vaguely familiar to me, but I sensed the memory of Brandr had no recollection whatsoever of this individual. With his knees slightly bent and his arms extended, he rode a standing wave in the middle of the fjord. The wave crested but never broke, keeping the rider in one spot.

"Brandr," he called.

I blinked, astonished the stranger knew my name.

"Now that I have your attention," the rider continued in a loud voice, "I believe you have something we want."

CHAPTER SIXTEEN

"I don't know what you are talking about," I shouted back over the screams of the fishermen. "I don't even know who you are." I gripped the railing fiercely when the boat shook in the monster's grasp.

"Perhaps not, but I am certain you could guess. My name is Aquous."

Judging from his ability to generate a wave in the middle of the fjord and tame the creatures of the sea, I assumed we had much in common.

"You're an Elemental," I surmised.

"I am; and like I mentioned before, you have something we need."

"Give him what he wants," shouted one man with an axe, who lunged at the monster.

"Spare us!" yelled another, who lay pinned to the bottom of the boat under the girth of the Kraken's arm.

My hand instinctively sought the parchment within the pocket of my cloak containing the prophecy.

"You can put them down now," Aquous said to the Kraken, and gave it a tap on the arm to quiet the beast. The three arms acquiesced and returned the battered boat to its original location.

"Praise be to Odin," heralded the men as the arms sunk below the surface.

The monster floated in the water nearby, waiting in case his master called upon him once more. However, I could not let down my guard. *We,* Aquous had said, meaning others stood nearby. The threat remained.

The boat gradually took on water from cracks in the compromised floorboards. Several men grabbed bailing buckets to keep the vessel afloat in the frigid waters. But I couldn't leave my spot at the railing, conflicted with emotion. The prophecy was meant to give me focus and clarify the reason for my existence as an Elemental. That served as the primary reason I had made the lengthy trip to visit the Oracle in Delphi. I'd thought the Oracle had intended the message for my ears alone. Only now, Aquous claimed otherwise. Did the incomprehensible prophecy actually concern us all?

"Hand it over and no one will get hurt," Aquous continued, and shot me a fierce look. He bent down to graze his fingers across the surface of the water. In an instant, the water froze to ice several feet thick. He clapped his hands together and the ice cleaved into thick plates.

I watched, attempting to guess his next move. Aquous clasped his hands into a strong fist, making the ice buckle and groan beneath us, lifting us twenty feet into the air. A collective cry of alarm passed about the men. I peeked over the side of the boat, to where large slabs of sea ice crushed the hull. *He doesn't plan to stop, does he?* Which meant I'd better figure out something else to counter his attack.

I reached over the side of the boat to touch the ice, heating its surface quickly, reducing his chunks of green sea ice to nothing but water. Within seconds we plopped into the safety of the liquid water, the boat relatively intact. The sides of Aquous's mouth turned down at my attempt to foil his plans.

I glanced at the faces of the men who had bravely fought off the Kraken and endured the cleaving ice pressing against the hull of the boat. The same men who now labored frantically to keep our vessel afloat and gather the supplies that had fallen overboard. Wasn't one piece of paper worth their safety?

Just as he stretched out his hand to contact the water's surface once more, a different voice—higher-pitched, but commanding in its tone—carried across the water.

"You're going about this all wrong," she said in a bossy manner. Though Brandr hadn't known her at the time, I recognized her voice in an instant.

Gaia stood alone on the far shore. Her untamed russet hair flowed freely about her. With a wave of her hand, she dredged sediments from the depths of the fjord to make a narrow land bridge that supported her weight; a feat only an Earth Elemental could achieve. From my vantage point on the boat, she appeared to walk on water, the small waves gently lapping her shoes with each step.

The men behind me gasped in surprise, but Gaia paid them little notice. Her emerald green eyes held my gaze. She extended an open palm toward me. "So let's see it," she said in a tone that left no room for disagreement.

Powerless to resist her intense gaze, I drew the parchment from my cloak and placed it in her outstretched hand. She tossed Aquous a conceited smirk to gloat in her success, and then unfolded the parchment before her.

At that moment, another young woman lightly dropped down from the sky. I assumed she was responsible for the rapid change in weather we had experienced upon entering the fjord. Her thick lips of ruby red contrasted starkly with her unblemished pale skin, ivory dress, and white fur-lined shawl. As she slowly descended, she ran her fingers through her hair, pulling her long bangs straight backward to clasp tightly at the top of her head and reveal her high hairline. Her flowing golden hair ended in fat curls that bobbed around the middle of her back. Her pale blue eyes trained on the parchment in Gaia's hand with great interest.

I stared at her in awe, captivated by her beauty and poise.

Feeling the weight of my gaze, she turned and acknowledged my presence. "What is it?" she snapped at me, quick-tempered.

"You're an Air Elemental," I stated, watching her hover over the water upon a pillow of air.

"Airis," she introduced herself. The side of her ruby lip curled up with disdain. "You must be a master of the obvious to deduce that all on your own."

I flinched at her cutting remark. How could she act so haughty and privileged when she knew nothing about me? I quickly learned her intrinsic beauty did little to diffuse her stuck-up personality.

"So what does it say, Gaia?" Airis asked, leaning over the Earth Elemental's shoulder.

Gaia flattened the paper, her mouth moving slowly as she read the Greek letters, "The ends must become the middle, or all will be lost. Five will rule four, unless...."

Gaia paused, her mouth dropping into a displeased frown when she reached the section of charred parchment. "So which one is it? Unless *there is* one? Or unless *they are* one?"

I shrugged. "Honestly, I don't know."

Gaia's eyes narrowed. "What do you mean you don't know? You're the one who heard the Oracle's prophecy!"

"And that's why I wrote it down," I explained. "So I could make sure I had every word exactly right. Which I did...until you cornered me in this fjord."

Gaia held the prophecy up in the air and aimed a long index

finger straight at my heart. "This is all your fault," she declared.

"Actually, I believe it is yours," I replied in a cool, steady voice.

Airis's nostrils flared, incensed by my accusatory—yet accurate—remark. "Give me that," she ordered, snatching the parchment from Gaia's hands. Her eyes scanned the Greek letters from left to right, her lips moving silently over each word. Then she paused. "Unless there is one," she stated, her eyes lit with revelation.

Gaia pointed at the parchment. "You can't be sure. You can clearly see that the prophecy's not complete since he burned the last section."

"But it makes perfect sense," Airis objected. "One of us is destined to prevent *him* from ruling us all."

I wasn't sure how much Brandr knew about the history of the Elementals at the time, but the way Airis spoke made perfect sense. She referred to Aether, The Fifth Elemental from the heavens, who wielded great powers over the future of humanity.

Gaia started, "Airis, I don't think...."

But Airis didn't listen. A malicious gleam consumed her pale blue eyes, clouding them in an opaque layer of white. "No time like the present," she said in a sinister tone, and then looked straight at me. Hatred filled her face, masking its prior beauty. She hovered above the water. Waves whipped wildly beneath her feet as she stirred the surface like the whir of a pair of rotating helicopter blades.

A swirling vortex blasted outward and Airis encapsulated Aquous in a bubble of air, lifting him high off the surface of the water to sever the direct connection with his Element. He pounded at the bubble's confining walls, impenetrable like thick glass. His struggle to fight back proved useless against her defenses.

Closing his eyes, he took a deep breath, focusing his energies outward. He called upon the sea below, sending a spout of water spurting upward suddenly, but it couldn't break through. He tried again, this time transforming the waterspout into daggers of ice thrust against the base of his cell. Once more, Airis's bubble deflected the icy daggers, breaking them into small shards that rained down like a blizzard upon those below.

I had to help. Summoning power from deep within my core, I shot a fireball straight at Airis. Only she contained it, preserving its heat and integrity in a second ball of air. The fire grew hotter and more intense, burning brighter than before, feeding off the reserves of oxygen contained within her bubble. I gasped in horror when she made the fiery bubble drift toward Aquous's cell and fused the two together. "Oh, God, no," I moaned, realizing my attempt to spare him from her attack would now cost him his life.

Aquous screamed as the fire raged. The heat intensified before it billowed into clouds of black smoke. I saw him cough and gag before the dark smoky mass obscured his face. "Sister!" Aquous cried, before the air extinguished from his lungs.

Airis's lips twisted into a malicious grin and she pointed one finger at Aquous's bubble, allowing a small leak for outside air to enter. Within seconds, his bubble exploded in a powerful, deafening backdraft. Flames shot forth at tremendous speeds, the heat and smoke spilling outward with a forceful detonation.

When the clouds and flames gradually died, I saw no sign of his body. Aquous was gone.

Gaia's gaze shifted to Airis. Shock registered across her pallid face, helplessly watching her kind eliminated one by one. A single choice remained: she could either retreat or suffer a similar fate. Without a word, she sprinted down her land bridge to the safety of the shore at top speed. Airis didn't notice, too consumed in her quest to annihilate Aquous.

Nearing the mountainside, Gaia raised one hand toward the

steep slopes, causing a landslide. I heard a thunderous sound when the cliffs broke apart and showered her with cascading rocks, obscuring her form in a cloud of smoke.

Airis snarled, realizing too late that Gaia had escaped beyond her reach. She whipped her head around, ready to unleash her fury on me.

I swallowed hard, cursing myself for dwelling on the answers of a doomed prophecy to the point I had lost control over the full extent of my powers. Would the fear that coursed through my veins now serve as enough of a catalyst to protect myself from Airis's attack?

With Aquous destroyed, the waiting Kraken issued a pitiable noise…his version of a mournful wail. He sunk back into the dark waters, spinning as he traveled downward. The vacancy left in his wake sucked everything with it, creating a huge whirlpool in the middle of the fjord. The men dropped their bailing buckets and scrambled to pick up their oars. With massive strokes into the water, they fought to oust the sinking ship from the monster's eddy, without success. The whirlpool swirled faster and faster, consuming everything in its grasp.

Unable to withstand the gyre's mounting power, the boat split apart, spilling all its passengers into the glacial-fed water, including myself. I splashed at the surface like a dog treading water, desperate to stay above the current that dragged me toward the Kraken's lair. Everything happened so fast in the churning water. I had no time to consider revving up my internal thermometer to combat the frigid cold when panic set in, making me hungry for my next breath.

One by one, the screams of the men fell silent. Nearby, I saw several bodies limply floating in the water. All of a sudden, I felt very isolated and alone. My head alternately submerged and exposed to the air, I choked on mouthfuls of the salty sea, struggling with desperation to not inhale it. I willed myself to escape; however, I couldn't conjure up fire while immersed in the icy water. I gasped for a breath to no avail. Before my head sunk for the final time, I caught a sight of the safety of my village lying just outside my reach.

I clawed at the cold waters above me, but could no longer touch air with my fingertips. Soon, I grew intolerant of the pain that blossomed in my chest…my lungs or heart failing, or perhaps both in succession. Water filled my ears, compromising my sense of which way was up and which down.

My body grew numb and unresponsive, and I prayed death would come quickly to spare me this suffering. Water closed in on me like a suffocating wall. And then I felt nothing.

Nothing at all.

CHAPTER SEVENTEEN

Northwest Wyoming, Present Day

"How ironic that we had been granted immortality within the realm of our own Elements, yet found ourselves in the wrong place at the wrong time," Brandr pined. "Had our places been reversed, Aquous and I would've survived. Instead, we unintentionally caused each other's death. From that moment on, I knew I could never trust an Air Elemental."

"But I don't get it. How could she do that to her own brother?" I asked Brandr.

"He was her brother in the sense they were all original Elementals, but not of the same flesh and blood like Hydros and Liam. Airis and Aquous did share a connection, only it wasn't deep enough to override her thirst for greater power, a thirst I learned led to Airis's demise soon thereafter. That's how you found Skye in Bora Bora."

I nodded. "Sad, but okay. I can see that in people. I used to think Gaia felt the same way."

"She doesn't, just so you know."

"Yeah, yeah. You and Liam keep saying that," I said, eager to change the subject. Talking about Gaia only made me think of

110

how much she liked Liam and how close I thought I was to losing him because of her. "I've got another question for you."

Brandr leaned back on his elbows. "Shoot."

"Why did Aquous disappear when he died? I mean, Hydros's body was still visible even when she was dying. I remember being so close to death when the rod from Skye's tornado impaled me outside of San Francisco, but my body was still there. Hurt, but there. And...." My voice trailed off, afraid to upset Brandr by describing his drowning.

"And?" he prompted.

"Well...." I swallowed nervously. "With you, your body remained even after your Essence had left." I glanced at Brandr to gauge his reaction. His facial expression barely changed. "I guess what I want to know is what happened to Aquous's body after Airis's backdraft. Why was there no sign of him at all?"

"I see what you're asking," Brandr said, running his fingers through his wispy hair. He took a deep breath before proceeding. "Sometimes, an Elemental may be hit with an extremely powerful blast of an Element outside of their own. In these cases, the Elemental's body will instantly separate into small particles of their Element and remain suspended there, surrounding the Essence like a protective sheath. It didn't happen to me, since I couldn't breathe. But for Aquous, his body broke up into millions of molecules of water."

"Which the fire from the backdraft instantly vaporized," I finished for him.

"Exactly. His water molecules protected his Essence at first, but the conditions weren't conducive to allowing him to reform. So his Elemental body died and his Essence lived on."

"Pele told me that Aether could destroy an Essence. What happens then?"

Brandr shook his head sadly. "Nothing. They are simply no

more."

My eyes grew wide. As much as Brandr irritated me like an unbearable older brother, he and I had been through a lot together. I couldn't imagine losing him. "That's not going to happen to you," I told him confidently. "Everything will be okay. We'll all make it through this together. I promise."

"We'll see," he replied in a melancholy tone.

"You'll be fine. I know it," I reassured him.

He forced a smile. "I hope you're right."

I searched my brain for something to change the subject. Or cheer him up. Or both. I went back to the start of his memory, riding on the boat at the entrance to the fjord.

"You have great eyes," I told him.

Brandr scoffed. "Don't you mean, 'had'?"

"No, I'm serious. I couldn't stop staring at them in your reflection in the water. They were so bright, so bold, so... *captivating*."

"Oh, shut up," he muttered. Still, I noticed a slight change of hue in his ghostly cheeks. At least I got his mind off Aether for a moment.

I let more pieces of this puzzle fall into place. "It was a mistake, wasn't it?" I wagered. "Losing you and Aquous at the same time."

"Airis didn't think so, but you could tell Gaia didn't agree with her decision."

"So that's why Gaia had to convert Hydros and me at the same time?"

"You got it." He sat quietly for a moment before continuing. "Now I bet you can understand why I can never like an Air Elemental."

"But Skye's nothing like Airis," I protested in her defense. "If you could just see past her Element—"

"Enough already," he said, his patience drawing thin. "Why don't you let it go, Jordan?"

"Fine. Whatever." I pouted. "I just meant—"

"Don't you think we have enough to deal with already without trying to match me up?" he complained.

"I was just trying to help. I thought it would give you something worth fighting for."

"I already had that," he said, and crossed his arms over his chest. "Thanks for noticing."

I furrowed my brow. "What do you mean?"

"You, Jordan. You." He shook his head, like having a conversation with someone as obtuse as a brick wall. "Aside from Aquous, you're the best friend I have. You gave me something no one else could…the chance to feel alive again. Sure, I had to deal with your head full of unresolved issues—"

I rolled my eyes at his backhanded compliment.

"…but it was worth it, just to have the chance to *feel* life."

"Brandr, I didn't mean—"

"No, I'm serious, Jordan. I've got plenty on my plate right now. Maybe you can let your heart reign supreme over your senses, but I've got other things to focus on. Aether'll be here in about a week, and if we're not prepared, none of us will survive this." And without another word, he left, his Essence drifting away like a pale orange ghost into the darkness of night.

That last sentence hung in my head with astonishing clarity. Brandr was right. Regardless of my disappointment with how things had turned out with Liam, or my frustration with Gaia's interest in him, none of that mattered now. There would be no future with Liam—no future at all—if we didn't work as a team to defeat Aether.

I crawled into my tent and pulled my sleeping bag up to my shoulders. I knew I should get some rest at this late hour to prepare for tomorrow's training. Still, my mind raced with questions, making sleep impossible. Why did Airis intentionally destroy her fellow Elementals, including her brother Aquous? Where was she now? I mean, I knew she wasn't an Elemental — that much was obvious since Skye had taken her place. If she were powerful enough to destroy two Elementals, then how did she die? Plus, Airis's Essence must be strong, like Brandr's. Would she be willing to help?

Rolling over on my side, I closed my eyes and willed myself to figure things out in the morning. Only the second my lids shut, I felt caught in a vicious whirlpool. Its swirling current dragged me downward into the depths of the fjord. I sputtered and coughed when the water entered my lungs in place of air. A great pain seized my heart until I felt no sensation whatsoever.

I flew out of my sleeping bag, adrenaline pumping through my veins as I struggled to settle my racing heart. Would my own death be similar when confronting a powerful foe? And how would it feel to be an Essence, destined to wander the Earth forever in a sort of half-living state?

Regardless of my fears, one certainty existed clear in my mind: I had to find Airis, the Air Essence. If she had proven that dangerous in her early Elemental form, I suspected her powers had grown since then. Meaning...I needed help.

There was no way Brandr would join me; reliving the harrowing pain of his death had sapped his strength. I completely understood his perspective. Even though so much time had passed, he couldn't possibly be ready to face the one who'd killed him.

I couldn't ask Skye. What if Airis tried to eliminate Skye in her quest for power?

And I wouldn't ask Gaia, for obvious reasons.

So it had to be Liam. I headed straight for his tent and

unzipped the flap. Kneeling beside his cot, I gently touched his shoulder. "Liam, wake up."

He pulled the sleeping bag up to his shoulders, covering his bare chest.

"Liam," I repeated, louder this time. "I just saw Brandr's death by the old Air Elemental, Airis."

"Yeah. So?" he replied, his speech garbled with sleep.

"I think Airis is the answer we've been searching for. The key to revealing the prophecy's full meaning!"

I lightly shook his shoulder to rouse him. He brushed my hand away like a pesky fly.

"Liam," I hissed, shaking his shoulder with greater force. "I need you to come with me."

"Huh?"

"It has to be you. I'm afraid to go by myself after seeing what Airis is capable of. Brandr won't come, and it isn't safe for Skye. And you know I can't ask Gaia. So it has to be you."

This time Liam didn't answer. Instead, his heavy breathing told me he'd drifted back to sleep in the short time it had taken me to explain.

"Ugh," I muttered, rolling my eyes. What could I do to jolt him awake? Then I remembered Pele's training. I waved my hands across the floor to warm the air beneath his cot, making it less dense like I'd done to enable myself to walk on air. With great concentration, the mattress eventually rose off the cot with the dozing Liam upon it. I snickered as he turned onto his belly, never suspecting a thing. He hovered a few feet above the cot when I stopped applying heat and let Liam's mattress drop suddenly upon the metal frame.

His face frozen in a startled expression, he flew up in bed and tossed his covers into a heap on the floor.

I wrapped my arms around my belly, hoping to stifle my

chuckle. It came out as a laughing snort instead.

"Geesh, Jordan. I was up already, okay?"

"Sure you were," I said, my voice still choked with tears of hilarity. "Get dressed. I need your help." I threw him an old shirt from off the floor and crawled back outside.

A minute later Liam joined me, his hair rumpled on one side. He rubbed the sleep from his eyes. "So where are we going?" he asked with a huge yawn.

"To get some answers." I took his hand and led him away from our camp, careful not to wake Gaia or Skye.

CHAPTER EIGHTEEN

"Do you know where she is?" Liam asked after I explained the purpose of our journey.

I closed my eyes, detecting her presence. I felt her Essence existing on an isolated volcanic island lying dormant in the South Pacific.

"Yes," I said with certainty.

We joined hands to ensure we ended up in the same location. White fire consumed my body and a wave of water flooded his, sending us spiraling off to a verdant island under the brightest of blue skies, nearly half a world away.

Easter Island, Present Day

We landed at the base of a sloping volcano. The entire place looked deserted, except for a lone figure in the distance.

"That's her," I told Liam, recognizing the golden hair from afar.

Airis looked straight at me the second I spoke, like she recognized my voice even though we had never met. Eager to greet us, she approached, her ghostly form growing more distinct with each step. My instinct was to run, remembering the devastation she had caused in the Norwegian fjord only moments before she killed Brandr. But I stood my ground, slipping my hand inside Liam's for support.

Her appearance captivated me, an aura of unspeakable strength fueling her raw beauty despite the fact that her form lacked the permanence of her former Elemental self. Airis wore a low-cut sleeveless dress of pure ivory that hugged her hips and flared at her ankles. The material sparkled like diamond dust with every movement in the bright sun. She had tied a scarlet red sash around her waist. Her broad shoulders were pulled backward with confidence as she treaded barefoot across the ground, unaffected by the short, coarse grasses and chunks of rough volcanic rocks that covered the landscape. Her long golden hair flowed freely behind her, dancing in the wind. Her ice blue eyes and ruby red lips never left our faces.

However, I noticed one remarkable difference between Brandr's memory of Airis from years ago and the Essence that stood before us now. Symmetrical tattoos decorated the middle of her chest in a faded blend of navy and green, typical in Polynesia. Her tattoos spread into a pair of lines that ran along the inside of each of her arms and touched a circular design on her palms. With each lengthy stride, I noticed the high slit in her dress revealed one ashen leg, where another pair of straight tattooed lines stretched down her thigh and ended in a similar circle upon the top of each foot. I stared at the intricate details marked across her chest, trying to decipher their meanings, when she stopped in front of us. Her Essence towered an imposing foot and a half above my head.

"Well, well, well. So Lir and Pyr have come to visit me." Her clear, crisp voice sliced through the breeze off the sea. "It's about time."

I gave Liam a sideways glance. He shrugged his shoulders

back at me. "You know who we are?" I asked, surprised to hear her utter our Elemental names.

"I knew you would come," she replied, a surety in her tone.

"Really? But how?" I hadn't expected her to catch me off guard so soon into our visit.

"The threat is near and you need some help. Naturally, you sought my aid."

"So you are willing to help us fight Aether?" Liam wagered.

A seductive smile snaked its way across her lips. "Everything will come in time, my dear," she said, tracing her long index finger across his jawbone. Her tongue licked her ruby lips before she continued. "But first, you must understand what you are up against."

Though Liam seemed unmoved by her advances, I squeezed his hand possessively. Airis's eyes caught my reaction and a pleased look registered upon her face. "Walk with me," she suggested, in a tone that sounded more like an order than an invitation.

Warily, I released Liam's hand and followed, prepared to defend myself if necessary. Airis didn't glance back at us, unthreatened by our presence. "So Brandr told you of our last encounter, did he not?" she began.

"He did." Blood boiled in my veins from her offhanded mention of his painful death...plus her complete disregard of Aquous's unintended demise at her hands.

"Um, hmm," she said in a casual way. "And did he mention the prophecy?"

"Not entirely," I admitted, settling my anger in hopes of hearing her side of the story.

"I see." She took a deep breath before continuing. "I assume you both know the Oracle in Delphi was renowned for her accuracy in prophesizing the destiny of certain individuals. So Brandr visited her to better understand his own fate. Unfortunately, his unwillingness to share his newfound knowledge ended in his downfall. But it provided the impetus I needed to better understand my powers."

I bit my lip, struggling to temper my emotions at her callous remark.

Liam shot me a warning look. "So how did *you* interpret the prophecy?" he asked, as if eager to distract me from dwelling on Brandr's death.

"In the most logical way, of course. Why, if Aether's powers could grow so great that he alone could threaten our livelihoods, then surely one of us could augment our own powers to defeat him single-handedly."

"And you thought you should be the one chosen to accomplish this task," I figured. The job seemed perfectly suited to her vain and arrogant personality.

"What other choice did I have?" she declared in an innocent tone. "Gaia refused, and Brandr and Aquous had proven no match. Of course, I accepted the challenge."

Had proven no match. Her words burned in my head. No wonder Brandr despised her. I was beginning to feel the same way already.

"So how did you accomplish that?" Liam inquired, interrupting my thoughts and returning my attention to our current mission.

She spun around to face us, her lips widening into a soft grin. Funny how his presence calmed her, while mine seemed to put her on the defensive.

"Alchemy provided the answers to my search," she replied to Liam.

I pinched my eyebrows together. "Alchemy? What's that?"

"Think of it like an early form of the study of chemistry.

120

Alchemists sought to transform metals into gold in a search for unlimited wealth. More importantly, they searched to find an elixir to prolong one's life."

I remembered Pele's explanation of the history of the Four Elementals, and how each of us had our lives prolonged indefinitely within the realm of our Element. But outside of that realm, our fate was the same as all other mortals. "How did it work out?" I wondered aloud.

Airis laughed in a regretful way. "I should think my existence as an Essence answers that question for you."

I blushed. Of course the life prolonging elixir had failed, otherwise she would still persist as the Air Elemental. A part of me wondered why she hadn't sought out the Atlanteans's secret Fountain of Youth, since they had achieved success in prolonging their lives. I figured there was no point in mentioning it now; it might provoke her anger to learn others had achieved that which she so dearly coveted.

"I was close, so very close," she continued, unfazed by my statement. "You see, the Octogram I have tattooed across my chest was meant to intensify the power of my Elemental body."

I stared at her eight-pointed star tattoo, like a perfect square overlapping a diamond of equal size.

"By taking in my own energy here," she said, pointing to a double semicircle at the top of the Octogram, "I can insert the energy back into my body." Next, she pointed to a similar shape with a needle-like point that pierced a circle at the base of the Octogram. The needle appeared to aim directly at her core. "Then these symbols in the middle can distribute my energy outward to the rest of the body."

"Almost like a battery cell powering an electrical circuit," Liam mused. I figured he'd made that connection from his time working with Marvin and Gerard at Lipoa's Hardware Store back in Hilo.

"Precisely. The current then travels down my arms and legs to my palms and feet, so I can concentrate my energy in these areas, amplifying the power of each blast."

"Without draining your power supply," Liam finished for her.

A sly smile coiled around her lips. "I like how you think."

"So what happened?" I asked, cautious of the attention she poured on Liam.

"It didn't work as planned. The power grew too great for my body, and you can imagine what happened as a result." Airis waved a pale hand across the translucent form of her Essence. "But I'm close to finding the answer to revert my powers and return to my original form."

"Is that even possible?" Liam and I exchanged nervous glances. From what Pele had said, only one Elemental could exist for each Element. Would her plan aim to destroy Skye so she could take over her position as the only Air Elemental once more?

Airis nodded. "I am confident it is possible to achieve my goal. That's the reason I came here to Easter Island. And the reason I'm glad you visited, so I can share my revelations with you."

"What's so special about Easter Island?" Liam wondered.

She slipped one arm over his shoulder. "Walk a bit further with me and I will show you." Strolling by his side, she guided him down a worn path that wound up a hill. I followed close behind, growing more and more suspicious of her behavior toward him. She whispered to him, though I couldn't make out a single word over the wind. I felt pretty certain she had manipulated the air to mask her voice, making me more irritated with her. Why had I bothered to bring Liam anyway? I would've been better off by myself than exposing him to her advances.

When we eventually reached the top of the hillside, Airis released her arm from Liam's shoulders. Turning to face us both, she announced, "Lir and Pyr, I'd like you to meet the moai."

"Moh? Eye?" I said, confused since the three of us stood alone on the hilltop.

A knowing smile crossed her lips. She pointed her tattooed arm across the desolate landscape. Our eyes followed the path of her index finger and met the most amazing sight.

Upon a rock platform, a group of monolithic human figures stood in a long row facing inland, their eyes directed upward to the skies. A backdrop of puffy white clouds against a sky of the brightest blue distinctly outlined the behemoth silhouettes of this army of rock statues. Each massive head perched upon a sturdy torso, their arms pressed to their sides and their hands resting across their round bellies. And each was carved with similar features: a broad nose, heavy brows, and angled jawbones, making them appear like towering humanlike pawns arranged in a line for a god's game of chess.

"They're humongous," I said with a low whistle, guessing each figure stood more than twice my height, and must have weighed ten tons or more.

"What are they?" Liam asked. "And where did they come from?"

"The Rapa Nui people who lived here carved them from rock in the volcano," Airis explained as we walked toward the base of the nearest statue. "They believe the spiritual essence, or *mana*, of their ancestors magically resides inside each moai."

I glanced across the landscape, spotting the volcano miles away. "But how did they get here?" I wondered, having counted fifteen of these figures standing at attention. I found it remarkable that these people could carve enormous statues from lava rock using simple tools. But even using ropes and logs, I couldn't

123

imagine how the people transported something that heavy such a great distance without machines.

Airis gazed proudly upon the row of monoliths. "One of their legends says a woman who lived alone on the mountain ordered the moai to march about at her will."

"I take it that woman is you," Liam proposed.

I stifled a chuckle behind my cupped hand, realizing the reason their eyes cast upward, always trained on the skies...and on the vain Airis herself. Personally, it would spook me out to have so many huge faces staring at me. However, she seemed to relish the attention.

Airis gave Liam a wink before continuing her story. "They all face inland toward the people and the woman on the mountain... except for seven along the coast, who watch the seas, helping travelers find the island."

Suddenly, everything made perfect sense. Airis had used the magical spirits of the ancestors housed within those moai to notify her of our presence and our identities. "So that's how you knew we were here," I exclaimed.

The Air Essence nodded, more to Liam than to me, I noticed. "Like I said before, you came at a good time. With the moai's help, I have recently mastered the skills needed to complete my transformation and grant me access to ultimate power — the power you seek so you can destroy the Fifth Elemental when he returns."

One eyebrow rose high up my forehead. "Really? How do you do that?" A wave of relief spread through my body, knowing she understood the importance of our trip, and how we needed all the Elementals and Essences to complete our final mission.

A disturbing look clouded her icy eyes. "I thought you'd never ask," she replied in a cold, calculating voice.

CHAPTER NINETEEN

The profound relief I'd experienced just a moment before faded in an instant. As Airis gazed up to the sky, the mild breeze quickly grew into a howl, making her golden hair whip wildly and the ivory dress billow about her legs. The puffy white clouds descended upon us, turning an angry shade of gray and obscuring the sun. The previously tranquil waters turned choppy, littered with whitecaps. The balmy temperatures dropped in an instant, sending a chill up my spine. When Airis's gaze met ours once more, I shuddered at her changed appearance.

The octogram tattoo upon her chest began to glow, first from the designs inside its center, then radiating outward, like the flow of electrons through the electrical circuit Liam had described. The glowing lines extended across her chest and down her forearms, igniting the circle inside of each palm and concentrating her powers in a particular spot. They spread down her legs to the circular tattoos on the tops of her feet.

"The alchemists told me it would be simple to reverse this process and make me whole again. All I needed was a volunteer. These moai were not enough, but they serve me well. You, on the other hand...." Her voice trailed off while a malicious gleam filled her eyes.

I glanced nervously at Liam, all too late realizing her intention. She had created a small army to do her bidding. And *we* served as the catalyst to complete her transformation to her former glory as a living Elemental.

"Not a chance," he spat, his hands balling into fists at his sides.

Her glowing eyes of glacial blue narrowed. "It's not like I need you anyway. In case you haven't noticed, one of the benefits of living on an island is that I have an abundant water supply. You see, I have already learned to harness the power of the sea on my own."

To emphasize her point, she swallowed her anger, channeling her rage into her core, and then directed both tattooed palms out to the ocean. A violent gust spiraled outward from each hand, picking up dirt and debris as they raced across the land. They soon reached the sea, funneling water upward in a pair of giant waterspouts that spun like ghostly twins. The twins then split, spawning more waterspouts that circled the island, churning the water's surface into a frothy blend.

Liam mockingly shook his head. "You are sadly mistaken, Airis. You only touch the surface, not the great powers that lie beneath." And to emphasize his point, Liam snapped his fingers with ease. I saw the waves behind him swell three times their original height, cresting over as they raced toward land and crashed loudly upon the rocky shore.

"Insolent boy," she sneered as her furious eyes turned a uniform shade of ghostly white. She directed one glowing palm at Liam's chest and blasted him with a gale force wind that knocked him off his feet and sent him flying backward at an incredible speed, straight into the torso of the largest moai. He crumpled to the ground in an immobile heap.

"Liam!" I screamed. I turned on my heels and sprinted after

126

him, desperate to see if he was okay. Yet I only made it half a dozen steps before my feet left the ground, kicking freely beneath me. I glanced over my shoulder with surprise, spotting Airis's face filled with derisive laughter. With a twist of her finger, her winds encircled me and locked my arms to my sides, spinning me midair to face her.

"Everything is falling nicely into place, just as I had planned," Airis declared with a malicious cackle. "I cared nothing for the boy. My affections were simply a part of my ploy to distract you."

"Me?" I shouted over the roaring winds that swirled around me. "What do I matter to you?"

"The alchemists taught me about the concept of an undying flame. How I could use my energy from the earth to create heat for the fire, making it remain lit forever. Yet without Gaia's earthly powers, the flame didn't hold like I'd expected." Her lips turned into a pout. I had a feeling the spoiled little brat was used to getting whatever she wanted. "But now that I have you, I don't need her at all, do I? Imagine the possibilities…fire at my fingertips!"

The gray clouds swirled around us like a vortex, lifting the moai clear off their platform. Their sunken eyes glowed red, as if Airis had awakened the spirits of the deified ancestors inside. The moai rose five…ten…fifteen feet above the ground, surrounding me in tight proximity. With a nod of her head, the moai began to spin in a circle around me like a wheel on an axle, faster and faster until their lava rock forms became a continuous blur of dark gray, punctuated by a line of laser red from their glowing eyes.

Despite the deafening roar of the vicious winds, my eyes held Airis's gaze in a peaceful sort of state, transfixed by her gleaming tattoos and captivating eyes. Every ounce of my body screamed to check on Liam lying below me, yet I couldn't force myself to look down. I feared she had knocked him unconscious, perhaps worse. Still I could do nothing to aid him. Not when I found her powers impossible to resist.

"And once I become immortal in the realms of air and fire, it won't be hard to take over water and earth as well, making me virtually unstoppable. Aether won't stand a chance against me. Not once I hold all the power."

Was this her destiny? To destroy all the Elementals so she could become a supreme being? To go beyond the alchemists' initial quest of finding a life-prolonging elixir?

"But you're not a god," I protested.

She sneered at me. "Not yet."

Biting her lip, Airis directed one tattooed palm at my chest, drawing the fiery glow of my translucent Essence from my core. I watched helplessly, my limbs pinned to my sides by the tremendous pressure of her gusts. The winds pushed harder against me, compressing my chest like a boa constrictor's coils wrapped in a death hug on its unfortunate prey. I gasped for a breath, and when I did, she began to pull a translucent orange tendril from my mouth. In a way, it reminded me of Brandr with his head of flaming red hair atop his ghostly form.

And then it hit me. *That's my Essence.* The long delicate tendril drifted outward in a slow moving stream, pulled on its own wind current toward Airis's greedy fingertips. *I can't believe she's trying to kill me!* I hoped the shock of that reality would embolden me with some unforeseen powers, yet I stayed fixed in my position. Nearing asphyxiation, the energy drained from my body, pain scourged my insides as she extracted my Essence and robbed my body of its soul.

In that moment, my brain could focus on only a single thought beyond the agony I endured. Once she completed her extraction, I wouldn't remain an Elemental or an Essence. I simply wouldn't exist at all, my body an empty shell, used and forgotten. Yet unlike when she had destroyed Brandr in the fjord, I would be gone.

Forever.

"Almost there," she announced, triumphant. Her whitish eyes widened, hungry for more, even if it ended with my demise.

I watched in helpless horror as she extended one hand forward, eager to touch my orangey Essence and claim it as her own. Her translucent form seemed to grow slightly opaque, like she gained permanence at my expense.

Then I detected a faint movement below me. *He's alive!* I cheered to myself, momentarily distracted from my pain at the sight of Liam's head rolling toward the sea. With great effort, he stretched out one hand to call upon the ocean. Soon, a huge wave formed, cresting high into the sky. The massive wall of water traveled far inland to our precise location without breaking. Only the wave stopped upon contact with Airis's ceiling of ominous clouds, as if the wave had struck an impenetrable brick wall.

His action diverted her attention. "Ha! Even your boyfriend is no match for my powers," she gloated.

From the corner of my eye I peeked at Liam, my mind filled with a new dread. He still hadn't left his spot. Had she broken his back during the impact and paralyzed him from the waist down?

Things weren't supposed to end this way. I'd thought this adventure would help bring us back together, not destroy us entirely. Especially when I had so many things yet to tell him. My eyes glazed with tears, knowing I'd never get that chance now. Not with my Essence uncontrollably hanging in the air before me, on its way to Airis's clutches.

For a fraction of a second, Liam caught my gaze. The side of his mouth turned up into a knowing smirk.

My heart swam with relief. *He's okay. And better yet...he has*

129

a plan to retaliate against Airis. I braced myself, waiting for an opportunity to break free of Airis's control.

Liam turned his palm upward toward the crest of the contained wave. Suddenly, its contents rained down upon Airis in a violent onslaught of golf-ball sized hail and sheets of horizontal rain.

"Aargh!" Airis screamed as the icy pellets pummeled her body. She threw her arms over her head to serve as a temporary shelter from the barrage of hail and heavy rain. Her concentration broken, the moai immediately stopped spinning and fell. With a deep inhalation, the orange tint of my Essence returned unharmed to my body, flushing my soul with a sudden burst of energy. Free of Airis's winds, I dropped to the ground, stunned but not hurt. I brushed my sopping hair from my face to search for Liam through the driving monsoon-like storm, which made it impossible to see more than a few feet in front of me.

Desperate to reach Liam, I crawled forward, staying low against the driving hail, blinding rain, and blustery winds. Hailstones littered the ground and puddles around him, and covered his chest in a layer of white. He shivered, but didn't call off the storm.

At that very moment, I wanted to say so many things to him, like *I'm so glad you're okay* or *That hailstorm was brilliant*, and even *I love you for saving me.* I wanted to throw my arms around him and cry in relief, but I resisted. All those sentiments would have to wait, since I doubted he could hold Airis at bay much longer. His counterattack had sapped his strength to the point where he could barely open his eyes. He certainly couldn't transport himself back to his tent in Wyoming, not in his current condition. Still, I couldn't risk leaving him here another minute. Enraged for foiling her plan, Airis would certainly destroy him if given a second chance.

130

"Protect yourself," I told him, placing a gentle hand upon his pale cheek. His weary blue eyes blinked once with acknowledgement.

"*No!*" Airis bellowed. "This was supposed to be my chance to return to the life I once had." Fury flooded her face, her mouth opening into a snarl. Despite hailstones pelting her body, she unleashed a last, brutal attack, sending forth a flash of wind that tore across the land at blistering speeds, so fast it turned the moving air a ghastly shade of gray.

If Liam could transport me to Atlantis and back using water, I figured I should be able to get him out of there with my white fire. I threw my arms around Liam. "*Ke ahi kea,*" I whispered in Hawaiian. A fraction of a second before Airis's barrage reached our spot, magical white fire engulfed both of our bodies in a sudden burst of superheated flames, purposefully keeping a barrier of cooler flames around Liam's injured form, just in case. I prayed the barrier would hold and protect him from the raging temperatures.

Sneaking a nervous glance over my shoulder, I caught a glimpse of Airis's displeased countenance and the moai scattered in a disheveled heap on the hailstone-strewn land. The blinding gray winds reached our spot at the same instant we rocketed back to the safety of our camp in the mountains.

CHAPTER TWENTY

The white flames diminished and the sweet smell of towering pines greeted us upon our return. I never thought I'd miss the forest so much, lit in the pale light of the moon. Airis's attempted extraction of my Essence had left a parched, burning sensation in my throat, making me feel like I'd swallowed a dozen flaming marshmallows. Still, I had survived the attack. I could worry about the recovery later. I hoped Liam had fared as well from our escape.

I laid my head on his chest, relieved to hear his heart beat. Somehow, my protective layer of cooler flames had held, shielding him from the intense heat of my white fire so he could return to this time unharmed. "You made it," I said with a smile, and lifted my head to gaze at his wearied face.

His eyes fluttered. "Thanks for getting us out of there."

I gripped his hand in mine in a show of appreciation. "I couldn't have done it if you didn't save me first." Dark shadows hovered over us, blocking the moonlight. "Are we ever glad to see you," I told Brandr and Gaia. They glowered back at us, their faces irate.

"Where have you been?" Gaia asked with a cracked voice.

"He needs help," I ordered. "Get Hina."

132

"Oh, my God. What did you do now?" Brandr asked with reproach. Meanwhile, Gaia took one look at Liam and disappeared like grains of sand blown in the wind, eager to find help.

"We went to find Airis," I replied matter-of-factly.

His jaw dropped. Before he had a chance to question me further, Gaia returned with the Hawaiian goddess of healing, Hina. She knelt next to Liam's prone body and placed one hand on his forehead, the other on the inside of his wrist. Chanting something I didn't understand in her native tongue, a glow began to radiate from her palms like the whitish shine of the full moon. She passed her hands over the length of his body, and then looked at me with her round face. "He should make a full recovery," she announced.

"I can't thank you enough," I told Hina.

"Treasure him," she whispered to me.

I cocked my head sideways, curious of her intent. Instead of elaborating, she gave me a wink and handed me a short cord of rope. Her work completed, she drifted upward on the back of a bright moonbeam.

I didn't have time to ponder Hina's cord of rope before Brandr went off on me. I stuck the rope in my pocket as he ranted. "Why don't you tell Gaia what you told me?" He sounded an awful lot like a father preparing to lecture his rebellious teenage daughter on the importance of thinking before acting.

Gaia stood right beside him, her arms folded across her chest in her typical confrontational style. She tapped her foot impatiently upon the ground.

"We went to find Airis," I said, my voice softer than before.

"Airis?"

"The Air Essence," I explained.

"Oh, for God's sake. I know who she is." Gaia shook her head sadly, like she remembered the misery Airis had caused in

133

her life. "I never trusted her. Not after the incident in the fjord," Gaia declared.

Well, that's a first. I never thought I'd agree with Gaia on anything.

"You two shouldn't have gone there on your own. You risked everything," she said, echoing his tone.

"Then why'd you tell her to go after Airis?" Liam asked Brandr.

"Airis?" Brandr asked. "It wasn't me, bud. I wanted nothing to do with her. Where'd you get that idea?"

"Jordan. She came to find me after she was with you," Liam told him. "She said we had to find the Air Essence. And you know what happened? Jordan almost lost all her powers. She almost got herself killed."

Brandr's jaw fell open. "You what?"

"I had to know," I explained. "You hadn't told me enough. None of you had. So I had to investigate a few things on my own."

"This isn't about us," Brandr began. "Gaia's right. How could you be so foolish as to think you could take on Airis?"

"Sorry, Mom," I snipped at Brandr. "Since when did you two start agreeing on anything?"

"Since you put our mission at risk," he replied. "What were you hoping to accomplish? To get Airis on our side?"

"Yeah, maybe I was," I admitted with a hint of regret. "But that obviously didn't work."

"You think?" Gaia hissed. "You almost got both of yourselves killed. And then where would we be? Short two Elementals before Aether arrives? How could you be so careless? That was such a waste," she huffed, blowing her russet curls from her face.

"It wasn't entirely a waste," I rebuked, irritated at her haste to pin blame on me like always. "We figured out a key part of the prophecy."

One eyebrow perched high on Brandr's forehead. "Go on."

"It wasn't 'there is one.' The prophecy never meant for a single Elemental to assume full power over all the Elements. Airis proved it. She tried to master all the Elements, but failed. Don't get me wrong; she's incredibly powerful. She has tattoos that use principles of alchemy to amplify her energies and focus her strength in her core. But her attempts to become immortal in the realm of all Elements ruined her. So we now know the final line of the prophecy. Gaia was right all along. It has to be a team effort."

"Unless they are one," Brandr said, a faraway look in his eyes. I imagined him envisioning the Greek letters that spelled out this phrase, moments before the other Elementals had surrounded him in the fjord. Startled, he had accidentally burned the parchment in a careless, unintentional act that ended in so many unnecessary deaths, including his own.

"Exactly. We must work as one—both Elementals and Essences—in order to defeat him," Gaia concluded. A satisfied grin settled across her face. "There is no other option."

CHAPTER TWENTY-ONE

Seven days until Aether's predicted arrival

The next morning, I woke before sunrise at Gaia's request. After throwing on a light jacket to ward off the brisk mountain air, I reluctantly slipped out of my tent and lumbered to meet the others by the extinguished campfire. I rubbed the sleep from my eyes and stifled a huge yawn. *Think positive. Act positive. You're here for a reason*, I told myself, even though I longed to crawl back into my sleeping bag for another few hours.

"Okay," I announced, trying to hide the reservation in my voice and accept Brandr's suggestion to believe in myself. "I'm ready to begin. So what kind of training is on the agenda for today?"

"With only seven days remaining, I've decided to change our tactics. Today, *we* will stop a waterfall," Gaia replied.

I noticed the way she said "we" sounded pretty exclusive. I couldn't tell if I was reading too deeply into her tone, but it almost seemed like she didn't consider "me" a part of the "we."

Get over it, I told myself during our hike up a series of switchbacks to the base of the falls. Gaia had gone through considerable effort to track me down through different periods, and to get Liam to convince me to join the team. Why would she have done all that if she didn't want me here now?

I heard the thundering falls long before I caught sight of the churning white water roaring over the edge. The waterfall's cool mist clung to my clothes and hair. Excited to begin, Gaia ran ahead with Skye and Liam at her heels. I trudged behind, my initial optimism already as flat as my moist head of hair. I shivered slightly in the weak sun. Its early rays had just begun to slice through the towering tree trunks that framed the river's edge, illuminating the valley below.

Intent on their work, Gaia talked feverishly with Liam and Skye, making animated gestures toward the top of the falls as she detailed her plan to restrain the water. Catching up to the others, I listened in on her ideas so I'd understand my role in the activity. The process sounded impossible, but so did stopping Aether, so I guessed it made a suitable training tool. In all the time she spoke, I noticed she never mentioned my use of fire. Not once.

"Let's do this," Liam said when Gaia completed her set of instructions. He sounded like an athlete rallying his teammates before the big game.

Waiting for direction, I watched from the side of the trail while Gaia and Liam worked together to dam enormous boulders at the top, preventing the flow of water over the edge.

"Almost there," Gaia announced, pleased with their progress.

I wondered if any of them bothered to notice that Gaia hadn't included me in their exercise. Had she intentionally neglected my help, like she did when Brandr and I watched them construct their replica of Stonehenge?

The shadow of a raven passed overhead and perched in the branch of a nearby tree. The raven looked down at me, its call resembling peals of mocking laughter, *Ha, ha, ha. Ha, ha, ha.*

"Oh, shut up," I grumbled at the bird, displeased with its

reminder of my lack of contributions to the team. Frustrated, I kicked a rock off the trail, sending it airborne until it splashed into the river far below.

Liam strained under the weight of holding back tens of thousands of gallons of water. Sweat beaded across his brow, running down his cheeks in rivulets and soaking his shirt. His face reddened as he gritted his teeth and leaned into the weight, his body tilting at a forty-five degree angle. His arms locked, but then began to give.

"It's too much for him. He's gotta let go," I said, worried about the strain his body endured.

"Not yet," Gaia said with a gleam in her eyes.

"Don't worry. I'm okay, Jordan," Liam grunted through staggered breaths.

"We could try it again, and I could chill the water enough to form an ice dam behind your rock wall," Skye offered. "Then Jordan could melt it to release the water."

"No. We're good," Gaia countered, much to my displeasure. "Stick to the original plan."

Holding back the great force of water, Skye and Liam's feet slid backward in the gravel. Skye locked off against the base of the rock to anchor herself in place, but Liam had nothing to stop his movement. I watched helplessly as his feet skidded backward as he struggled to restrain the water from bursting through the barrier prematurely.

I couldn't take it anymore. "That's enough," I screamed at Gaia.

"Just a little longer. I've got this, Jordan," Liam protested through gritted teeth.

"At what cost?" I replied. Furious with Gaia, I ran behind Liam to bear some of his weight. Wrapping my arms around his back, I dug my feet into the ground and pushed with all my might. Still, it felt like a towering wall pushed back, threatening to collapse upon us.

We held that position for what seemed like forever. I glanced upward, noting only a mere trickle escaped. *Come on. What are you waiting for?* A thin misty cloud hovered at the top, evidence of the wind whisking the huge mass of water restrained high above.

Finally Gaia nodded her head, belatedly pleased at the result. "Release," she commanded in her irritatingly authoritative tone. Liam and Skye's hands simultaneously dropped to their sides as the massive wall of water gushed forward. The boulders exploded under the weight, allowing the water to rush over the side and thunder upon the rocks far below. Down below, fallen tree trunks embedded in the current tossed and turned, unable to escape the torrent. Pulses of spray shot high into the air when the water cascaded over the falls.

Liam bowled over backward, knocking me to the ground.

Skye stood at the top of the waterfall, using her stiff wind to help restrain the water's path. She added her artistic touch with stilling the air, allowing a magnificent double rainbow to appear in the spray. She didn't seem as drained as Liam, confirming my belief that he had done most of the work.

Meanwhile Liam panted, gasping for breath as his exhausted limbs quaked, his muscles depleted of all reserves. I wrapped my arms around him, willing him to recover quickly. Then I turned and glared at Gaia.

She watched the waterfall proudly, satisfied with her work. But when she turned toward me, I noticed a smug smile written upon her face. It was a test. She hadn't needed that much time to carefully place her boulders upon the ledge, had she? Instead, she was testing him to see whose side he would choose. Even though he now lay safely in my arms, he had waited for *her* signal to release the water, despite the agony he'd endured.

She had won this time. The realization made anger boil through my veins. After all Liam and I had shared, after I had forgiven him for withholding his true identity and betraying me to Gaia, I still couldn't trust him…not fully, at least. I released my arms from him and stood to leave.

"I'm no teacher, but I'd say you all earned an A-plus for effort." I applauded them, my voice laden with sarcasm. Aggravated, I sulked away from their magnificent creation, needing some space from him…from them. From everything.

CHAPTER TWENTY-TWO

I had only made it a few steps before I felt a gentle hand upon my shoulder. "So much for a break," I muttered to myself, too upset for tears.

"Jordan? Is something wrong?" Liam asked with concern.

I stopped in my tracks as my jaw gaped wide. Was he blind? Or did he actually believe Gaia's every word?

"What did I do?" he prodded when I failed to respond.

His hand slipped from my shoulder as I wheeled on him, my face flooded with frustration. "Seriously? What did you think just happened?"

Shock registered in his eyes, but he quickly defended her. "Gaia's only trying to challenge us to prepare for what's ahead."

"Not *us*," I clarified in a sharp tone. "You. She's challenging *you*. Because I didn't see anything back there that said 'team effort,' that's for sure. While you and Skye were pushed beyond your limits, Gaia purposefully took her sweet time to stack those rocks, like she wanted to prove my worthlessness. So I get it. I'm not needed. But I can't believe I was such an idiot for believing you." I let out a bitter chuckle. "You know, after our fight on the beach, I actually thought I had something to contribute. Now, I know I was wrong."

"You don't know what you're talking about," he objected.

I placed my hands on my hips. "Maybe that's because I don't feel like I know who you are anymore. I thought things were different after Mexico, with Gaia gone and all. I mean, I know you surprised me once with that quick kiss in the woods, but otherwise, I've hardly spent any time with you since we've gotten here."

Liam rolled his eyes. "It's not like it's been easy to spend any time with you when Brandr was always around."

"Well, excuuuuse me. The guy was freakin' occupying my body, thank you very much."

"See, you've spent so much time with him that you're even starting to talk like him. I can't believe how much you've changed."

I narrowed my eyes. "Don't even start. Because if there's anyone who's changed, it's definitely you. And to believe I actually thought I knew you so well...and all that time we spent together was a lie. I can't believe Gaia put you up to it, just to get me to buy into her plan. How stupid could I be?"

"Get real, Jordan. You know for a fact that I wasn't the only one hiding things. You conveniently neglected to mention that you were an Elemental, too."

"Only because I was ready to give up all of my powers for you! *I* didn't choose this life. But *you* embraced it. You even took on your Elemental name right from the start."

He shook his head. "No one chooses this life. Besides, what did you think I was going to do? Just sit there and ignore my responsibility?"

"Not when Gaia can be so convincing," I grumbled, pointing at his chest for effect.

His jaw dropped. "What's that supposed to mean?"

"You know perfectly well. You certainly didn't seem to mind

one bit when Gaia kissed your cheek. Which makes me wonder how much went on between you two before I met you."

"You should talk. You and Brandr have gotten pretty close lately."

"Eww," I squealed. "I can't believe you said that. Like I had a choice when he took over my body."

"You two are always together, even after he left your body. You couldn't have minded all that much."

"Ohmigod." I cupped my palm over my lips. Suddenly, it all made perfect sense. "I can't believe you're jealous."

He nonchalantly blew the hair from his eyes. "Jealous? Me? Oh, please."

"Let me make this perfectly clear for you: Brandr acts like an obnoxious older brother. I don't like him...not like that, at least."

He nodded, accepting my answer in silence.

"And Gaia?" I prodded, expecting him to disclose his true feelings in reciprocation.

He let out a low sigh. "It's complicated."

My mouth fell open. "That's all you can say? That 'it's complicated'? All this time, I thought you actually liked me. But now the truth comes out; it was only an act."

His face wore a wounded expression. "Is that what you really think? That I faked my feelings for you?"

"Actually, yes. Why else would you have let me find out this way?"

"Come off it, Jordan. You killed my sister! What did you think I would do...forget all about that?"

My arms dropped to my sides and my face flared red. I clenched my fists, struggling to keep my temper from flaring. I couldn't believe I'd ever thought I loved him. Because now I saw Liam for who he really was: vindictive and self-righteous.

Suddenly, I couldn't stand to look at him anymore. What

began as a minor argument had escalated into a blame session, with each of us spilling grievances that had burdened our shoulders for far too long. I whirled around, tears stinging my eyes. I really didn't know him anymore, did I?

How could I be so stupid? How many times had I told myself to guard my feelings, to avoid getting close? Every time I'd found happiness, it had ended with pain. And now, the cycle repeated itself once more.

"I hate you," I muttered, the angry words tasting bitter on my tongue. My chest heaved with pent up hostility.

"Jordan, listen." Liam reached out for my hand, as if trying to simmer my temper. "Please."

"No. I tried before, but it was a huge mistake. I can't trust you anymore. I can't trust anyone," I grumbled. I pulled my hand from his and marched away, wanting nothing to do with him anymore.

I only made it two steps before Liam pulled me into a spontaneous kiss. I pushed my arms against his chest, trying to free myself, but his arms locked around me and his lips intensely pressed against mine. Conflicted thoughts flew through my head. I struggled between my current anger and my past feelings for him. Still, he kissed me harder, attempting to vanquish all of our differences in this single act.

Gradually, something in my brain shifted, validating the effectiveness of his methods. In an instant, my anger fled, replaced with an unexpected pleasure that coursed through my body. I'd forgotten how much I longed to be close to him and how I'd hungered for the touch of his lips against mine. My heart overruled the logical side of my brain, and I responded with a deep, ravenous kiss.

His familiarity invaded my senses. My fingers greedily clung to him and my mouth moved on his. I soaked in the scent of his body, the stroke of my fingers across his chest, and the sensuous taste of his kiss. I felt Liam loosen his grip around my back, allowing his hands to softly trace the contours of my body, refreshing his memory since our last contact far too long ago.

Time lost meaning as we clung to each other, like quenching a desperate thirst. Liam's hands slowly traveled up my back and through my hair, until they settled on my face. He pulled away for a moment, cupping my cheeks in his palms while he studied me with a look of silent admiration. His face read compassion, honesty, and best of all...love.

Inside my chest, my heart pounded fiercely. My ragged breath came out in fast, heavy pulses through my parted lips that yearned to reunite with him once more.

A faint smile graced his face. He looked at me intently through his amazingly bright blue eyes. The past no longer mattered. I only desired to look ahead to the future...a future that guaranteed we would remain together.

My fingers leisurely drifted toward the back of his head. I returned his smile. I closed my eyes and leaned forward, ready to bridge the gap between our lips. When I rose onto tiptoes to meet him, a cool, moist air enveloped my body, like I'd stepped inside a cloud. All of a sudden, his fingers turned icy cold on my cheeks. My eyes flew open and an alarmed gasp escaped my mouth, stunned by his rapid change. The affection I'd seen only moments before faded to jealous rage in a flash. But before I could react, his frigid fingers wrapped around my throat and silenced my scream.

CHAPTER TWENTY-THREE

"Li…am," I gasped, frantically struggling to pry his fingers from my neck. I wanted to scream, *What're you doing?* But the words lodged inside my throat, my head growing light with dizziness.

A despicable sneer snaked its way across his hardened face as he lifted me off the ground. I coughed and sputtered in his iron grip while my feet kicked wildly, meeting nothing but air.

"You're…hurt…ing…me," I wheezed, imploring him to stop. When my brain turned fuzzy, I forced it back to an alert state so I could scour the clues for an explanation for his rapid transformation. Only seconds before we had shared the most amazing kiss of my life. Now uncontained fury filled his gaunt face, dictating his every action.

"Li…am…*stop*," I begged, my eyes searching his dark blue ones with desperation before spots obscured my vision. In that instant, my legs halted their flailing. I blinked, remembering the time I had seen that same wild anger on the top of Gallows Hill in Salem, moments before William Mills's blood spilled across the ground.

Though Liam's body stood before me with his clenched fingers depriving my intake of air, I realized this wasn't exactly

146

Liam. I stared back at the wickedly blue eyes, as if gazing into the past to confirm my suspicions.

"Hy...dros," I panted, certain the Essence of Liam's departed twin sister Shannon—a.k.a. the former Water Elemental, Hydros—had fused with his body to assume complete control, much like Brandr had done to mine to foil my escape. Only Brandr had occupied my body for the purpose of guaranteeing my cooperation with the team.

Whereas Hydros intended to kill me.

I suddenly understood why Pele had warned me about Hydros's bitterness in an attempt to discourage me from apologizing to Hydros's Essence. Not only did Hydros despise me for destroying her outside of San Francisco when her incoming wave swelled to enormous proportions and threatened many innocent lives. Hydros also loathed me for another reason: she knew I liked Liam.

"Please...release...me," I begged, desperate for air.

I never thought she'd listen. Her icy fingers opened and I immediately dropped to the ground. I hunched over, gasping for breath, my hands futilely stroking my throat. Unable to speak, I glanced up at Hydros, her face contorting his features into a malicious version of his former self.

Hydros aimed Liam's hands at me. Before I could react, stinging, serrated shards of ice lashed my cheeks and pierced my flesh, like thousands of needles stabbing my skin hard enough to draw blood. In that one violent act, she turned me into a human pincushion.

Think, Jordan, think. I tried to block the pain by forcing a quick burst of heat from my core to combat the sting, but I still lacked the energy to fight back.

She made Liam stomp his foot upon the ground. Crystals radiated from his sole, fanning out like a giant snowflake that quickly hardened into a thick sheet of ice. Somehow, between when I'd destroyed her in California and now, she had taught herself to summon moisture from the air itself and turn it into ice. I swallowed hard, watching her spin the ice into sharp points like daggers. I raised my arm to shield my face from her onslaught, but couldn't form a heat shield fast enough to melt the daggers before they hit. In a primordial battle of fire and ice, her frozen daggers sliced through my flesh, leaving wounds on my forearms. I winced in pain, the coppery smell of my blood hanging in the still air.

Before I could wipe the blood from my arms, Hydros showcased her newfound skills by fashioning a sharpened blade of ice, launching it straight at my heart.

This is getting way too serious. I forced heat outward in a sudden, unconscious response to protect myself from Hydros's wrath. The intense wave of heat shielded my body, melting the blade to a dull, rounded point as it neared. I watched with relief as the weapon grew smaller and smaller, yet could not penetrate my defenses.

Hydros made Liam's face drop into a scowl. She narrowed his eyes, preparing for another attack. With steadied resolve, she directed both of her palms straight at me, sending a powerful blast of ice toward the ground that breached my heat shield and encased my feet, locking them firmly in place. Before I could focus my energies outward once more, her arms rose, and with them the stream of ice, sealing my legs, then hands, then chest in an attempt to prevent any form of retaliation. The ice crackled as it restricted all movement and overpowered my heat shield, making it impossible to melt the ice faster than it crystallized around me, imprisoning me in a cone shaped cell.

"Shannon, please," I begged, crippled of my defense.

She paused, confused. "What did you call me?"

"Shannon," I continued, hoping that hearing her given name would soften her temper.

She shook her head, ridding herself of past memories. "That name means nothing to me anymore."

"Liam doesn't think so. Otherwise he wouldn't have become an Elemental to try to help you."

Still, she pressed harder, making the layers of ice build at a rapid pace until they sealed around me like a cold conical coffin. The ice crackled as it restricted all movement. My reactions slowed to a sluggish pace, preventing me from fighting back. Seconds before her ice shielded my head, I heard the most amazing sound....

Liam's voice.

"Jordan, on the count of three," he instructed. His words came out weak and stifled, but I knew it was him, nonetheless. And in that moment, I understood the battle he waged to oust her from his body and regain control of his actions. He wanted to help me. Otherwise, he couldn't have gone through that much effort to overrule his irate sister.

And that gave me new hope.

"One," he said.

I took a deep breath, channeling my energy inward to warm my core.

"Two," he continued, struggling to project his voice.

But before I heard him finish his count, crackling ice robbed my next breath. Completely encased in a freezing world, time slowed. So did my heart. Her vicious attack quickly drained my reserves as coldness seeped into my core.

I guessed by now Liam had reached my cue of "three," but I couldn't hear his confident voice, couldn't see if he'd met success in expelling her Essence from his body, and couldn't feel anything beyond the pervasive cold. I could only make out a hint

149

of a darkened form where Liam had stood.

I wondered what Brandr would tell me in this situation. I had to admit, I'd grown accustomed to hearing his criticizing comments on my every move. Things seemed strangely quiet without him, and deep down, I wished he could help me escape before this became my icy tomb.

Break free. The memory of Brandr's voice echoed in my mind. I knew he was right. No other options existed to guarantee my survival.

Time slowed.

Until I turned…frozen.

Solid.

My mind drifted from consciousness, and I quickly lost all sense of purpose for breaking out of my icy shell. A peaceful sensation enveloped me. I lost sensation in my hands and feet, but it no longer mattered. Nothing mattered, in fact. I forgot where I was and why I was there.

Until I heard a familiar noise: "*Three.*"

I gasped, uncertain if I'd imagined that word or if Liam's voice had penetrated my dome of ice.

Whatever the source, the sound of his voice snapped me back to reality, reminding me of the importance of my role in our team. Or perhaps, reminding me of my importance to him. In my heart, I'd like to think it was the latter that snapped me back to reality. I let the word repeat in my sluggish mind, over and over again until it provided enough motivation for me to channel my energy outward once more.

Three. Three. Three. It's go time, Jordan.

Radiating a spontaneous explosion of heat, I transformed my icy prison into a cryo-volcano that ejected huge masses of liquefied ice instead of molten rock. Water came down in buckets upon me and sloshed around my feet as I freed myself.

Hydros made Liam gnash his teeth to show her displeasure.

"Get out," he roared, seeking to gain control of his body. "Do it now, Jordan," he commanded.

I nodded, understanding his intent: hit her with all I had. Mopping the hair from my eyes, I focused all my force directly on her in a rush of fire and heat aimed straight for my foe. Only Hydros willfully expelled herself half a second before my fire made contact. I gasped in horror at what I'd done. Worse, I was powerless to restrain my fire once it had been set in motion.

"Liam," I screamed, but my warning came too late. The fiery blast hit Liam's chest dead center. I stared in disbelief at his body, now broken apart into about a billion water molecules. Suspended in air, the molecules preserved Liam's recognizable form, like a fuzzy, imperfect version of his former self, just like Brandr said had happened to Aquous when Airis hit him with a powerful blast outside of his Element.

"Oh my God, oh my God, oh my God," I stammered, my heart frozen with fear. "Liam...*Liam!*" I started to hyperventilate.

Liam looked back at me, blinking in stunned surprise. Then the molecules began to separate and drift apart, leaving his watery blue Essence behind.

What else had Brandr told me? I frantically tried to remember the rest of my conversation with the Fire Essence. Something about the conditions weren't right for Aquous to reform. But they could be with Liam, if I acted quickly.

"I can't believe this is happening. Hydros," I panicked. "You have to do something!"

Hydros stood there, unresponsive.

"Do something," I wailed. "He's dying."

She blinked, her body immobilized with fright.

Particles began to disperse into the air, making his form less recognizable with every passing second.

151

"You have to save him," I begged. "You're not like Airis. She killed her brother for power, but you...don't you remember how you used to be? A peasant girl by the name of Shannon, who spoke to the salmon in the river and rode the Cata monster to freedom? You're a good person...I've seen it. Which is why you need to do the right thing now and save Liam."

He slowly began to dissolve and drift away...and disappear. Soon, he would no longer exist at all.

"You have to save him," I repeated, hoping my words would register with her this time. I wanted to shake some sense into her, but she had nothing tangible for me to grasp. "Cool down the water," I told her. "Condense it. You *can* bring him back."

"But what if I don't?" she said in an unexpectedly chilling tone. "What if I can absorb his powers if I don't save him?"

"How can you say that?" I screamed, knowing precious seconds ticked away. "How can you even *think* that? This is your twin brother we're talking about! You'll be much stronger with him than on your own."

"How can you be so sure?"

"I know. I've seen it. I've even lived it. When Brandr died, Ignis didn't double his powers. Instead, they both existed as Essences. But when Brandr fuses with me, my powers swell. I'm much stronger with him than on my own. And you'll be the same, I guarantee it."

Hydros nodded, my argument sealing her decision. "Then there's no time to waste." She stretched out her hands and spun a puffy cloud around all his particles, bringing them back together. The cloud cooled and condensed until it took on the shape of Liam. Then Hydros zapped an icy blast at his shape, shocking the cloud back into a solid form.

"You did it!" I cheered, gazing upon Liam in the flesh once more.

152

Slowly, she let his body drop to the ground.

I ran to him and knelt by his side. "Liam. It's all over now. You'll be okay."

But Liam didn't respond. I placed my hand upon his arm, shocked to find it as cold as ice, and prayed he would be okay. I wouldn't let myself think beyond that, knowing I'd never forgive myself if he was worse than hurt.

I glanced up at Hydros. "What do we do?" I asked, hoping she had the answers I sought.

"It didn't work?" Hydros hissed, her face steaming with renewed rage. "You promised me, and it didn't work? This is all your fault."

I glared back at her, tears welling in my eyes. I hadn't meant to hurt him. And if I didn't convince her to save him, his body would have already vanished, leaving only his Essence behind. "Shannon, remember why you agreed to Gaia's demands in the first place…to protect your family, especially your twin brother."

Her anger faded as tears filled her eyes. She knelt beside her brother with worry, her ghostly face washed with guilt, knowing she shared my blame.

"Shannon, I hadn't realized how much you were like me," I confessed. "I was just so mad at you for taking William from me in old Salem Village…and worried you'd repeat that action against my friends in California. I had no other choice, no other way to stop you. I'm sorry. I didn't know. I had no idea that you weren't any different than me until Pele showed me your past."

The willowy form of Hydros's Essence bent over her fallen brother. "I'm sorry," she wept. "I never meant for any of this to happen. And I never, ever, wanted *you* to get hurt," she told him. "You must believe me."

Liam's inert body remained upon the ground, unable to produce a single response.

Tears streamed down my cheeks and splashed onto his face. I pressed my cheek to his cold skin so my lips could speak to him alone. "Liam, I need you," I admitted, begging for a sign of consciousness to confirm his safety. I wept in a small, broken voice, "I love you." I wrapped my arms around him and desperately wished I could reverse this cruel twist of fate.

He lay still and unresponsive.

The tears fell harder, blurring my vision. "I'm so sorry, Liam. You have to believe me. I never even had the chance to tell you that. Not once. And now it's too late." I pumped heat from my core into his cold body. Long seconds passed, every one spent praying I could alter the past.

Despite my efforts, nothing changed.

Finally, I raised my head. "I don't know what else to do," I admitted to Hydros.

She looked back at me, quietly, helplessly. Anxious, she wrung her hands, making me feel worse than before. She wasn't a monster like I'd originally thought, not when we both held Liam first in our hearts.

If only I had never lashed back at her. If only I had convinced her sooner to save him. If only I hadn't gotten mad at him before. If only I'd trusted him explicitly, then none of this would have happened.

If only….

I dropped my head again and squeezed his motionless body, refusing to lose him. All my thoughts of a future with him began to fade. I clung to our past memories, regretting my mistakes and previous anger toward him. I could've had so many other opportunities to spend with him if I hadn't dwelled on Gaia's interest in him or the secrets he hid from me. My body shook with uncontrollable grief. "I love you," I whispered to him once more, the words barely distinguishable through my sobs.

Then I felt his chest rise.

I froze, uncertain if I had imagined the action in my inconsolable state. I stopped moving, waiting for another sign, when I heard his faint breath.

I fell backward onto my hands. "Hydros," I exclaimed, "did you hear that?"

She sat up on her heels, her full attention focused on his chest.

I twisted my hair out of the way, holding it behind the nape of my neck, and hovered over his face, listening for a breath. I heaved a huge sigh when a faint exhalation brushed my cheek. "He's alive," I whispered to Hydros, my voice choked with fresh tears.

A profound sadness glazed her eyes and a faint smile graced her lips, like we'd reached a tacit agreement to set aside our differences for Liam's sake. "Thank God," she breathed, clutching his hand.

Liam's eyes fluttered open. He squinted for a moment, letting his eyes adjust to the light.

I wiped my tear-stained cheeks on the back of my hand. "You really had us worried," I told Liam with a sniffle. I couldn't erase the huge grin of relief from my face.

"Us?" Liam asked. He looked from me to Hydros and back. The corner of his lips turned up weakly.

I cupped his cheek in my palm, grateful to have his vivid blue eyes hold mine again. "I'll be right back. I'm going to get some help," I said, and stepped backward, letting Hydros share a private moment with her twin. Still, I couldn't take my eyes off him, knowing how close I had been to losing him forever. At one point, Liam's gaze left his sister to find me. And for a brief second, I saw hope in his expression. I smiled back and turned away.

Hope. *That was definitely something worth fighting for.* I ran

155

down the path to find Pele and Hina.

CHAPTER TWENTY-FOUR

I had killed Liam.

Even though Hydros had saved him and Hina deemed him completely healthy, I still couldn't free my mind of the image of him broken into particles, his washed-out Essence staring at me with a miserable look from his lifeless eyes.

After Hina had completed her assessment of his condition — *again* — we returned to camp, a trip I was grateful Liam could make on his own. Hydros protectively slipped her long, ghostly arm over her brother's shoulder while they walked. Everyone hovered around Liam, anxious to understand how and why this had happened. But I lagged behind, my mind consumed with a truth that would haunt me forever: *Liam had died because of me.*

And to think we had grown so close in such a short time leading up to that night on the beach when Gaia and Skye appeared. Now I understood the meaning behind Auntie Lulu and Liam's hushed disagreement outside my bedroom window. Lulu had expressed concern over his romantic involvement with me, worrying he might sabotage the future dynamics of our team.

I couldn't say for sure. He must have spoken to Gaia and Hydros after we'd first kissed by the reef, and they'd surely reminded him of the importance of his mission. Only he took it a step farther than they'd expected; he'd gained my love, something neither of them seemed to appreciate. Not a single bit.

True, Liam had tried to explain, but I didn't listen. I'd been too eager to tell him I'd fallen for him. Funny enough, that moment never arrived. So even to this day, he didn't know the truth behind my feelings. Worse, we'd reached a point where I might never be able to share that information with him. How could I, when we never had more than a minute alone?

I wobbled on my feet, finding it increasingly difficult to focus. I pressed my fingers to my temples, hoping to soothe the stabbing pain in my head. I'd spent far too long dwelling on the past, yet those thoughts continued to corrupt my mind. I knew I needed to forget it all; my personal desires should carry little weight so I could focus my efforts on protecting my friends back in California and guaranteeing their future. But it wasn't that easy.

Suddenly, I found it unbearably difficult to stand. My head throbbed like a large, abnormal growth was pressed against the nerve at the base of my skull. A blast of pain shot up my spine to the nape of my neck, then radiated outward, threatening to cleave my head in two. My throat grew parched and raw, making me force every swallow. My eyes burned in the stagnant, dry mountain air, wildfires raging inside each pupil. I blinked repeatedly, but couldn't soothe the burn.

Wobbling on my feet, the world whirled around me at a dizzying rate. I clutched my belly and doubled over with pain, a pitiful groan escaping my lips.

Brandr slowed down to check on me. "What's with you?" he asked, sounding uncharacteristically concerned.

I sank to my knees. "I dunno," I managed in a small voice. "I just hurt."

"Gaia said they were going to let Liam rest, but the rest of you were all supposed to meet at her tent in ten minutes," he said. Like I wanted a personal secretary.

"It doesn't matter," I grumbled, not even certain I could make it to her tent from here. "It's not like they need me anyway."

"Whatever. You know that's not true."

"It is," I protested. "They don't think of me as part of the team."

Brandr crunched his nose. "Where'd you get that harebrained idea?"

"Oh, gee. I dunno. Maybe 'cause everything they've practiced doesn't involve *fire*," I snapped.

Brandr recoiled, stunned by my harsh words. Only they weren't harsh enough to deter him from pressing the subject. "You don't seem like yourself. Did you eat something strange? Because you look like you're about to puke."

"Thank you, Captain Obvious," I said with a heavy dose of sarcasm, and realized I sounded a whole lot like Brandr with my snippy tone. I prayed for a slight breeze to cool my face. Or a stiff gust to blow Brandr away and rid me of his endless stream of questions.

"Maybe you're allergic to the pollens in the woods," he suggested.

"Just go away," I begged, trying to ignore the heaves that ravaged my stomach.

"Is it that time of the month?" he wondered aloud.

"For the love of God," I barked. "Don't you have someone else to bother?" I placed the back of my hand to my forehead. The amount of heat that spewed forth from my skin surprised me.

Brandr laughed. "Nope. Just you. That's my job," he teased.

His lighthearted mood grated on my nerves. "I'm serious. I don't want any more of your help. That's what got me here in the first place."

"So now you're blaming this all on me?"

"If the shoe fits," I muttered, clenching my eyelids shut to alleviate the infernos that raged within.

"Then, how about I get someone else to help you?" Brandr suggested.

"No," I replied with a swift shake of my head. "All I want is to be left alone."

"Fine. Have it your way," Brandr grunted, and stalked away as loudly as he could in his Essence form.

I knew I should regret snapping at Brandr. But I couldn't see past the pain that corrupted my every thought and action. I only wanted to lie down and make everything disappear: the overwhelming responsibility, the insufferable guilt, the grating jealousy, and the agonizing burn.

A slow trail of tears trickled down my hot cheeks, reminding me of how close I'd come to losing Liam. A few seconds more and I would never have had a second opportunity to look upon him, to embrace him, or to kiss him in his tangible form. He would have spent the rest of eternity drifting from place to place like Brandr and Hydros, existing in a sort of half-life stage. Not really feeling, but not really dead, either.

Unless Aether destroyed his Essence.

A jolt of reality jarred my senses. I decided at that very moment my personal desires no longer mattered. No future would exist for any of us if I continued at this rate, wrapped up in my confounding personal issues. Liam would be better off if I pushed him aside; then, I could never risk his safety again. Gaia would be happier without my competition for his heart. Plus Brandr would be relieved not to listen to more of my longings for a life I couldn't have.

I fell over beneath the sweeping branches of a Ponderosa pine. A shaded bed of dry needles blanketed the knobby roots. It wasn't exactly what I'd call comfortable, but I lacked the energy to care. Between Airis's attempt to extract my Essence, nearly dying inside Hydros's icy prison, and blasting Liam into droplets of his Element, my body and mind couldn't handle much more abuse. Unable to move from my spot, I rested my feverish head upon my folded arms and gritted my teeth to stifle the pain until I entered a fitful sleep.

CHAPTER TWENTY-FIVE

I tossed and turned in a heated battle against the demons that infiltrated my mind. From above, a thick black cloud descended upon the land, obscuring the lofty branches of the tree in impenetrable darkness. A frighteningly wicked voice spoke through the cloud, "You think you know so much, when in fact you are nothing but an ignorant, naïve child."

I couldn't distinguish his features through the blackness above, but knew his identity in an instant. *Aether.*

Trying to scramble to my feet, his strong force of gravity pinned me to the ground. "You still perceive me as a threat," I countered, sounding braver than I felt. "Otherwise why would you have come to challenge me alone?" I glanced out the corners of my eyes, searching for someone to come to my aid. I kicked myself for my previous insolent behavior toward Brandr. I'd give anything to have him fuse with me now and enhance my powers to break free of Aether's force.

The forest stood unnaturally quiet and still. I alone must counter this attack.

Calling upon all of my strength from within, I acted in the most extreme method I could imagine. I turned my palm upward and focused my power on the top of the tree, shooting it with a stream of fire that ignited the canopy.

Aether chuckled at my pathetic attempt. "Your friends will be next," he threatened.

"Not a chance." I'd promised Sully I'd return to Pacifica one more time, and I always kept my promises. Thinking fast, I looked beyond the flaming treetops and spotted a bright point of light gleaming in the distance. Directing all my strength toward that very point, I made the star swell to enormous proportions, like the expanding sun I'd envisioned back in the Visitor's Center of Meteor Crater when I imagined the death of our planet. Within seconds, the star quintupled its size, its radiant glow shifting to a brilliant red in the night sky. Out of fuel to burn, the star collapsed upon itself, its tremendous gravity sucking everything toward it in a massive stream of particles. Nothing could escape the black hole I'd created, not even light.

Desperate to anchor myself to the tree, I twisted my arms beneath the knobby roots, locking myself to the earth. Aether's massive arms stretched from his cloud in an attempt to drag me with him.

"*No!*" I screamed and thrashed madly, engulfing my body in a sudden burst of flames to ward off his attack.

He yelped and retracted his burnt palms. The intense gravitational field of the collapsing star's black hole reached outward to his very spot. In a powerful vortex, it sucked Aether away inside his dark cloud, transporting him to another time and dimension through a wormhole of space, and ridding my mind of his poisonous thoughts.

I was safe, for now at least. Panting from exertion, I cautiously unwound my arms from the shelter of the tree roots. The danger had passed…and I had survived. We had all survived.

A profound relief surged through my veins. Buoyed with confidence, I leaned backward on the soft and cushiony ground, like a mattress of air supported my weary body. Nearby, a cozy campfire crackled and its white noise soon lulled me to sleep.

I rested for only a few minutes before I was woken by Brandr's riotous laughter. "I knew it!" he cheered, and stuck his face right in front of mine.

"Go away," I told him, and rolled over on my side.

"You did it! Right on," he exclaimed over the crackling fire, and popped his head in front of mine once more.

I opened one eyelid halfway. The smell of a campfire filled my nostrils. "I know. I defeated Aether. All by myself," I said in a groggy voice, exhausted from the ordeal.

"Aether? What are you talking about?"

"He was here, like a dark cloud," I explained. "And I banished him out into distant space through a black hole."

My response made Brandr laugh louder. He doubled over in hysterics, clutching his belly. "Maybe in your wildest dreams," he hooted.

I blinked, wondering if I had imagined everything. "But it seemed so real," I said in a soft, confused voice.

"Nice try. Actually, I came to compliment you for your great show, courtesy of me, of course."

My brow furrowed. "My show?"

Brandr's looked at me proudly, his face and flyaway hair backlit by tall flames. "I knew my guilt trip would work," he boasted.

"What are you talking about?" I asked, propping myself up on my elbows on the mattress. Just then, I realized what he was talking about. I hovered nearly ten feet above the ground, resting on nothing but air. I peeked upward, shocked to find the treetop consumed in raging flames.

"Aaaahhhh!" I screamed, completely shocked. The fire licked my body and whipped through my hair. "What did you do to me?"

"Not me, sweetheart," he replied, his smile growing wider. "I mean, I will take credit for starting the process. But to be honest, this time, it was all you."

Overhead, branches creaked and cracked, succumbing to the burning flames. "You set me up?" I seethed. My eyes fueled with rage, burning like...well, like everything around me at the moment.

"Hey, babe. The methods don't matter as much as the results. This is awesome!" he exclaimed, pumping his fist with excitement.

"What do you mean, 'awesome'? The whole freakin' tree's on fire."

"You have no idea how perfect this is," Brandr explained.

"Are you telling me that I wasn't really sick?"

"Think of it more like a much-needed, perfectly-timed transformation," Brandr said. "Everyone will be so psyched. And Liam...." He hesitated, searching for the right words.

"What about him?"

"Let's just say Liam will notice a difference."

"What's that supposed to mean?"

"Your face...," Brandr began.

"Go on," I said, narrowing my eyes to prepare myself for another one of his snide remarks.

"It's glowing."

"It *glows*?" I pressed my hands to my cheeks, trying to notice a difference.

"I mean, you radiate a glow like I haven't seen before."

"Of course I'm radiating," I roared. "I'm still on fire."

"A glow of confidence, I mean," Brandr continued. "Like you're no longer concerned with the pettiness of the past."

"So now you're saying I was petty?" I shook my head,

refocusing my thoughts. "It doesn't matter. I can't like Liam anymore. It's over."

"Why?" Brandr asked, sounding like a teenage girl eager for the latest gossip. "What happened? Oh, wait! Let me guess. Now you're into hot guys like me instead?"

"Oh, shut up," I snipped, deliberately ignoring his pun. "We've got a war ahead of us, and I don't have time for distractions any more, okay?"

Brandr laughed. "Ooooh, this gets better by the minute. I think I'm gonna like hanging out with the new you."

"I hate you," I said, though I couldn't wash the wide grin from my face. "And one more thing...don't ever call me 'babe' again."

"You got it, Pyr." He laughed louder this time, visibly pleased with himself for achieving what I'd previously deemed impossible. And in his typical flamboyant show of enthusiasm, he let out a loud whoop that rang through the night air, and then held up his fist to knock my knuckles in congratulations.

For the first time in my life, that name didn't upset me. Instead, it sounded perfect. I wasn't just Jordan, the girl from my past who craved a normal existence. I was Pyr, the Elemental of Fire...my destiny.

Just then, Liam sprinted out of the path. "I heard fire and screaming and...oh, my God, Jordan! Are you okay?"

"I can't make it stop," I shouted over the noise of the fire. Strangely, my voice came out calm and strong.

"Here, let me help," he offered, and aimed his hands at me. Like a fire hose, a powerful stream of water shot forth, making the fire sizzle into a huge cloud of gray smoke. Liam doused my body then the entire tree, from its trunk to its canopy, and all the smoldering debris that coated the forest floor. With my body temperature lowered, I slowly sank back to the ground and walked away from the smoke. My hair sagged limply around me, and my wet clothes clung to my frame.

"Thanks," I said to Liam.

Despite my haggard appearance, Liam stood there speechless. He blinked, like he was seeing me for the first time. Mopping the hair from my face, I gave him a faint smile.

Brandr leaned over and whispered in my ear, "Thought you said it was over."

I nodded and took a step away from Liam, locking my emotions deep inside.

A hurt expression passed across his face. "Are you okay?" Liam asked, concerned. He reached out to me, then reconsidered and retracted his hand, appearing confused by my actions.

Sometimes if you love someone, you have to let him go. It's better this way, I reminded myself, remembering Aether's threat from my nightmare. There wouldn't be a future if we didn't win. I needed to direct all my attention toward achieving this goal, or I would never have a chance to be with Liam again. Never.

Liam gauged me with uncertainty through his deep blue eyes, trying to determine the reasoning behind my elusive behavior. "What happened?" he asked with reservation.

Before I had a chance to explain, Gaia and Skye ran up the path. "We saw the smoke! How did this happen?" Gaia shrieked. She crossed her arms over her chest and stared from the blackened, smoldering tree to Liam to my dripping face and back.

Brandr threw an arm around my shoulder like a teacher presenting his prize student. "Gaia," he said with a formal air to his tone, "I'd like you to meet Pyr."

Gaia unfolded her arms, removing her imposing barrier between us, and rested her hands on her hips instead. "Just in time," she declared. A thin smile wound its way across the Earth Elemental's face. And for the first time since I'd met her, she appeared secretly pleased. Because of me.

CHAPTER TWENTY-SIX

Six days until Aether's predicted arrival

The side of Gaia's mouth turned up in a small, satisfied grin. "We'd better get to work," she said. We'd never be friends, that much I knew for certain. However, her change in behavior after I woke as my Elemental identity, Pyr, was definitely a start in the direction of civility toward me. And I decided I'd take what I could get for the sake of the team.

"Is Pyr up to this?" Liam wondered aloud. "I mean, she just went through a pretty major experience, and might be a little wiped out to start training all over again."

"I'm fine," I blurted. I didn't need him to stand up for me. "And by the way, I may have accepted my Elemental identity, but you can still call me Jordan."

Liam's eyes cautiously flickered toward me.

"Really, I'm fine," I repeated, wishing he'd drop the subject. It would be so much easier to stop thinking about him if only he'd ignore me back.

He gave me a skeptical glance, clearly unconvinced, before looking back at Gaia. "Okay then. So what did you have in mind?" he asked.

Gaia's face lit, like she'd been rehearsing this proposal for some time. "I think we should create a supervolcano."

I covered my mouth with the back of my hand and whispered to Brandr, "What's a supervolcano?"

He whispered back, "Basically, it's a super-sized volcano that has the potential to unleash an incredible force that could cover nearly all of the continental U.S. in a layer of ash."

"Oh," I said, stunned at the idea.

Meanwhile, Gaia elaborated on everyone's role in carrying out this task, "Skye could contain the ash and carry it out of harm's way on the back of her winds. The lava that mixed with water from Liam and the earth from me would generate superheated mudflows. Pyr could heat up a massive amount of rock below the surface, then wait for my signal to release it all in a mammoth explosion."

Her plan sounded grandiose indeed, but I wanted nothing to do with it. Was this exercise worth the risk and potential loss of life? I remembered the devastation that had rained upon the vacation villas of Pompeii when she'd made Mount Vesuvius erupt.

"Bigger than Vesuvius?" I wondered aloud.

Gaia nodded. "Much," she said. A hungry gleam filled her eyes.

Regardless of what Liam thought of her, Gaia still seemed bent on destruction. What was she thinking? Was this her way of "including" me in their little sessions? Or was she gloating about her powers surpassing mine?

My eyebrows pinched tight together. "I'm confused. Aren't we trying to protect these people?"

"We won't have anyone to protect if we're not prepared," she countered.

"No. I can't," I said in a small voice. Fresh tears stung my eyes.

She placed her hands on her hips with defiance at my attempts to spoil her plan. "Well, what else do you have in mind?" she asked.

Too consumed with grief, I looked to Brandr for help. "What about a geyser?" he suggested.

I liked his idea. It could be violent, like she wanted, and hot, which required my help. And it didn't have to affect anyone outside of our small area. *It's perfect.* I flashed Brandr a wide grin.

"A geyser," Gaia repeated slowly, letting the idea take root in her mind. "Not bad, Brandr. Not bad. But let's make it a big one."

"You got it," he replied. He shot me a quick thumbs-up when Gaia wasn't looking.

We hiked a short ways from camp until we found a clearing in the woods near a trickling brook. With a sweep of her hand, Gaia covered all the vegetation with a layer of rock, like a clean canvas for her masterpiece.

"We'll need some water to boil deep underground," Brandr advised, "then add gas to the mix."

Gaia tapped her toe to the ground. I watched with amazement as a hole opened in the earth. Liam pulled water from the brook and filled the hole, and then I touched the water to quickly raise its temperature to near scalding conditions. With a twist of her finger over the hot water, Skye infused the pool with air.

We stood back to watch our bubbling, spitting, splashing creation. A pool of brilliant turquoise…but only a pool.

"It doesn't look like a geyser," Liam observed. "Aren't they supposed to spurt out water?"

"You're right. We must've missed something along the way," Gaia added.

"Forcing water through a narrow opening should in theory

shoot it higher into the air, right?" Brandr suggested.

"That makes sense to me," I said with a nod. Once again, he surprised me with his vast array of knowledge concerning our Element. Who knows, maybe I'd have learned all that too if I was an Essence as long as he was.

Gaia shaped her hands like an artist molding a lump of clay, creating a tall, narrow opening around the pool.

"But we'll need to add the heat from beneath the ground." Brandr gave me a knowing look, meaning it was time for a trip beneath the surface.

"Then here goes nothing," I muttered under my breath, and tried to recreate the conditions that Brandr had used to travel inside the Earth's crust.

"Why don't you use that sun-core thing you did to me on the beach?" Liam offered.

His comment twisted my heart in a vicious grip. I hadn't meant to hurt him when I'd fought him on the beach in Hawaii… not that bad, at least.

Closing my eyes, I turned up my core to levels exceeding anything I had accomplished on my own. Soon, I glowed bright and hot like the sun. The ground beneath my feet began to melt and I slowly sunk downward, leaving a puddle of molten rock around me.

I moved through the rock with ease in my white-hot body until I found the spot below Gaia's opening. I stared at the turquoise blue opening above me, trying to figure out how to heat the water without having to stay trapped in this spot.

From under the earth, I imagined Pele's voice echoing in my ear, "Focus, child. You can do this." I glanced over my shoulder, expecting to see her, only no one was around. No one but me.

Suddenly Brandr appeared by my side, his vaporous form barely discernible against the backdrop of rock around me.

"C'mon, Pyr. You can do this without my help this time."

He was right. I could do this. Touching my hands to the rock beneath the pool, I transferred my own heat to the rock, effectively melting it. "It should take a while to cool, right?" I asked Brandr.

"At those temperatures, yes, I would think so," he said with a satisfied smile.

He reached one hand toward me and together we drifted back to the surface. While I cooled my body's core, Gaia created a series of shallow earthquakes to open channels for the water to accumulate, and Skye pressurized it. The ground thumped when water jetted out of the narrow, cone-shaped hole, blasting two-hundred, and then three-hundred feet into the air. Its superheated contents rained upon the earth with tremendous force. Then Skye controlled the winds, directing the sulfurous steam high into the sky.

Gaia looked pleasantly surprised by the display of our unified power. Personally, I agreed with her. This geyser was *amazing*. It spewed superheated water into the air for several minutes before it began to run out of steam. Just when it seemed to exhaust its water supply, another charge of water thrust upward and began the cycle all over again. Three times in a row we watched the geyser eject its steaming contents high into the air before it coughed and sputtered, ready to rest until its water channels filled once more.

Skye turned to me, her face lit with excitement when I slapped her an enthusiastic high-five. I looked at her, and in that very moment my heart ached, reminding me of my little sister, Sarah's, unbridled joy. I couldn't bring Sarah back, but I felt like a part of my departed sibling still lived within me. And no one could ever take that away.

A wash of guilt reminded me that I hadn't congratulated Liam first. After all, a geyser was nothing without water. The guilt left instantly when I noticed Gaia had already wrapped her arms around him in a warm, admiring hug.

My memories of Sarah faded in an instant, replaced with awkward, jealous pangs. Pains I'd intended to banish forever once I became Pyr. Maybe my plan to end things wouldn't work as easily as I'd hoped.

When Gaia released him, Liam turned to me, beaming. "You nailed it!" he exclaimed. He flashed me his most amazing smile... the one that used to make my heart skip a couple of beats in a row.

Only I found it difficult to return his smile after seeing him with Gaia.

"It's just one geyser," I replied in a grumpy tone, downplaying our achievement. "It's not like it's enough to save the whole planet." Before waiting for any of them to respond, I stormed away, needing space from Gaia and Liam.

CHAPTER TWENTY-SEVEN

To celebrate our team's unified success, Gaia suggested we hold a campfire after sunset.

Brandr sat deeply engrossed in conversation with Skye, making me think he'd forgotten all about his vendetta against Air Elementals. I wanted to be happy for him, especially since I'd encouraged their blossoming relationship. Instead, his happiness gnawed away at my own, knowing I'd had something special with Liam before Gaia stepped in and messed up my life.

I considered returning to my tent to leave the uncomfortable scene altogether. Still, I stayed. Not because I was a glutton for punishment, but because I didn't trust Gaia with Liam alone.

Gaia tossed her locks of russet hair over her shoulder and scrolled through her iPod, searching for some background music. Satisfied with her selection, she set the device on the log next to her, letting it pipe its tune loud enough for us all to hear. She swayed back and forth, giving the impression that not a care burdened her soul.

Before the song fully ended, she flipped to another title. The lead vocalist sang in a melancholy tune about remembering the past. I knew the lyrics were meant to sound uplifting, but suddenly I couldn't stop fat tears from welling up in the corners

175

of my eyes. Of course I remembered…all too well. In fact, I couldn't rid my head of thoughts from the past or the love I'd lost at her hands. First my family, then my friends: Lucius in Pompeii, William in Salem Village, and my friends in Pacifica. Every time she'd ripped me away from the ones I cared for most, and left me alone in an unfamiliar land. Even now she managed to repeat my misery by stealing Liam's heart right in front of me.

I squeezed my eyes together, telling myself to disregard the words and focus on the rhythm instead. It only made the songs pulse louder through my head, repeated over and over until their lyrics drove me mad. "Block them out," I whispered to myself when the next new refrain began to play.

Had Gaia purposefully composed this playlist? I could only focus on a few select words from each song that repeated in my head, dwelling up fresh pain from the past. Everything screamed of unfairness. How I wished I could've told Sully I planned to return to school with him this fall. Or met Liam under different conditions, rather than discovering he was the twin of my enemy after I'd fallen in love with him.

"Ooh, I love this song," Skye exclaimed after Gaia changed to a different tune.

By the time Skye's favorite boy band started singing, I lost control of my emotions. The lead vocalist's words echoed my pangs of regret about the story of *my* life. Perhaps he intended this song to give him renewed hope. But for me, it washed every ounce of encouragement away.

Suddenly, I found her playful teasing with Liam impossible to ignore. The way she ran her fingers through her thick hair and let it bounce off her shoulders. Or how she laughed unnecessarily hard at his weak attempts at humor.

I shaped a fireball in my palm, envisioning myself lobbing it straight over the fire and onto Gaia's iPod to drown the annoyingly

176

romantic music and distract her from Liam. Somehow I resisted the urge, despite her single-handed attempts to sabotage my future with Liam.

There won't be a future for any of you if you don't stop Aether, I reminded myself.

Unfortunately, that thought didn't prevent my eyes from glazing over. For long minutes I sat there, staring at nothing but the flickering flames. The heat stung my teary eyes. I tried to hide the sniffle behind my hand, but my stupid nose dripped like a leaky faucet.

"Are you okay?" Brandr asked from across the fire, eyeing me with concern.

Instead of responding, I bit my lip and turned away.

Nearby, coyotes yipped in the darkness, their calls carrying loudly over the music.

Gaia's eyes grew wide. She scooted closer to Liam on the log and placed her hand on his knee for comfort. I rolled my eyes. Like she needed protection from the wild noises; she was the Earth Elemental, for God's sake. I'd never seen true fear in her emerald eyes.

For a split second Liam caught my glance and shrugged his shoulders, suggesting I had nothing to worry about. But I was tired of letting my feelings go. Things would've been so much easier if I didn't care about what he did or who he liked.

I knew I'd admitted that I was over Liam. And Liam sensed it too, puzzled by my sudden disinterest in him after I'd become Pyr. But that didn't stop a streak of jealousy from pulsing through my veins just now when Liam didn't shy away from Gaia's affections.

I purposefully crossed my arms over my chest to show my displeasure. Then I stood up and left altogether.

My face steamed as I exhaled short breaths, unable to diffuse my temper. Pain and guilt seeped into my soul, reminding me of what I wanted but couldn't have. I was angry with Pele for getting me into this mess in the first place, and infuriated with my heart for letting me get too close again. Only this time, I didn't have to worry about the three other Elementals harming him like I did with Sully or Micah. I didn't have to worry, because he was one of *them*. This time, the damage affected me alone, even if it hurt just as bad.

I wanted to run far, far away. But regardless of how far I ran, I knew I couldn't escape the painful memories I kept locked deep inside.

CHAPTER TWENTY-EIGHT

Three days until Aether's predicted arrival

We spent the next several exhausting, but successful days training as a team. Still, I felt an inexplicable emptiness inside, reminding me of a promise I had to keep. Sully had said they went to the beach every Friday night. Exactly one week had passed since I last saw him, so it had to be tonight.

After dinner, I pulled Liam aside to confide in him. "There's something I have to do."

Liam seemed puzzled. "What do you mean? We've already accomplished everything; we came together as a team. What more do you need?"

"Closure."

He gave me a sideways look. "Huh?"

"I know this is hard for you to understand, but before I met you...well...." I paused, searching for the right words to convey my thoughts. "I had some friends on the outside. And I need to see them one more time, just to keep everything in perspective."

A saddened look filled Liam's eyes.

"It's not you," I told him reassuringly. "It's got nothing to do with you."

"Funny, 'cause I can't help but think that it does."

"Believe me, it doesn't."

He gave me an unconvinced half-smile.

"It doesn't," I repeated. "This is my last chance to tell them goodbye."

Liam nodded, the half-smile disappearing from his face.

I couldn't stop to think about Liam's emotions right now; all my attention must focus on the rising threat, or there would be no future. Period. I closed my eyes to focus, training my concentration toward the bonfire on the Taco Bell beach, willing my body there. White tongues of fire danced about my palms, then grew into higher flames that licked my limbs and soon engulfed my form. Spitting, crackling, snapping flames glowed around me and stirred my hair. Then the world faded to black as I sped through the dark recesses of space, confident as much in my destination as my reasons for returning.

From inside the burning fire, I saw Sully sitting nearby on a driftwood log, scrolling through his cell phone.

"Do you have a minute?" I asked, feeling the precious second ticking away in my mind. It had to be now. No other time remained. I stepped out of flickering, crackling flames.

Sully swore loudly as he tipped backward off the driftwood log with surprise. "God, Jordan! What're you trying to do? Give me a freakin' heart attack?"

"But you invited me back," I reminded him. "You told me to come any time."

"Ever hear of advance warning?" he asked, righting himself back on his seat and tapping the spot next to him, just like I'd done on that rocky ledge overlooking the ocean. I accepted his invitation, careful to leave a noticeable space between us in case Bethany was nearby.

"Here, Cam wanted me to show you this picture he drew for

you," Sully said, sharing his phone with me while he scrolled through thumbnails of his photos. I couldn't help but notice he skimmed quickly over pictures of him and Bethany Donovan.

"How is Bethany?" I asked politely, ignoring the ache in my heart that remained from the time I'd learned he'd broken up with me to date her instead. Granted, Pele had played a considerable part in sparking their relationship to make me vulnerable to Liam's advances. Still, I'd be lying if I said his rejection didn't hurt.

"Um, yeah," Sully said, shifting his eyes uncomfortably. "About that. We kinda broke up a couple of days ago."

"I'm sorry," I automatically replied, secretly wondering if it had something to do with me. She had looked less than thrilled to see me talking to him at the bonfire on the beach. I knew I shouldn't like him, but I couldn't help myself. Sully represented a connection to the normal teen life I'd so desired. Though I had learned what type of harm might befall him for getting involved in my life, I still felt drawn to him. And drawn to normality.

A normality I couldn't have.

"I shouldn't have bothered you the last time. I only needed to remember what it was like when I was here. I'm sorry if I ruined things for you."

He shrugged. "No biggie. It would've happened sooner or later, I suppose. Anyway, it's good you came back. Micah wanted to see you. He'll be here in a minute or so."

"Micah doesn't want to see me," I objected.

Sully looked me straight in the eyes. "Actually, he does."

My mouth dropped open. That made no sense. Here I'd come back to say goodbye to Sully, my last connection to the real world I fought so desperately to protect.

"I don't think it's a good idea."

Sully's phone buzzed in his pocket. He pulled it out and read the screen in two seconds flat. "Too late. He's on his way."

"Sully," I started to object. "I don't have much time."

"It'll only take a minute. I promise." And to prove it, he replied with a short, five-letter text. I glanced at the screen, catching a glimpse of his reply that said, "Hurry," before he left that screen.

"Besides, I still have to show you that drawing, remember?" He scrolled through photos once more, but my mind dwelled on his response. Why was it so urgent for Micah to see me all of a sudden?

Sully found Cam's picture and tapped his finger once on the screen to enlarge the image. I squinted at the screen depicting little Cam's marker drawing of three people. The first two wore wings like angels. Only one major difference existed between the glorious ones that sung by heaven's gates and the individuals here…one had long black tresses that swirled like molten lava about her feet, the other shone silver like the moon. I recognized the figures in an instant from the time Pele brought Hina to his bedside at the hospital, healing the wounds Gaia had inflicted when her earthquake toppled the upper lanes of San Francisco's Bay Bridge.

But the third figure captured my attention. Cam had drawn a picture of me balancing a ball of fire in my palm; wide, caring smile, short silky black hair, cropped from his mom's haircut when I'd first arrived. He even added a warm glow around me, using whimsical strokes of orange and yellow that mingled together like dancing flames.

My eyes glazed with a fresh coating of tears.

A car pulled up into the parking lot and the door slammed shut. In the dim light I could make out the familiar contours of Micah's silver Nissan Sentra, the one that had knocked me off the road by mistake and thrown me into his life. So much had changed between us since that first day, and now I only had a few minutes to see him for the very last time.

I barely had a chance to compose myself before Micah rushed across the beach to catch me.

Sully looked from Micah to me and then back again. "I'm just gonna grab a bite to eat. Can I get you anything?" he said in a casual way, but I understood his implications.

I had to admit, I wasn't sure what to expect. Would Micah yell at me for all the destruction I'd brought to his hometown? Would he criticize my lovesick heart for not heeding the warnings and departing before the situation grew dangerous? After all, the last time I saw him he'd acted like a complete stranger, as if forgetting everything we'd been through. Unsure of his motive, I waited for Micah to make the first move.

Micah opened his mouth to speak and then shut it again, like he'd rehearsed his words countless times before, yet suddenly blanked. He looked at me, blinking, as if rethinking his next move.

"How have you been, Micah?" I said to break the awkward silence.

He took a deep breath to relax. "Not bad. And you?"

His question didn't seem to warrant a response. The kind people asked to be polite, rather than to know the actual truth. He didn't want to hear about my upcoming mission or my conversion to Pyr, or that I almost destroyed Liam's Elemental form.

And to be honest, I didn't want to share any of that with him. Instead, I held my breath as my eyes traced his features, trying to forget how attractive I'd previously found his bright, hazel eyes, or his short hair that spiked slightly in front and trailed into thin sideburns down his cheeks.

He took a step toward me and reached for my hand. I didn't

pull away.

"I'm sorry," he admitted in a soft voice.

"Sorry?" I asked, never expecting *him* to utter an apology. Wasn't I the one who should be apologizing to him for ruining our friendship, his life, his town, and almost killing his brother... all because I let my selfish heart cloud all logic and reason?

"Yeah," he replied as his shoulders slumped forward. "I'm sorry things ended up this way. It's not your fault, though. I know you were only trying to keep us safe."

I gazed at Micah, my eyes moistening with a fresh coating of tears. Ever since I woke up in the hospital, surprised to discover I'd survived my wounds, I'd thought he hated me. But now I felt a huge weight lift from my heart. He'd forgotten the near tragedy of the past and forgiven all our differences. I knew in that moment that he still cared, and that knowledge buoyed my spirits. This was exactly what I needed to affirm my belief that I made the right decision in accepting my Elemental name of Pyr and the powers it bestowed. All to protect the ones I loved, like Cam, Micah, Sully, and most of all, Liam.

I forced myself to think about the present with Liam rather than dwelling on my past crushes. I wasn't normal, would never lead a normal life. It only made sense to distance myself from Sully and Micah to allow them to move on with their lives, as hard as that might be. I never had that option with Lucius or William, since Gaia and Hydros killed them in front of me. But Sully and Micah had a chance at leading long, safe lives...so long as I didn't allow myself to be a part of it.

"You'll be great. You always are." He kissed my cheek. "Good luck," he said, a twinkle in his soft hazel eyes. Then he flashed me his most charming grin...the one he'd always reserved for Tessa, the one that twisted in a cute way on one side as it revealed his teeth. "So, I guess I'll be seeing you around," he said.

I couldn't bear to contradict him. Instead, my fingers subconsciously drifted toward my cheek, where I could still feel his kiss.

Micah gave a small wave and walked away, making me feel more alone than ever.

I wiped my eyes on the back of my sleeve as a new wave of emotions washed over me. My chest heaved as past memories flooded my mind. Not that things should've worked out for us anyway…not with him dating Tessa and me constantly on the run from the Elementals. But life had changed. Sure, he was still with Tessa, and deep in my heart, I knew I loved Liam. But a small piece of my heart still belonged to Micah and Sully, in different, inexplicable ways. I accepted the fact that I would truly miss never seeing them again, especially considering they grounded me to the normal life I'd so desperately craved.

But there was no looking back. I had accepted my role as Pyr…and must look forward from here on out.

If only it was that easy.

I wiped a stray tear from my eye. Why did goodbyes have to be so hard? *One more to go*, I reminded myself, and walked off in search of Sully.

I found him waiting alone on the side of the beach wall, purposefully away from his friends. I couldn't tell if he'd been watching me with Micah. Not that it mattered. I'd never see either of them again after tonight.

"Walk with me?" I said to him. It was more of a request than a question.

"You look a little different," he started.

"I feel a little different," I admitted.

"Are you still afraid?"

I nodded. "A little, but not like before."

"C'mon, Jordan. I know that look. Everything'll be all right.

185

I just know it."

A doubtful expression clouded my face as new hesitation choked my breath. "I hope to God you're right."

We walked in silence for a while, but I didn't mind. I needed the time to clear my head and focus on the future, even if it seemed short-lived. There were so many things I wanted to say, but refrained. Just being with him was enough for now.

"Bethany and I didn't have as much in common as I'd thought," Sully explained once we were out of earshot of his friends.

"I know what you mean," I agreed, more to myself than to Sully. "Sometimes I feel like Liam and I are polar opposites. Sometimes I'm not really sure what I saw in him in the first place."

Sully jammed his hands deep inside his jeans pockets, like he did whenever he searched for words to break the awkward silence.

I wasn't sure if he expected to hear more from me...perhaps an admission that I'd missed him during my absence? So I voiced the foremost thought in my mind. "I know you don't understand everything I've been through," I started, hoping the words would come out right. "But I wanted to thank you for always being there for me. I feel like you're the one person I can always count on. The *only* person I can count on."

The side of his mouth turned up in a satisfied, lopsided grin. Perhaps not the exact words he longed to hear, but they would suffice.

We walked together in silence, a couple of "exes" enjoying the comfortable company of each other. I let my mind wander as we strolled the beach together, the numbingly cold water bathing my feet with every incoming wave, and erasing the trail of our footprints, leaving no visible evidence of our path.

For long minutes, I listened to the rhythmic roll of the waves up the beach that punctuated the quiet. I watched several immature gulls of speckled down and their white-headed parents with bright red bills skitter along the water's edge, searching for bits of food. I remembered how I'd feared the ocean before, hesitant even to let the tip of my toe graze its surface lest Hydros detect my presence. Now I strolled across the sand without concern, knowing my biggest threat came not from the Water Elemental, but from above. If only I could decipher the remaining part of the prophecy...then I could remove that threat altogether.

The phrase replayed through my mind: *The ends must become the middle.*

Strange how this one part continued to perplex me, as if it contained the final clue to the puzzle; a clue that could guarantee our success, or doom us to failure. What did the Oracle mean? And if it was supposedly that important, why couldn't she be more direct?

The sun started to fade as we neared the end of the beach, where quaint cabins on stilts lined the water's edge. Decorated with old fishing buoys and gathered nets, residents stored battered fishing boats and beginner surfboards on their wooden decks to protect their possessions from the rising surf. I recalled the pounding tsunami Hydros had unleashed upon this town after the other Elementals had discovered my location. We possessed a common bond against a shared enemy. So much had changed in that short amount of time. I'd gone from being Jordan, who craved a normal existence, to acknowledging my roll as Pyr, the Fire Elemental. Still here I stood, next to Sully, like I'd had the opportunity to travel back in time. And gazing upon these reminders of my time in California, all of a sudden I wished things never had to change.

I wasn't ready to return to my version of normality with no more answers than I had since I arrived. I'd run out of distance to separate me from my obligations, and I felt hesitant to return, knowing my time here had ended all too soon.

Sully seemed reluctant to return, too. Rather than heading back to the party and the awkwardness of being around Bethany, he bent down and picked a smooth, flat rock from the sand. Staring out to sea, he absentmindedly lobbed it side-armed with a *skip, skip, plop* before it disappeared into the incoming surf.

He frowned at his disappointing attempt and then reached for another flat, round stone. I envied his carefree attitude, always finding a moment to play despite his concerns, like getting over Bethany while his best friend, Micah, was still with Tessa. All too often, I dwelled on the thoughts clouding my mind.

Spinning his hat backward over his short, light brown hair in his characteristic way of concentrating, Sully let the rock sail toward the surf, where it skipped across the dark water. A look of satisfaction filled his face as he plucked a third stone from the beach.

"Sometimes I think it seems easier to live in the past, but maybe it's time to move forward." He paused for a moment, letting his eyes linger on mine.

Under different circumstances, I probably would've realized he referred to the possibility of our future. Only my mind fixated on the round stone clutched in his open palm. Bold white veins spliced its flat, smooth surface of a uniform black matte color. And in that instant, I flashed back to the beach with Liam, where black lava rocks mingled with bleached white coral fragments, giving the appearance of oversized grains of pepper interspersed with salt crystals. I knew fire and water didn't mix, and yet something had drawn us together.

Sully cocked his arm backward to release the skipping stone.

"Wait!" I exclaimed, grasping his wrist before he could hurl the stone and lose it in the waves.

"What's wrong?" he asked, but I couldn't answer. Ideas zipped through my mind as I traced the smooth surface with my thumb, a circle of opposites fused into one.

"The ends must become the middle," I said aloud to myself, and dropped to my knees, setting the stone on the sand beyond the surf's reach. I removed from my pocket the cord of rope Hina had given me and placed it around the stone until the frayed ends touched, forming a perfect circle. Her words rang in my ear, *Treasure him.*

A gasp escaped my lips. I rose to my feet to study my work from a distance. *Of course! How had I neglected to notice this before?* Fire and ice might exist as polar opposites, but we had to come together to make our team become one entity. Meaning, I needed Liam...and he needed me.

We'd have to put our differences behind us; it was the only way we could defeat Aether. The Oracle had foreseen it so many ages ago, Pele surely knew, and Liam had probably even guessed the solution himself. Yet I wouldn't have believed any of them if they had told me directly. Instead, I had to discover the truth on my own.

The entire prophecy ran through my head with astonishing clarity:

The ends must become the middle,
Or all will be lost.
Five will rule four,
Unless they are one.

How had I ignored the clues? In the ancient Maya marketplace, I had watched the local children play their version of "Rock, Paper, Scissors." But it wasn't just a game, was it? The contest served as a physical reminder of the Oracle's prophecy. I held

189

my left hand flat, five fingers together like a piece of paper, and then formed my other hand into a fist, the thumb tucked neatly beneath my four fingers. *Five will rule four.* I moved my flattened hand over the fist, the five fingers shrouding the four Elementals in darkness here on Earth, spelling our doom when the threat of Aether returned from the heavens.

The fist of four might have won over the single blade like a rock could break the scissors, yet instead of shattering the scissors, the fist broke apart into four separate entities.

Unless they are one. The final line sang in my ears, confident in its wording. Airis was wrong in assuming she could concentrate her powers in a single being to defeat Aether. We had to come together, not just learning to work together as a team, but to unite our Elements as one. I changed my right fist into the single blade the Maya children used in the marketplace, my lone index finger projecting outward to slice open the flattened five fingers and win the game.

"That's it!" My face widened into a broad smile of reassurance, relieved to fully grasp the Oracle's meaning.

Watching me with bewilderment, Sully cocked an eyebrow high on his head.

I slipped the stone and section of rope into my pocket and leapt to my feet, my face lit with an exuberant grin. "Sully, you're a genius," I exclaimed, and threw my arms around him in an elated hug.

His look of confusion quickly transformed into a smile of pleasant surprise. His hands caught me and lifted me clear off the ground. He spun me around twice before setting me down lightly, the soles of my feet resting once more upon the cool sand. Yet his palms didn't leave the bare patch of skin by my waist. I slowly unwound my arms from his neck until they rested upon his shoulders, but didn't release him entirely. Confused by his expression, my smile gradually subsided.

His pale blue eyes held my gaze, our chests pressed together against the chill of the ocean breeze. At that moment, I realized I had an unmistakable connection to Sully. Why else would I find reasons to keep coming back to him?

Sully swallowed hard before daring the same question that stood foremost in my mind, "So what does this mean?"

I knew how I wanted to reply, but couldn't risk exposing him to the inherent dangers of my lifestyle again. "What do you want it to mean?" I asked.

"I...um...," Sully started.

While I waited for him to complete his thought, past feelings of longing stirred inside my body. I remembered the closeness we'd shared before: the motorcycle ride along the coast, when I'd wrapped my arms securely around his waist as we zipped over the rolling hills outside of Pacifica. The smell of his jacket wrapped around me to ward off the cold when he'd found me stranded in the storm, then asked me on our first date at the pizzeria. The night he'd brought me to his house to spare me the ridicule of wearing Micah's hand-me-downs. How he'd looked at me in a sensual way before we fell onto his bed, our lips inseparable. And how he'd said goodbye at the airport, allaying my fears of traveling to Hilo with his sweet farewell kiss.

Feeling safety and comfort in his arms, I wished this moment could last forever. Sully represented a connection to the past, a connection I'd yearned for so long, an opportunity to be like everyone else, if only for a short while.

But Sully was right: I must look ahead, must move forward. If for nothing else but to guarantee a future for him, even if it meant I'd never see him again.

"I guess this means goodbye," I whispered sadly. My eyes released his. Slowly, I slipped my arms from his shoulders and backed away, ready to depart for the last time. I didn't permit myself another glance in his direction; it would only make things harder. Besides, now I had the answer I'd searched for. Only moments before that answer had brought me profound joy and relief. So why the sudden change?

I took a deep breath, acknowledging the reason: a portion of my heart would always belong to Sully, but I could never give him more. It wasn't fair; he deserved better.

With a heavy sigh, I closed my eyes, ready to summon the white fire to return me to the team of Elementals, when I felt Sully's fingers reach for mine.

"Jordan, wait," he instructed in a soft voice. Despite my plans to avoid looking back, I paused, my feet suddenly rooted in the cool, moist sand. I closed my fingers around his and let him spin me to face him.

"When will I see you again?" he asked.

I let my eyes drop and shook my head, unable to vocalize the truth. Suddenly *never* seemed too painful a word to admit, especially after everything he'd done for me.

A lone tear slid down my cheek, missing him before I even left.

"Then how will I know you're okay?"

"Believe me, you'll know." I couldn't bear to admit what possible fate the planet might have in store if we didn't succeed in our mission.

Sully looked back at me in a way that made me think he fully understood my intentions. "So…I guess this is goodbye."

"Yeah," I admitted with regret. "I don't know what will happen, but…."

"Shhh," Sully said, silencing my apprehensions with a warm embrace. "I do. You'll be great." His hand caressed the back on my head. "Good luck," he whispered, letting his forehead touch mine.

A small smile graced my lips, but my throat choked on tears when I replied. "Thanks." It seemed too simple a word to describe the gratitude I felt for everything he'd given me since we'd met, yet I didn't trust my voice to utter another word.

Slowly releasing his grip, Sully took a step backward to let me go. I nodded, knowing the time had come and that I had his goodbye to sustain me through the mission that lay ahead. I walked a few paces away, grasping the stone and the corded rope in my palm to serve as tangible reminders of Sully. He gave a small wave as I summoned white flames to devour my form, whisking me away from the familiar sights of Pacifica.

It has to be this way, I reminded myself. But that assurance couldn't erase the pangs of loss that consumed my heart.

CHAPTER TWENTY-NINE

Two days until Aether's predicted arrival

First thing in the morning, I shared the news of my discovery with Gaia. She stared at me in silence for a long while, as if processing the idea and selecting a course of action. I expected our training to increase in intensity in the short time that remained. Instead, Gaia called us together. I plopped down on one of the logs by the dead campfire; my arms and hands were sore, my muscles fatigued from overuse. I saw lots of weary faces when I glanced around the circle of my teammates: Hydros and Aquous, Brandr and Skye, Liam and Gaia. I appreciated knowing I wasn't the only one exhausted from our rigorous training, but worried for the sake of everyone else if we couldn't pull off our mission.

"I'd like to thank you all for the hard work and effort you put into our training," Gaia began.

I scrunched up my nose. Since when was she so formal and appreciative of anyone?

"And thanks for meeting today," the Earth Elemental continued. "You've probably figured this out," she said, pointing up at the sky. A foreboding line of thick black clouds spiraled overhead, obscuring the midday sun. What little light that filtered through cast an eerie greenish glow. "We don't have much time left."

I noticed she conveniently omitted the part about the Maya priest's prediction Aether would arrive on the tenth day. None of us could forget that. None of us lost track of time. Even without looking at the sky, we knew as well as she did that Aether would be here very, very soon.

Liam perched on the edge of the log with anticipation. "Do you think we should attack him when he least expects it?" he suggested.

Gaia contemplated his suggestion for a minute and then shook her head. "No. We'll be better off fighting him from here, where we're each closer to our Elements."

"So, what did you have in mind for today?" I asked, hoping my body could withstand another day of physical and mental strain.

She slowly looked around the circle, seeing the toll the training had taken on everyone. "Today...you have the day off."

Brandr's jar dropped. "Say what?" he asked in disbelief.

"It's like we're training for a marathon," Gaia explained. "And we need to taper before the race."

While the others whooped and slapped each other high fives of celebration, I sat quietly by myself on the log. Her logic made sense, but deep inside I was convinced she had a different underlying meaning. If we didn't survive our encounter with Aether, she wanted to guarantee we had a positive memory of our last days on Earth. And that morbid thought kind of put a damper on my ability to have fun.

Liam went to talk to Gaia while Aquous, Hydros, and Skye darted off. Hina's words came to mind again: *Treasure him.* How did she think I could do that when I couldn't spend a moment alone with him? Unsure of what to do for the next few hours, the best decision would be to clear my mind to prepare for the upcoming battle. And the best way to accomplish that task was to get away from camp for a while. I walked over to Brandr and asked if he'd like to join me for a hike.

Instantly the blush rose high in his cheeks. He shifted his eyes nervously from side to side, and scratched his head, contemplating his answer. I'd never seen him act quite like that before.

Puzzled, I asked, "What's gotten into you?"

"Well...um...yeah. About that," he stammered. "Skye already invited me to roast hot dogs with her over the fire. And you know, I'm the guy to go to when you need fire," he said with an anxious chuckle.

I shot him a hard look.

"I mean, you are, too, of course," he added belatedly. "You can join us if you like. I'm sure Skye won't mind."

"Thanks, but I think I'll pass," I said, and walked away. I was happy for him, but missed his constant companionship. Lately, his friendship had grown on me to the point I considered him one of my close friends. No, scratch that. He was my *best* friend. Sure, I could've asked one of the Water Essences to join me, but I didn't bother to think of anyone else. Obviously, Gaia had given us the day off so she could spend her time with Liam.

I hadn't made it far when I felt a rush of hot wind by my side. I turned, surprised to see Brandr. "Why are you here? I thought you had a date with Skye."

The D word made Brandr's face turn crimson in an instant. He shook his head of flaming red hair, trying to refocus. "I had to tell you something before you left."

"O...kay," I said slowly, confused even more than before.

"I wanted to apologize," he began. His eyes gauged me with a tinge of regret.

196

"For what?"

"I think I've been a little too hard on you. I don't know if you've noticed, but Liam hasn't been acting quite like his normal self. And I was wondering what harm could come of it now? We've already accomplished what we needed to do."

I shifted my weight to my other foot. "So what are you saying?"

"Jordan, you know I want you to be happy."

"Yeah, 'cause that would look pretty hypocritical right now if you were happy because of my encouraging you to get together with Skye, and I wasn't happy because of you telling me not to be with Liam?"

"Um, I'm not really sure I got all that, but I guess that's basically what I'm trying to say."

"Like I said before, I'm good."

"Jordan, I just think you should—"

"Thanks for thinking of me. Really. I've got this. I'm good. Besides, shouldn't you be getting back to Skye?"

His mouth turned into a small frown. With a saddened nod, he drifted back down the path, his orangey Essence a shade paler than normal.

I knew I shouldn't venture too far, but I couldn't convince myself to turn back around and return to camp. Continuing down the bed of pine needles that lined the path, I mindlessly let my feet lead the way. Overhead, the black clouds grew thicker, adding a slight nip to the mountain air.

I also knew from experience I needed to make noise to alert wildlife—especially bears—to my presence. All the refrains from Gaia's melancholy mix at the campfire suddenly inundated my mind. I belted the words I could remember and made up the rest, making my singing sound more like a bad medley than a string of distinct songs.

197

It didn't matter to me...no one was around, and the singing actually lifted my spirits, allowing me an opportunity to vent at maximum volume without bothering a soul. To be honest, I kind of liked it that way.

Looking back, maybe this should've been my path all along: living on my own, far from the reaches of civilization. Lucius and William would have lived full lives, well into their adulthoods. I never would've risked Cam or Micah or Sully's safety if I'd never met them.

I stopped for a moment, the gravity of those thoughts weighing deep on my soul. I never would've experienced any of those acts if I'd been a recluse all my life like Ignis, who chose to live on his own even though he didn't seem to enjoy it. He bottled up rage from an event that occurred hundreds of millions of years ago in Earth's past, and still hadn't overcome his grief of losing the battle to Gaia.

I resumed my hike at a slower pace, my feet willing me to return. *Not yet*, I told myself. *Just a few more minutes on my own.* How would I feel to go back and interrupt Skye and Brandr's impromptu date? Or worse, catch Liam and Gaia making out?

The thought made my stomach churn. Despite knowing the prophecy stated Liam and I needed each other, I couldn't figure out how to make that happen. I also didn't understand why Brandr had made a point of chasing me down to give me permission to get together with Liam again. Had Liam asked Brandr to speak to me? Or had Brandr made that decision on his own? It was impossible to say.

Before long, I found myself at the overlook to the falls Gaia, Liam, and Skye had worked to hold back. I closed my eyes, overwhelmed with the magnitude of our responsibility. I released a deep sigh, a small teardrop sliding down my cheek. It didn't matter how I felt or what I wanted. I couldn't let the team or my friends in California down.

I stayed there for long hours, watching the water drop in sporadic pulses. The sky darkened and I heard the sound of footsteps behind me. I turned, feeling the blood drain from my cheeks and fearing Aether had arrived unnoticed and I wasn't ready. I still craved more time here on Earth. And though I considered Brandr a close friend, I didn't wish his Essence lifestyle for myself. I swallowed hard, waiting for Aether to climb out of the undergrowth and enter the clearing.

Only no one emerged.

I'd admit that during my time spent at camp, I'd grown somewhat desensitized to the natural noises of my surroundings: the chirping crickets, the yipping coyotes, and the cawing ravens. But this was the first time I'd heard things that didn't exist. Maybe fear had settled too deep within my veins. Or maybe I'd been alone for so long that I craved some form of contact.

I looked behind me again, but still saw no one. Could my active imagination have been playing tricks on me all along?

CHAPTER THIRTY

Beneath the darkening clouds, a blood red moon rose early, hanging low on the horizon, distorted and unnaturally large at this high elevation. Its appearance added to my uneasiness while I listened for the footsteps to return.

The moon looked completely different from the pure white light that had illuminated the tropical sky, perched high in the velvety night when I first met Hina and the Fire Essence, Brandr. That event seemed like eons ago. So much had changed since then, but I still felt ill prepared for my upcoming fate.

Despite my reservations, I knew the time had come and I must return to camp. Before I turned to leave, I felt a pair of hands — strong and determined at times, yet surprisingly gentle — slip around my waist. My eyes flew open. So I hadn't imagined those footsteps after all. Had he merely waited until I wasn't looking to surprise me?

I spun in his arms. "Liam," I breathed. A wave of relief surged through my body, followed by a small smile that slipped across my face. At that very moment my confidence returned, knowing I wouldn't face our upcoming challenges alone. Relaxed with that knowledge, I decided to heed Brandr's advice and spend a moment with Liam, without reservation. I leaned into Liam's warm chest. He rested his chin on my shoulder, letting his cheek brush mine. I closed my eyes again as my body slowly relaxed in his embrace.

"I couldn't find you anywhere back at camp," he commented.

I caught a hint of worry in his tone. "You were looking for me?"

"Yeah," he said in a way that made it sound like he wanted to add, *obviously*.

My smile widened. He'd been looking for *me*. Meaning he really must care more about me than Gaia, otherwise I'd still be here by myself.

"You doing okay?" he asked.

"I guess so," I replied, not wishing to give him too much credit for allaying my nerves. Before I could have unconditionally leapt into his comforting arms and have him hold me tight, but things were different now. And I'd spent enough time questioning his feelings lately to abandon my hesitation altogether.

But tonight, he'd sought me, for reasons I didn't understand.

"Tomorrow's the tenth day," he observed.

"I know," I replied in a glum tone.

"Are you ready?" he asked. His hands seemed to subconsciously grip me tighter, wanting to protect me from Aether and whatever he might throw at us.

I didn't know how to respond. Since when was anyone ready to meet one's potential doom? So I bounced the question back at him. "Are you?"

"Yes...and no, I guess." His hands released their grip while he lifted his chin from my shoulder.

With hesitation, I looked up into his eyes, trying to decipher his emotions. Suddenly, I found I couldn't release his gaze as his eyes held mine in a deeply personal way.

"You've been crying," he noted, breaking the silence. His

thumb brushed my cheek.

I leaned into his chest. "Nothing is perfect. Not me, not you, and certainly not our team of Elementals. What will happen to everyone, everything we know, if we fail?" I asked in a small voice.

Liam's arms tightened around my back, drawing me closer. He leaned toward me until I felt the warmth of his chest pressed against mine.

"We won't," he reassured me.

The certainty of his response startled me. Didn't he share some of my fears? "But how do you know?" I ventured.

"Because I believe in us," Liam said in a confident tone. "We *can* defeat Aether. We have to. There is no other way."

I frowned as my eyes left his, wishing I shared his optimism.

"You doubt us?" he asked.

"It's not that," I managed. "It's the uncertainty. There's so much we don't know. So many things could happen that we haven't practiced. That we can't possibly predict...." My voice trailed off, worry clouding my thoughts.

"Then we'll work together," he suggested with unwavering faith.

I gave a small nod, hoping I hadn't ruined his view of the upcoming events. His optimism might be all we had to last the day.

And if we didn't survive, then this might be the last opportunity I had to tell Liam how I really felt about him. Before I lost my nerve, I blurted, "There's more." But when I opened my mouth to explain, I froze. What if he didn't want to hear what I had to say? What if I jeopardized everything we'd worked so hard to achieve simply by declaring three little words?

"Is this about Brandr?" he guessed without waiting for my explanation.

"Brandr? What do you mean?"

"I…um…well, it just seems like the two of you have been spending an awful lot of time together recently, and —"

"Ohmigod!" I interrupted him. I chuckled with hilarity. "I thought we already went through this. Brandr acts like a brother to me…and an annoying one at that. Besides, I think he's got a thing for Skye."

Liam scrunched his face, giving the impression of surprise and disapproval. "He shouldn't lead her on. Especially since he's an Essence and she's not."

"She liked him first. Plus, she could become an Essence herself some day. They're not very different after all. So in the meantime, why not let them be happy?"

He nodded, understanding my reasoning even if he didn't agree with it. "Then this wasn't about Brandr?" Liam asked, sounding relieved.

"No, not at all. I wanted to tell you that I'm afraid because…."

"Because?" he prompted, waiting.

I stared into his eyes, sincere and caring. He deserved to know. *And this might be your last chance*, I reminded myself. I swallowed hard and tried again.

"Because I love you," I started, surprised to find the words I'd struggled to voice for so long suddenly roll off my tongue with surprising ease.

Liam replied with a casual, "I know."

My jaw fell open. "What do you mean, 'you know'?"

"You already told me."

"Wait, *what?*" My brows pinched together, certain I had saved that choice of words until this specific moment.

"Back when you were fighting Hydros, right after you'd exploded from her trap like an icy volcano."

"But…but…," I stammered, "you weren't even conscious.

203

You couldn't have known what I was saying."

A sly grin snaked its way across his lips. "Hydros told me afterwards. She wasn't happy about it, but she got over it. Besides, I had to do something extreme to get you both to work together."

"Oh. My. God. What were you thinking? I almost killed you."

"But you didn't."

"But I could've, if Hydros hadn't been there to condense you back. What would I have done then?"

Liam shrugged. "I hadn't really thought that far ahead."

I heaved a sigh of exasperation. "How could you be so brainless?"

"So now you think I'm brainless?" he asked, cocking one eyebrow high on his forehead.

"Uh, yeah," I said, and rolled my eyes. "Why else would you take that kind of a risk?"

"I had to take the chance," Liam said. "I couldn't think of anything else to do. A few minutes longer and you would've died."

"Oh, please. I had things under control, thank you very much."

"Whatever," Liam objected. "You were completely covered in ice."

I opened my mouth to protest, but Liam silenced my retort with a spontaneous, unexpected kiss that squelched my desire to be alone, and instantly rekindled all my feelings for him. My anger at his unnecessary risk quickly dissolved when his lips shaped mine...deeper, and more intimate than ever before. I cherished this moment, preserving the smell of his hair, the touch of his lips, the warmth of his smile, the heat of his touch. I wanted to remember every detail and the satisfaction I drew from our closeness...in case this proved the last time we were together.

Liam pulled away sooner than I would've liked. His deep

blue eyes held my gaze, like something remained on his mind. He kept me locked in his embrace when he spoke. "I wanted to tell you before, but I couldn't."

"Tell me what?"

"How *I* still felt about *you*," he admitted. "With everything we're up against, I kept telling myself that my wants and needs would have to wait. I didn't want to mess things up and make Gaia blame you for anything. Plus, I didn't want to make you feel like you owed me anything...you know, in case I didn't make it in the end."

I put a finger to his lips. "Don't say that. Of course you'll be fine. We'll all be fine if we work together. You said so yourself."

"I know. It's just that time's running out. And I feel like I've missed out on spending time with you."

I shook my head, thinking about the times I'd neglected him for fear of upsetting Gaia. "But you didn't. You spared us in Mexico by bringing rain to the land. You saved me from Airis on Easter Island when she tried to steal my Essence. We trained together here in the mountains. And you even tried to tell me that you still liked me."

"Yeah, but then my sister fused with my body and tried to kill you." He let his eyes fall. "I should've told you sooner. I thought you already knew."

My lips crept into a small smile. All of my doubts from the past ten days washed away in an instant. Liam had never stopped liking me after all. Ironically, all those doubts had originated from inside my own mind. "I don't want to lose you," I whispered, tears filling my eyes.

"You won't," he said, a smile widening across his lips. "Which is why I won't let anything happen to you or me." He leaned forward until his forehead touched mine. My heart pulsed loudly inside my chest. I found it impossibly difficult to breathe. I waited, eager to see what he did next.

"I mean it, Jordan. I love you. And I won't let you get hurt."

All the anger and frustration I'd felt toward him since he'd revealed his identity as Hydros's twin faded in that instant. *He loves me. He said it.* The words floated through the crisp night air, hovering about my ears, replaying themselves again in my memory. I could tell in the sincerity of his tone that he wasn't simply echoing the sentiment I'd voiced…he meant every word.

A wave of elated relief spread through my body.

I leaned forward, ready to finish our kiss, when a deafening noise rang through the air. A searing streak of light ripped open the sky, blinding in its intensity. My face froze with fear as I looked at Liam, wondering what to do. The air held an unsettling stillness for a short second before the shock wave hit, tumbling us off our feet. I landed on top of Liam, his arms cradling me protectively. Thinking fast, he threw a thick ice dome around our fallen bodies to shield us from the flying debris. Trees toppled outward from the blast, their tall trunks snapping like matchsticks. They crashed upon his dome of ice, cracking its surface but not breaking through. Dust hung in the air. Trees creaked and heaved until they found their final resting places.

From inside the shelter of his ice dome I stared at him, my eyebrows poised in the form of a question I was too afraid to voice, waiting for confirmation of my worst nightmare.

Liam swallowed hard and returned my gaze. His eyes filled with dread when he whispered, "He came early."

CHAPTER THIRTY-ONE

After the initial blast ended, Liam dropped his ice dome and helped me to my feet. We dodged the debris and tore down the path leading back to camp, my pulse thudding inside my throat, desperate to find our team of Elemental fighters. Luckily, we bumped into them halfway back. Brandr said they'd also seen and felt Aether's initial greeting, and realized our time had run out sooner than we'd expected.

"He's this way," Brandr said.

We made good speed at first, but gradually our progress slowed. Felled trees lay strewn in all directions outward in a radius from the blast, tumbled like matchsticks from the tremendous power of his landing. We scrambled over them, eager to contain Aether in this very spot before he shifted his focus to other regions of dense population.

Sure, it would've been easier to use our Elements to transport us there in less time, but Gaia stressed the importance of us remaining together. "Remember the prophecy," she professed as she leapt over an obstacle in her path. "Five will rule four, unless we are one. We're stronger together than we are apart. Whatever happens, we must stick together. No one takes him on alone. Are we clear?"

We all grunted some sort of agreement.

"And it'll be difficult to resist his gravitational pull," she coached us, "so we'll need to anchor ourselves to our own Elements here on Earth."

"Got it," Brandr said.

A minute later, Gaia stopped and held up one hand in a fist, her elbow bent at a right angle: our signal to proceed with caution. No one spoke a word. We moved silently over the last stretch of ground. The destruction intensified with each passing step. I covered my mouth with one hand, trying not to reveal my location by coughing on the powder and debris that hung in the air.

The dust cloud slowly settled, revealing an enormous gaping hole: a crater blasted in the middle of the forest. And right in the middle stood the largest, most massive and muscular person I'd ever seen. His stature easily reached over seven feet tall. His arms and legs were as thick as some of the tree trunks I'd clambered over on my way to the site. He had a shaggy head of the blackest hair, thick bushy eyebrows, and a dimple in the middle of his pronounced chin. I had difficulty making out other features in the dim light, but the starry backdrop of the night sky clearly outlined his colossal form. He reminded me of the strong gravitational force of the black hole in my nightmare when I'd woken as Pyr. His intense personal gravity would not allow light to escape.

Gaia gave a low whistle. "He's gotten bigger and denser since the last time. He grows larger and more destructive with each pass toward Earth."

Brandr nodded. "You're right. It definitely seems like that dude's amped up his mass while he's been gone. What do you think he bench presses now? Two-fifty? Maybe three hundred pounds? Look at those arms."

"Quiet," Gaia hissed, her patience running thin.

Fear rippled up my spine, thinking of how vulnerable I was to someone of that magnitude.

I hurried to Brandr's side in case we had to fuse his Essence with my body to amplify our powers. I gave him a nudge in the ribs to get his attention because I didn't dare utter a word. But Brandr's eyes never left Aether. "You won't like me when I'm angry," Brandr mumbled in his toughest voice.

"Who are you talking to?" I whispered.

"Huh? Oh, nothing," he replied. "In a way, he reminds me of a dark version of *The Hulk*."

"Only bigger. And scarier," I added.

"Good point."

From the corner of my eye, I watched Aquous reach into the pocket of his baggy shorts and remove a hair tie. He pulled his long blond hair back and tied it off around the nape of his neck. He tucked his long sleeved T-shirt into his shorts and pushed the sleeves up to his elbows. Then he stepped forward, ready to work.

Gaia watched him out of the corner of her eye. "Aquous, no," she cautioned. "We stay together, remember?"

"I'm with Gaia on this one. I don't think that's a smart idea," Brandr warned.

"No worries, man," Aquous said with a wave of his hand, like brushing away a pesky fly. "I've got this. It's all good." And without another look behind, he strode toward Aether.

I bit my lip, praying he was right. My eyes flitted to the right and left like an athlete's sense of field awareness in the middle of a soccer game. I had to know and remember everyone's location in case we had to act suddenly and defend ourselves.

"Aether, brother," Aquous began in his casual, non-confrontational way. "It's been a long time." He opened his arms and held out his hands to embrace the last of the original Elementals.

Aether turned and took a step toward Aquous. From my perspective, the night sky seemed to distort around his body. When he moved, the background seemed to move with him. Normally, I imagined the fabric of space lay flat and untouched. But now, it appeared the stars and planets in the velvety sky curved around his massive force like a bowling ball making an impression on a bed's clean linens.

"You weren't so complacent the last time I saw you, Aquous, when you banished me from your world," Aether began in a steely voice. "But you were significantly less transparent," he chortled with a deep, malicious laugh.

"You are quite observant," Aquous replied with his own backhanded compliment. "So what brings you our way?"

Aether's laughter died in an instant. Overhead, the clouds closed in, pulled by his force of gravity into a dark mass above his very spot.

Beside me, I saw Hydros fuse with Liam in precaution of the dangers that lay ahead. I hoped their fusion would provide enough protection for Skye and Gaia, who stood alone.

"You know perfectly well, I'm afraid, my *brother*," Aether sneered, the final word rolling off his tongue with patronizing disdain. "I was born of this land, and I am here to reclaim what is rightfully mine."

"Rightfully yours?" Aquous questioned. "I'm sorry, but this is no place for you and you know it. Your presence here proved too disruptive to nature."

"Then let nature suffer. I will return and claim this for my home, even if it means I must live in a world devoid of other life."

"Why must you sacrifice others for your own desires? Surely there is another, more prudent course of action you could take,"

Aquous countered.

"You dare challenge me?" Aether roared. "I am certain you realize that I will stop at nothing this time. And I will not hesitate to eliminate anyone who stands in my way."

"This isn't looking good." Gaia expressed her fear. Liam grabbed my hand, whirled me by his side, and then reached for Gaia and Skye. Combining his powers with Hydros's, they constructed an ice dome around us in case Aquous's methods failed.

Aquous and Aether's conversation went back and forth for a few more minutes, but I couldn't make out their words inside Liam's shield of ice. I squinted through the frozen, translucent dome, watching intently for either to strike.

When Aquous said something I couldn't hear, Aether's mouth contorted with rage. His brows drew low over his darkened eyes. Suddenly, the fabric of space snapped back to its original resting point for the briefest of moments before Aether's wave spread outward in all directions from his body. The pulse knocked us all off our feet faster than one of Gaia's seismic waves, because it traveled through empty space at the speed of light. We had no warning, but luckily we'd had the foresight to protect ourselves from this danger.

"What was that?" I asked Brandr, alarmed at the power produced in such a quick act.

"A gravitational wave, I think," Brandr replied. Desperate, he looked around, searching for something.

I peered through the ice shield to follow Brandr's gaze. Blinking at the spot where the original Water Essence had stood seconds before, I asked, "Where's Aquous?"

"He's gone," Gaia said in a low voice.

"Where'd he go?" I scanned the entire crater, looking for a sign of his presence.

"He's gone," Brandr repeated softly, sadly. A chill ran through the mountain air and seeped into my core. In that moment, I fully understood Brandr's intent. Aquous's Essence was no more.

Aether cackled a deep, low laugh that reeked of pride and arrogance. He turned toward me alone, staring with a look so fierce I couldn't break away from his gaze. His thick eyebrows narrowed, drawing his eyes into thin slits that pierced my mind.

Suddenly, I no longer saw Aether but a different scene altogether. Out in the far reaches of space, I watched two glowing orbs encircle each other: one a hypergiant mass of blue plasma, the other a fiery red color reminiscent of the setting sun. Each eclipsed the view of the other as they spun, locked in the inseparable embrace of two immense soul mates. Their tug on the other accelerated when their proximity increased, forcing them closer and closer together.

A battle of titanic gravitational forces existed between the pair of behemoth stars. In the final seconds before they touched, an unparalleled burst of energy pulsed outward, stronger than anything else measured in the universe. Their massive gravitational wave distorted the fabric of space and time. Then the stars finally touched, ejecting immeasurable quantities of gas and matter into the darkness of space. In that precise moment, both stars shed their gaseous outer layers in an explosive burst of light and profound heat, leading to their premature deaths. Nothing remained to remind us of their former glories except a pathetic dark spot in the deep recesses of space.

I swallowed hard, recognizing the shape. It wasn't just a pathetic dark spot, but a black hole. *The blackest of blacks.* An object so dense and with a gravitational force so strong, not even a pinprick of light could escape its domination. In that short moment of time, he had reduced my fiery kin into nothingness.

Aether's gloating voice echoed in my mind. *Don't you get it?*

I will win in the end. You cannot stop me this time.

I remembered how quickly he had destroyed Aquous and how easily he could eliminate the rest of us the same way he had decimated the massive stars in my mind. My mouth gaped in shock and awe, certain he was right. My skills seemed miniscule compared to the supremacy he wielded over the universe.

"What's wrong with you?" Liam asked, a note of concern in his voice. "Why are you just standing there doing nothing?"

"I can see it," I stated slowly, paralyzed with fear. "He's projecting his thoughts into my head."

"Well, block him out," Liam ordered.

Still, I fixated on the image of the stellar collision, powerless to stop it from recurring in my mind and unable to heed Liam's advice.

CHAPTER THIRTY-TWO

"Brandr, help her. Do something," Liam implored.

Brandr leapt into my body before Liam completed his request. "Fire Essence in the house!" he declared and booted me from the controls, erecting a swift mental blockade against Aether's corrupting thoughts, purging him from my mind but not from my memory.

I trembled, the image of the exploding stars lingering, fresh in my head.

"You've gotta help me out a little here, Jordan," Brandr encouraged me. "Think of this to distract you." He flooded my mind with dozens of images of Liam over the past ten days: on the ball court in Mexico, in front of the waterfall and geyser, sitting by the campfire, even inside the tent when Liam had almost kissed me before Brandr suddenly expelled himself from my body, disgusted by the prospect.

I laughed despite myself. *You may try to act tough,* I told Brandr, *but deep inside, I know you're a softie.*

As long as it works, he replied to me alone. *Glad to have you back. Now, let's get started.*

Whatever you say, boss.

"She's good now," he announced to Liam. "We've got

everything back in control."

A brief wave of relief spread over Liam's face.

"So what's the new plan?" I asked, grateful to rid my mind of Aether's horrific thoughts.

"Unlike Aquous, Aether's made of carbon," Brandr mused.

"And?" I said, trying to find a connection between Aquous and the immense force that remained before us.

"And diamonds are made of carbon," Brandr continued.

Gaia nodded. "I will extract the carbon from his body. Then using intense heat," she said, pointing at me, "and intense pressure," she pointed at Skye, "we can change the carbon. Diamonds may be formed underground in nature, but I bet we can replicate those conditions here inside this crater if we try."

"Then we should be able to form one heck of a gemstone," Brandr concluded.

"And after, Hydros and I could blast it into space," Liam offered.

"Or break it up and sell it for trillions of dollars," Brandr suggested.

Gaia nodded. "Or that."

"Ready? Let's win this for Aquous," Liam said.

"High temp. High pressure. Got it," I reminded myself, shaking out my arms in preparation.

"Yep," Brandr agreed. "Then the carbon atoms should bond together and begin to crystallize."

"It's times like these that make me glad to know a science nerd like you," I told him.

"For God's sake! Are you two done yapping so we can get to work? Geesh!" Gaia grumbled.

Funny. I think she's starting to sound a little like you, I told Brandr in my head to avoid further upsetting her.

Don't say that, Brandr thought back with a shudder. *Don't*

215

ever say that.

"Follow my lead," Gaia ordered.

Liam dropped his ice shield and we exited. We quickly spread out side by side in the crater, waiting for Gaia to begin the extraction process.

Gaia pulled the carbon out of him, black in its raw form. Skye surrounded Aether with a mass of air pushed inward with unspeakable force. She squeezed him tighter and tighter until the pressure inside grew intense, like inside the earth. Skye infused the hyper-oxygenated air to make my fire burn hotter than possible on my own. Liam added a wall of water behind, intentionally preventing him from breaking through Skye's box of air.

"Then cool him really fast," Brandr recommended. "It'll lock the diamond's structure into place. Otherwise, he could turn into graphite instead."

"Like a giant pencil lead?" I asked.

"Yes, like a giant pencil…oh, for crying out loud," Brandr snipped. "Just do it!"

Hydros and Liam switched their wall of water into an icy cloud that enveloped Aether's body, preserving his form in a solid layer of diamond crystals. What little light filtered through Aether's black clouds struck his body and made it sparkle like a million miniature suns.

"Wow," I breathed, impressed with our efforts. "It's beautiful."

For a few minutes we waited in silence, hoping and praying we had fully contained the threat.

"Huh," Brandr said. "I'm actually a bit surprised. That was a whole lot easier than I'd expect—"

"Jordan, watch out," Liam shouted, interrupting Brandr's premature congratulations.

With a sudden, unexpected force, Aether burst through his outer layer, transforming his diamond exterior into a shower of glittering gems. Hydros and Liam threw up an ice shield. Gaia erected a wall of rock from the ground beneath her feet. With one hand, I created a raging wall of fire. Brandr used my other hand to aim the fire in front of Skye, guarding her from the shower by disintegrating those parts at extremely high temperatures before they could rupture her protective bubble of air.

Aether closed his eyes in concentration. Amazingly, his form began to swell in size. I had a bad feeling things were about to get a whole lot worse.

The Fifth Elemental crouched low and then leapt into the air. His landing generated a shock wave, knocking us off our feet.

I scrambled to right myself before he unleashed a second wave.

Laughing at our helpless reaction, Aether spun in circles, pulling his arms closer to his core with each rotation.

"This isn't going to be good. Anchor yourself!" Brandr advised. We fled toward the forest, grabbing onto the nearest tree branches to avoid Aether's tug. Loose particles of dirt and debris flew toward him, collecting about his body in an armored shell.

"He's using his gravity to increase his mass," Brandr noted.

Meanwhile, shell upon shell accumulated around him, sealing Aether in protective layers, leaving only his face exposed. Satisfied with his work, he gave a sly sneer.

My feet soon drew toward him, tearing me from the branch. "I'm losing my grip!" I screamed over the noise of the particles sailing through the air toward Aether. I struggled to maintain my hold. Sucked closer to Aether's intense gravitational pull, my fingers slipped from the tree branch.

"I've got you," Liam shouted. He grabbed my wrist, pulling me back to safety. I smiled a thanks and locked my arms securely around the branch, hanging on with all my might.

"We need some help to stop him," Skye said. She gave Liam and me a knowing stare and displayed a square stone carving in her palm.

Liam agreed. "Activate the stones."

I wrenched one hand from the tree to pull the Maya priest's gift from my pocket, and doused it in a quick burst of flames. The stone emitted a greenish glow. The jaguar's spirit rose from the rock and took form. He stood at attention with my hand resting between his shoulder blades, ready for action.

I glanced at Liam and Skye, noticing the greenish tints of their animal spirits had already coalesced by their sides. Liam gave his plumed snake a nod and it darted forward, sliding across the earthen ground in a serpentine motion toward Aether's massive feet. Intently focused on gaining mass, he failed to notice the serpent's silent approach. When the spirit latched on to Aether's calf, the jaguar lunged forward, ramming Aether full force, knocking his tremendous girth off balance. The eagle grabbed Aether's shoulders in its strong talons and helped throw him to the ground. He landed with an ear-splitting bang. In the blink of an eye, the slithering serpent bound the Fifth Elemental's calves, then body, in a snug coil reaching all the way to Aether's neck.

Aether's dark face reddened, his cheeks puffing with fury as he battled the serpent's tightening grip. The jaguar and eagle stood nearby, ready to pounce should Aether break free.

The serpent slowed Aether's spinning. With the spirits distracting him, Aether's gravity diminished and we regained our footing on solid ground.

Aether counteracted the serpent's tight grip, kicking and thrashing with surprising speed. Unable to contain Aether any longer, the plumed serpent dissolved in a green burst of light.

Angered at the loss of their own kind, the jaguar and eagle

spirits latched on to his outer shells, ripping off pieces with their claws and talons. Aether swung his thick arms, trying to brush them away, but the spirits moved too quickly for him. They removed more bits and chunks, further angering Aether. He growled and then smashed his massive fist, connecting with the eagle's keeled breastbone. The eagle disappeared in a green poof of mist.

"Oh, no!" I gasped when Aether clubbed the lone jaguar straight in the heart. With sadness, I realized the spirits of the Maya were no more.

"It's not enough," Gaia declared. "We need more help." She clapped her hands twice. Seconds later, I heard a rustle of movement in the undergrowth behind us. I turned toward the noise, surprised to see the tridents and aqua plumed helmets of two dozen Protectors from the Lost City of Atlantis. Each wore a shiny chest plate that gleamed in the moonlight, and a short blade strapped to his calf muscle.

I never thought I'd be so happy to see them again, especially after my last encounter ended with a trio of tridents pointed at me, ready to defend their kingdom from my blasphemous claims.

On cue, the Atlantean Protectors dropped to one knee and wrapped a handful of dried moss around each trident in a tight wick. They stood up and extended all twenty-four pointed tridents straight at me. I gulped, sweat beading across my brow. I remembered the last time one of those sharp points had grazed my jugular, and wondered what I'd done to provoke their anger this time.

Gaia huffed and tapped her foot impatiently. "Well, what are you waiting for? Ignite them already!"

"Oh. Right," I replied, relieved I had misunderstood their intentions.

I snapped my fingers and produced a hot tongue of fire in

the palm of my hands. Skye twirled her index finger and a gust of wind carried the fire in a circle around me, rapidly setting each trident's wick aflame.

With blazing tridents, the Protectors fanned outward, each aiming his three sharpened points at Aether's outer shell, waiting for the Atlantean captain's command.

"Strike!" the captain hollered, and two dozen flaming tridents released simultaneously at Aether. His shell caught fire and fractured upon impact, dropping into blazing chunks about him. The inferno rose higher and set the next shell on fire. Aether howled, stomping on the flames with his massive feet, but could not extinguish them. Next, the Protectors reached for the hilts of their short blades strapped to their outer calves. On the captain's count of three, they cocked their throwing arms backward and launched the knives at Aether's fiery form, cleaving the shell into small pieces that fell to the ground in a flaming pile.

Aether's face reddened with fury. He cupped one fist in his hand and then pushed his hands outward.

"Antigravity," Brandr quickly warned us. "Shields up!"

We erected shielding versions of our Elements around us. Aether shot out a powerful wave of flaming tridents, blades, and blazing fragments of his former shells toward us. I closed my eyes and focused my power outward. I heard the *ping* of weapons deflecting off my shield, followed by the blood curdling screams of the dying. Fearing the worst, I peeked out from the safety of my wall of fire after Aether's antigravity blast had passed. Fortunately, the other Elementals remained unharmed. However, the Protectors were not as lucky. Each lay motionless upon the ground, slain by the Atlanteans' own weapons. The aqua plumed helmet rolled off a nearby Protector, revealing the triangle shaped tattoo on his forehead. The Fountain of Youth could extend their life for a few millennia, but could not heal their mortal wounds.

Gaia heaved a defeated sigh. Her alliance with the people of the lost city had proved no match for Aether's strength.

CHAPTER THIRTY-THREE

Aether crowed at our feeble attempt while the sky turned gray and angry, the clouds darkening into a thick wall as they condensed above our very spot. A chill ran down my spine, whether from the drop in temperature or a sense of foreboding, I couldn't say. I sensed the tide was about to change in this war, regrettably in Aether's favor.

Remembering the last time I'd experienced this sudden change in weather back on Easter Island, I gazed upward. Overhead, Airis hovered with her army of moai statues trailing in orderly rows. The immense moai appeared to march through the air in stoic support of Airis, their faces expressionless except for their lips drawn in thin pouts. Their sunken eyes focused on Aether, gazing intently on his form down the bridges of their long, broad noses.

Meanwhile, the full force of the wind whipped outward from Airis, making her ivory dress and golden hair flap behind her back like a flag waved proudly in battle. Her alchemist tattoos glowed a pale blue, beaming off her chest and down her bare arms and legs. With an air of superiority she passed above us, not even bothering to acknowledge our presence as her contemporaries.

I shot Liam a nervous glance. "What's she doing here?"

He didn't reply. His eyes warily trained on Airis's form lest she turn her powers against us like she had before.

She rode her wind currents right up to Aether. "You have finally returned to us, brother," she declared in a resounding voice that carried over the wind.

He narrowed his thick eyebrows at her. "How dare you call me your brother? You cast me from your world, making me seek an existence among the stars."

"I fear you are mistaken," Airis replied calmly. "You desired a greater power than what we possessed here on Earth. You left of your own free will."

Aether scowled at her, his dark features harboring unresolved bitterness toward the Air Essence. "If that is how you perceived it. You treated me like an outcast, the four of you banding together to select the precious earthly Elements. What other choice did I have? So now I have returned, to make you pay for the callous mistakes of your arrogant youth."

"Brother," she said in a pacifying tone, despite her troop of rock monoliths, whose aggressive red eyes aimed directly at Aether. "You did not know what I now do, that this tremendous power is achievable here after all. Forget your battle with these unworthy foes and join me. I can show you the true venue for your powers here on Earth."

It surprised me to see Aether pause for a moment to ponder her proposal. He scratched his mane of dark hair, contemplating the new future she suggested. A future where he would be accepted by the other Elementals and remain here on Earth, instead of wandering the far reaches of space…alone.

Yet his minor hesitation provided the opportunity Airis sought to launch her attack. She glanced behind, her eyes turning a milky white. With a wave of her glowing palm, her monolithic figures assembled in a tight circle around Aether.

"It was all a ploy," I breathed, thinking how she had also tricked me by preying on my feelings for Liam. Before Aether could react, Airis rotated the moai statues into a swirling vortex to restrain his arms and legs. The winds picked up dust and debris, lashing these fragments and particles at his shells and face. The wounds on his cheeks oozed with blood, but she persisted, intensifying the magnitude of the winds until the moai's figures became a uniform blur. Aether howled in pain as the violent cyclone ripped away bits and pieces of his outer shells.

Airis gloated, "It was so nice of you to come home so I could complete my transformation." With a despicable sneer, she stretched her insatiable fingers toward him.

"She's doing it again," I told Liam in a voice barely perceptible over the wind. "She's planning to steal his Essence."

Airis reached closer, extracting a wispy stream of the deepest blue from his mouth, dark like the midnight sky. Her ravenous eyes widened with delight at the sight of his Essence. She licked her ruby lips, eager to wield unlimited powers once the extraction was complete. With a malicious cackle, she snatched a portion of his Essence and wound it around her index finger, marveling at her accomplishment. The wisp of midnight blue clung tightly to its new home.

Aether watched in horror as Airis held her finger in front of her nose and inhaled deeply. The small portion of his Essence entered her nostrils and infused her with an instant burst of adrenaline. Her translucent figure gained in permanence, making her features more distinguishable against the darkened clouds above.

"It's working," Airis boasted, stretching her limbs in front of her to admire her changed arms and legs. Her eyes hungry with desire, she reached toward his Essence again, tugging a huge handful of the deep blue stream from his mouth.

I understood Liam's initial concern; we now faced a new and unexpected threat should she succeed. If Airis had destroyed Aquous and Brandr before, what was to stop her from taking out all of us once she possessed Aether's Essence?

In a desperate attempt to stop her, Aether summoned a tremendous burst of gravity inward, fusing the severed bits of his outermost shell and drawing the Essence into his body with a loud suctioning sound. The shells quickly reconnected, sealing his wounds and pulling his Essence back inside.

Airis grew irate, spinning the winds about him at higher and higher speeds.

With a fatal glare at his foe, Aether locked his thick hands together with a thundering clap. A startled look froze on Airis's face before his massive force of gravity pulled her and the army of moai inward at an unstoppable rate. The sudden collision generated a shock wave that knocked me from my feet. A ring of shattered fragments of lava rock exploded outward from its source and into the blackness of space beyond.

As an automatic defense mechanism, I erected a heat shield to protect my body against the flying shards of volcanic rock from the pulverized moai. Chunks of rock melted in an instant upon contact with my shield. Locking off my elbows to withstand the brutal force, I peeked out of the corner of my eye, noticing Skye, Liam, and Gaia had similar shields from their Elements. Skye had created a thick-walled bubble around herself, ricocheting the particles off her protective sphere. Liam had generated a wall of ice six inches thick, like an impenetrable warrior's shield. And Gaia had ducked behind a pillar of rock she had thrust instantly from the ground.

When the fragments finally diminished, I peered out from behind my heat shield. Nothing remained but the blackness of space. Aether had completely destroyed Airis and her moai army.

225

"Figures," I muttered, cursing Airis and her selfish ways. "She could've helped us if she hadn't been so greedy." Now she had nothing. Nothing at all.

"No," Gaia objected from behind her rock shield. "She still helped."

"How so? She's gone," I said. "Completely gone."

Gaia looked hopeful. "She is. But she gave us the key to defeating him."

CHAPTER THIRTY-FOUR

Hopeful, Gaia said, "We'll just need to try something else."

"But what? We're out of options and he keeps getting bigger and bigger. How can we contain him?" I didn't mean to sound so pessimistic, but nothing seemed to work. Our bodies taxed and strained beyond our limits, the outcome of this battle did not look promising.

What do you think, Brandr? I asked him alone.

We can't give up, Jordan. We'll figure something out. We just have to keep —

Skye cut him off. "Look!" she exclaimed.

I turned my head, noticing a wide stream of lava winding into the clearing.

That's odd. There's not an active volcano nearby, is there? I asked Brandr.

Instead of answering me, he let out a loud whoop. "Yes!" he shouted. "Reinforcements have arrived."

I stared at the unexpected lava flow, trying to decipher Brandr's meaning, when a section of the molten material cooled into the recognizable features of a human face with thick full lips, a broad nose, and wise glowing eyes. Long flowing tresses spilled around the face. For the briefest of moments, one of the eyes winked at me before disappearing back into the streaming flow of molten rock.

A wide smile lit my face. *Pele*.

A translucent, orange glow of another robust figure trailed behind the Hawaiian goddess. My jaw dropped at the sight of Ignis. "*You* came?" I declared, astonished. "But I thought you said there wasn't anything we could do to get you to help."

"I know, I know," Ignis replied with a heavy sigh.

"So what changed your mind?" Brandr wondered aloud.

Ignis shrugged. "Pele stopped by and told me Aether had returned, and well...I figured the two of you still had a lot to learn, so maybe this was my chance to show you a thing or two," he bragged, puffing out his chest.

I couldn't believe he had the audacity to be so arrogant after blowing us off before. But I didn't dare voice the thoughts I kept locked inside my head, afraid he might leave when we really could use his help.

Brandr didn't hesitate in teasing Ignis openly. "Oh, really, old man? Or is it you're afraid of us getting all the glory and recognition for our work?"

Ignis's chest deflated slightly. "Or that. C'mon now, let's get this party started."

Brandr chuckled. "I couldn't have said that better myself."

While our exchange took place, Pele had decided to fire things up a bit. The goddess split the earth, unleashing a fiery pit of molten rock that spewed a thick black cloud of fine ash into the air. Skye shifted the winds so the black ash cloud spread toward Aether.

"What are you trying to do?" Aether taunted, coughing on the polluted air. "Choke me to death? I'm not afraid of you, Pele. I'm not afraid of any of you. I'll destroy you all, then lay waste to the planet you banished me from so long ago. Nothing will survive. Nothing." He ended his rant with a deep, malicious cackle.

Pele responded with a series of flickering sparks. Soon, the sparks transformed into bolts of lightning, bright flashes illuminating the interior of the billowing cloud. "Now," she commanded.

Ignis reached toward the cloud to extract the lightning, carrying the charges high into the air until they made an ionized ring over Aether's head.

"Let's do this," Brandr said, "as one."

"As one," Gaia agreed. She placed her hands upon the earth, sending out a series of seismic waves. The tremors rattled the ground beneath Aether's feet and disrupted his concentration. At the same time, Skye funneled the air into a swirling vortex, blasting and battering Aether. Between Gaia's earthquake and Skye's fierce winds, Aether struggled to remain upright.

"Your turn, Liam and Hydros," Gaia said with a nod. Together the Water Elemental and his twin covered the ground in a slippery sheet of ice, leaving Aether with no traction to prevent the attack.

"It seems his gravity is dependent on his mass," Brandr noted in a voice too low for Aether to hear.

"I was thinking the same thing," Gaia said. "And if we can reduce his mass—"

"Then we reduce his gravitational powers," Brandr finished for her.

"Exactly," Gaia replied.

"So what are we waiting for?" I asked, grateful for a new logical plan that might actually work this time.

Brandr and I combined our powers to shoot a burst of superheated fire at the ionized ring, converting it into a blindingly bright ball of electrified charges. It exploded, showering Aether in energized sparks, shocking him momentarily and causing him to shed his outermost layer.

"That is so sweet!" Brandr proclaimed. "With Ignis and Pele's help, we made St. Elmo's Fire."

"If you say so," I replied, focusing my efforts on sustaining the stream of fire. I didn't care about its name, only that it worked to stop Aether.

The ring of lightning struck the Fifth Elemental again, causing another protective shell to drop away from his body.

"Destroy the shells," Gaia instructed.

Liam and Hydros shot a ray of ice at one shell, freezing it solid. Skye immediately funneled a whirling wind at the frozen shell and sent it flying into the thick trunk of a tree, where it smashed into a million pieces. Liam and Hydros aimed their freeze ray at the next shell to repeat the process.

"Colder," Gaia cried, desperate to end this mêlée. "Try cryo-cold."

"Got it," Hydros and Liam answered together.

The surface of Aether's shell instantly turned frost-nipped red, followed by a frost-bitten white, and eventually a deadened black. His outer layer froze solid, restricting his movements altogether.

"Now break it apart," Gaia coached. While she hurled rocks and boulders at his outer layer, Hydros whipped a barrage of sharpened blades of ice at his form, fragmenting the brittle exterior and breaking it down into pieces that each of us could destroy.

"The cold makes his body brittle," I observed with a low whistle.

Aether howled while his body cracked and cleaved from the abuse.

"Again," Gaia ordered. "Again."

I couldn't remember how many times we repeated this process, whittling down his form little by little to reduce his powers before he could retaliate. Gaia had likened this fight to a marathon, meaning I couldn't relent. One minor mistake or lapse of judgment could mean the end for any of us, especially after seeing how easily Aether had eliminated Aquous and Airis forever.

Except I realized a serious problem with their methods. True, Liam and Skye could whittle his body into fragments of his former self, but Aether could use his gravitational powers to pull these shards back together again, the way he'd healed himself against Airis.

Unless....

Finally, I understood why fire proved the necessary component of our team of Elementals.

Brandr, we have to destroy the pieces, I told him, *before Aether melds them back together again.*

You're absolutely right. By the time he finished that thought, a few of the shell fragments had already attached into bigger parts, attracted by the gravitational pull of their close proximities to each other.

We'd better act fast, Brandr cautioned while more of the shell particles amassed into growing chunks.

Without hesitation I extended my arms, sweeping a raging blast of fire and heat across the ground, incinerating the shell fragments into smoldering cinders and pieces of ash. I channeled all the fury and fire I had inside of me. My eyes burned like never before. Unbelievable amounts of heat radiated from my core and down my arms, ready to explode. Brandr and I unleashed a colossal stream of flames from my hands. Our fire destroyed his pieces, turning them into glowing embers, chemically changed in composition and unable to return to their original form. Meaning he could not rebuild these parts.

Unfortunately, Aether quickly realized this as well. "*No!*" he roared, infuriated with our success in reducing and eliminating his mass.

Pele's volcano raged, fueling Ignis's ring of lightning with a continuous source of power.

Aether struggled to fight back against our St. Elmo's Fire, but each lightning strike tore away another shell, making his mass fade. Before long, we had reduced Aether to his original size. A wave of relief filled my heart when Brandr and I burned the remnants of his final protective shell.

Aether glowered at me, his face filled with fury and disdain. He glared at us with beady eyes and laughed mockingly. "Don't you remember your precious prophecy? The ends must become the middle, or all will be lost. Five *will* rule four. The Oracle knew it. And you have all learned the truth as well. You cannot defeat me," he sneered. "Not in this lifetime. Not ever. I have overcome all of your defenses, so now it is your turn to bow to my rule."

Aiming toward us, he stretched out his hands and pushed them downward. An irresistible field of gravity instantaneously locked my feet to the ground. I felt an invisible force push upon me and shove me to my knees. I peeked out of the corner of my eye. Gaia, Skye, and Liam had also succumbed to the same fate, forced into a subservient posture before the supreme Fifth Elemental. The gravity increased, pressing upon my head until I stooped in deference, powerless to resist. "Bow before me," Aether gloated, "just like the prophecy stated. Five will rule four."

In a sudden burst of strength, Brandr prevailed against Aether's gravitational field. He lifted my head and glared back at the dark being. "Unless they are one," Brandr challenged in a fierce tone.

I remembered Hina's cord of rope in my pocket. We didn't

just have to work together as a team. The prophecy ran deeper than my initial understanding. The extremes had to come together to make the ends become the middle. And that couldn't happen unless we unified our Elements.

Brandr, we have to lock together and concentrate our powers. It's the only way, I told him.

Using all his might, Brandr screamed, fighting against the intense gravity as he reached out toward Liam and Skye. Understanding his intent, I helped him defy Aether's gravitational field and make physical contact with our teammates.

The instant my hand touched Liam's, a blinding light shot outward, directed straight at Aether. Fire and ice spat and crackled violently, our polar opposites uniting as one to maximize and strengthen each Element's inherent power. Brilliant colors of bright purple, blue, and white of the hottest fires fused with sharp shards of ice to create a concentrated beam. Still, Aether surprisingly held his ground, battered but refusing to acquiesce.

Brandr and I pulled Skye closer, letting her hand rest on top of our joined hands. Suddenly, a rushing gust of wind infused the beam of fire and ice. Aether's field of gravity weakened, allowing us to regain our footing. Together, we stood with locked hands aimed at Aether's core, refusing to relent.

"Now, Gaia!" I exclaimed. Freed of Aether's formidable gravity field, Gaia stepped toward us and placed her hand on top of ours. The unified beam widened and intensified, filled with battering chunks of rock and earth materials.

Aether raised his hand to shield his face from our crushing discharge of pure Elemental powers, but couldn't defend himself from our deadly blast. In hindsight, I should have expected Aether would target me. If he had the chance to take out just one of us, he'd obviously pick the one he perceived to be the biggest threat...namely me. Unlike the others, my powers existed outside of this world, within his realm in the depths of space.

So intent on my work, I failed to notice Aether had devised a back-up plan of his own. While shielding his face with one hand, his other reached toward the ground, extracting specific chemical elements from the rocks and bonding these together. He laced his weapon in a coating of fire and launched it at my heart. At the same moment his weapon released, Aether's Elemental form fractured, separating into distinct dark entities that hung suspended in space.

I wanted to congratulate Brandr for finding the strength to override Aether's gravity and link us together as one. I wanted to tell Liam how thrilled I was that we'd both survived this attack. And I wanted to apologize to Gaia, Hydros, and Skye that I misunderstood their intentions all along and wished I had trusted them sooner.

But I didn't say any of those things. Instead, I silently watched Aether's flaming weapon approach at an alarming rate. In the past, I'd heard stories of people witnessing their lives pass before them. In near-death experiences, I imagined time slowed to a leisurely pace to cherish their final seconds before the end.

Only for me, this phenomenon occurred at super-speed. In a single millisecond, I saw the faces of those who'd departed before me: my parents, my little sister Sarah, Lucius from Pompeii, and William from Salem Village. And for that briefest of moments, a sense of peace surrounded my body, ready to reunite with my loved ones once more.

I knew I should apologize to Brandr; I'd promised Aether wouldn't destroy his Essence, and now I'd let him down. Unable to prevent the inevitable, I began to close my eyes, ready to succumb to my fate, when Gaia leapt in front of me to intercept the blow. The weapon sunk into her chest, containing the fire and all its materials inside.

"*Gaia!*" I screamed.

"Don't worry about me," she shouted in her last remaining burst of strength before her body crumpled to the ground. "Finish it."

"My pleasure," Ignis said, and blasted Aether's Essence with a supercharged lightning strike. The bolt blasted his dark entities of gravity and transformed them into a solid black mass that swirled for a moment, desperate to coalesce. Ignis delivered a second charge, more powerful than the first. "Just in case," he said with a sly grin.

The eyes of Aether's Essence grew wide for a fraction of a second before I lost him from view behind a billowing cloud of smoke. Ignis's tremendous electricity knocked me backwards off my feet, and expelled Brandr when my body landed on the ground ten feet from where I'd originally stood. The massive shard of light silenced Aether's scream with a deafening boom, instantly obliterating the rest of his particles of gravity.

Instantly, the swirling black clouds overhead dispersed. The smoke settled, revealing only a pile of gray ash where Aether had stood. Particulate matter dropped from the sky like glowing charcoal ashes by a campfire.

I glanced over at Brandr's Essence, slowly prying himself off the ground. His flaming red hair stood on end from the electricity in the air. I covered my mouth to keep from laughing. "Yeah, but you should see *your* hair," he teased me back.

Instinctively, I felt the top of my hair, singed and frayed and standing in a wild mess atop my head. Not that it mattered at the moment. "We did it. *We did it!*" I cheered. A huge grin filled my face.

Brandr let out a whoop of congratulations and slapped me a high five in the air. I stared at him, thrilled with our success. "He may be gone, but his power of gravity still exists," he reminded me. "The Element will search for a new residence."

"Next time, we won't let the Fifth Elemental's power grow out of control. Next time, we'll form an early alliance," I stated with confidence.

I glanced over my shoulder, happy to see Liam and Skye slowly recovering from Ignis's final strike. But the thrill of our victory suddenly vanished when I turned and saw a body, unmoving, in the very spot where she had saved my life.

Oh. My. God.

Gaia.

"Call Hina. Hurry!" I shouted, and sprinted to the Earth Elemental. Already, Gaia's physical form had begun to separate into distinct particles of her Element; the first step of her transformation into an Essence, unless we could reverse the process.

Hina arrived much faster than I'd expected, sliding down a moonbeam to appear by Gaia's side. Perhaps after all the incidents from our training, she knew not to venture too far from us tonight.

"What happened?" I asked the Hawaiian healer and moon goddess.

Hina shook her head sadly. "It seems Aether extracted the chemical elements of iron ore and radioactive uranium from the rocks, fashioning them into a poisonous barb that lodged in her heart."

"But Gaia's the Earth Elemental. Shouldn't she be able to withstand anything within her Element?" I countered.

"Not in that lethal of a quantity in such a vital organ, I'm afraid," Hina replied. "Worse, Aether encased the barb in flames to hide it from your detection. And as you know, Gaia is not immune to fire."

I swallowed hard, knowing Aether had manipulated my fire

to mask his poisonous barb.

CHAPTER THIRTY-FIVE

If Hydros could save Liam by cooling and condensing his water molecules, then there had to be a way to do the same for Gaia. Only pieces of her Element remained, leaving a crystallized outer shell in the shape of Gaia's body. Her hair and skin had fragmented and fractured, like grains of sand stacked upon one another. They wouldn't congeal back into her Elemental form on their own.

"Don't worry, Gaia, we'll find a way to save you," I said, and slipped my hand into hers.

A faint smile wrapped across her lips. "It's too late for me, I'm afraid."

I shook my head. "Don't say that. Hina can still help. You'll be all right, you'll see," I said with surety.

Gaia placed one crystallized hand upon mine. "There isn't much time. Stay with me. Please."

"Gaia, I don't understand. It worked for Liam."

"Liam also had the Essence of his Element to help. The same is not true for me, I'm afraid."

I knew in that instant she was right. Gaia was the first and original Earth Elemental. None existed to aid in her time of need.

"Then can't you do it on your own?" I suggested.

"Not now. I don't have the strength."

My head fell, knowing her time drew near. A time she chose to spend with me alone. "I don't understand," I spoke, tears filling my eyes. "Why'd you do it? Why bother to save *me* of all people?"

Gaia's voice grew weaker. "In all the time I'd spent on this planet, I'd never known a love like the kind you two share."

I looked up at her with surprise.

"You can imagine how I felt when I realized I could never win Liam's heart, no matter how hard I tried to prove I was better than you." She emitted a slightly bitter, resentful laugh. "He was right...you were the best bet to halt Aether's advances. Still, I saw the way Liam looked at you, the way he stood protectively by your side whenever you confronted danger, and how he defended you above all the rest of us."

"Gaia...," I began, my heart filled with guilt.

Her green eyes held mine with earnest, willing me to hear her final thoughts. "This was the only way I could prove my love to him, by giving him the one person he couldn't live without... you."

I didn't know how to respond. A part of me wanted to apologize for all our differences and misunderstandings over the years. Another part wanted to hold her like she had consoled the dying Hydros during our battle outside of San Francisco. And the last part wanted to thank her for giving the ultimate gift — her life — so that Liam and I might have a future together.

It wasn't fair. None of it. Why did things have to end like this? For a long minute I sat in silence, staring at her until I couldn't see past the tears, imagining how I would have felt had our places been reversed. Would I have had the courage to act like she'd done? To sacrifice myself for someone else's happiness?

All these years, I was wrong about her, wasn't I? She no

longer desired power or fame of an adoring population grateful for her protection. When it came down to the end, she was moved by one factor alone: *love*. A love that wasn't reciprocated. A love she couldn't truly have.

"My time is done, Jordan," she admitted. "But don't worry. I'll still stop by to pester you from time to time."

After all we'd been through, her humor made me smile with sadness.

Gaia looked so very weak, so tired and ready for the end; so unlike the Gaia I knew, who had prevailed like an indestructible force over the millennia.

"You're in good hands," she told me, her eyes wistfully flicking to Liam in an act that tugged at the strings of my heart.

My lower lip quivered. "I'm sorry, Gaia. I never gave you a chance to explain."

"It had to be that way. You needed experience in order to fully understand."

"You don't have to do this," I objected. "You don't have to leave us, you know."

A faint smile graced her wearied face. "It's time for another to take over. I've completed my mission, my purpose on this planet."

"No." I shook my head and threw my arms around her crystallized body in a fast embrace. My hair spilled around my cheeks, masking my tears. "Don't do this," I begged.

Gaia laid a weakened hand over my back to return the hug. I was surprised at how quickly her strength had faded.

Liam leaned over her passive body, placing a soft, innocent kiss upon her cheek. I believed he hoped his gesture of appreciation would help her pass more easily into the next realm of her existence. In the short remaining moment she had with us, Brandr, Skye, and Hydros each said their own goodbyes.

In all the times I had wished to rid Gaia from my life, I now greeted her passing with sweet sorrow.

Gaia's exterior shell crumbled away into a pile of sparkling crystals where she had lay. The russet tint of her Essence hovered over her body for a moment, viewing its earthly remains. Her untamed hair flowed freely behind her, framing her face in a striking way, showing an innate beauty I had never before noticed. She glanced back at me, her washed-out emerald eyes fixed on mine with a sentiment I hadn't expected: *respect*. In all the time I'd known Gaia prior to our team's training, I'd perceived her as a terrible foe, causing insufferable damage. But in the end, she'd proven a trusted ally when I most needed her support. My eyes softened, watching her now in the purest form. My face brightening, I gave her a slow nod, hoping she understood that she meant more to me than words could express.

Satisfied with the resolving of our past differences, Gaia's Essence shot straight up into the air, and then rocketed back toward us. She paused for a brief moment in front of our faces. Her wispy form rapidly encircled both of us, wrapping us tighter together in the wake of her vaporous trail in a show of approval. I leaned my head against Liam's shoulder and slipped my arm around his back, needing to hold him, needing him near. He returned my embrace with a light squeeze.

A profound sadness filled my eyes. Blinking back the tears, I watched her coppery spirit trail zoom back up into the sky, hover for a moment, then plunge down to the earth and disappear into the soil. Seconds later, the ground trembled violently, shaking us from our feet.

I had to smile. Even in passing, she wanted to depart with her own version of a goodbye.

CHAPTER THIRTY-SIX

Liam wrapped his arms around me, holding tight until my tears ran dry. He ran a soothing hand over my head, but it couldn't erase the memory of Aether's poisonous flaming dart aimed at me until Gaia intercepted the blow.

A clear, crisp voice rang through the air, interrupting me from my thoughts. "Well done, Pyr." I looked up to see Pele approaching. The ends of her flowing black hair glowed like molten rock.

"I can't believe Gaia's gone," I told her, wiping my eyes on the back of my hand. My throat grew tight.

"I am sorry," Pele said, setting a sympathetic hand on my shoulder. "We suffered many losses today, but triumphed in the end. I am so proud of all of you. Really, I am."

In an uncharacteristic show of affection, Pele gave Liam, Skye, and Hydros a hug. She held up a fist in front of Brandr, pausing midair to knock knuckles with his translucent hand. Then she wrapped her arms around me, giving me a strong squeeze. "I knew you could do it," she whispered in my ear.

"Thank you," I told her, letting my cheek brush her long tresses that held a slight scent of molten lava. "For everything."

"You had it in you all along," she said softly, "you just needed someone to show you how to use it."

Pulling away from her hug, I flashed a huge smile. "I'm glad that person was you," I told her.

Behind me, I heard Brandr clear his throat with unnecessary force. I glanced over my shoulder and noticed him waiting, his arms crossed over his chest. He tapped his foot impatiently upon the ground to remind me.

"And Brandr, of course. I couldn't have done it without him, either," I added, making Brandr puff out his chest.

"Of course you couldn't've," he said, and swept me into a hug that lifted me off my feet.

"How are you doing that?" I asked, astonished his intangible Essence could actually sweep me off the ground. I glanced at Liam, puzzled.

Liam looked back at me with a shrug and mouthed, "No idea."

Brandr set me down on my feet once more and flashed me a knowing smirk. With a wink, he said, "You think I've already taught you *everything* I know? There's more where that came from, babe."

I laughed. "I thought I told you to never call me that name again!"

He tousled my hair with his ghostly fingers. "Oops," he said in a playful tone. With a smile I'd expect from a proud older brother, he stepped backward to take his place by Skye's side and gave us a nod.

Hydros threw her arms around her brother. "We did it," she smiled at him.

"*We* did," he agreed. I noticed he placed more emphasis on the first word, and thought of how close he'd come to dying in order to gain Hydros's support in accepting me as a member of the team.

"I'm going to find Gaia," she told him, "to make sure she's okay."

"You don't need to explain. I understand," he reassured her.

Hydros glanced at me and then back to Liam. "You'll be fine. I'm not worried about you."

"Take care, sis," Liam said with a small wave goodbye.

"You, too," she replied. Her watery blue Essence drifted off into the distance, in search of her old friend.

"What about the next Earth Elemental?" Liam asked Pele after we lost Hydros from view. "Are we supposed to make contact once that person is chosen?"

I had originally desired a different destiny. And the girl, Shannon, had wished for a normal life with her family in ancient Ireland before she accepted her identity as Hydros. How did we know this new Earth Elemental felt any different?

Pele opened her mouth to respond to Liam's question, but I spoke first. "Why not give him or her a chance to lead a normal life, now that the threat is gone?" I suggested. "We can always find Gaia's replacement later if we need to."

I contemplated the choices others had made for me. If I could go back to my family's home outside of Jerusalem, would I exchange all that I'd experienced since then for my old, normal life? That day when Gaia first appeared so very long ago, I had been completely naïve about my powers. There were people I never would've met had I stayed in that old life. I could have prevented so many unfortunate sacrifices if I'd lacked these powers. Then again, I never would've known the happiness I expected to have with Liam.

I waved to Pele, Skye, and Brandr, pleased to notice his vaporous arm had affectionately draped over Skye's shoulder. Though I'd miss them, I felt certain they'd be okay. And I knew I'd see them again. Soon, I hoped.

"So where do you want to go now?" Liam asked.

I considered his suggestion for a moment, realizing I had no reason to go back to California. Inside my heart, I knew I needed to let my friends live their lives without my involvement or interference. Instead, I shrugged. "It doesn't really matter to me, as long as I get to be with you."

My response brought a smile to Liam's face.

"How about going back in time to my home in Ireland? I want to explain to my parents what happened to Shannon. To tell them how brave she was. To let them know how her spirit lives on." His voice choked with pride for his twin sister. "And to introduce them to you, of course."

Funny how with all the danger we'd encountered today, I suddenly felt surprisingly nervous at the thought of meeting his parents. It seemed like a big step, heavy with implications about my importance in his life.

Liam looked at me intently, waiting for my answer.

I had spent so much of my time on this planet living in fear. And in that time, I'd discovered it wasn't my fate to lead a normal life. I'd learned that despite my valiant efforts, I couldn't change the past. Now, my life of fear had ended. A sense of excitement and adventure filled my soul, eager for the promise of a bright future. And I chose to spend that future with Liam...whatever our destination.

"Sounds good to me," I told him. I took a deep breath, and then asked, "So, are you ready for this trip?"

"I'm ready for a new beginning," he corrected me. "With you."

The time had come to stop living in the past. This moment marked the start of a new chapter in our lives.

Our journey seemed vastly different from our trip to Atlantis inside Liam's air bubble, and our quick exit from Easter Island when I'd thrown my arms around him and used my white fire to return his injured body to camp. This time, heat and cold clashed, making a cloud of white steam rise from our joined hands. A stream of water and white fire swirled together, mingling, steaming, and sizzling upon contact.

I opened my eyes long enough to see the faces of our friends fade to black. Liam and I departed this world, shooting through space and time to our new location. I wasn't sure how long we'd stay…perhaps a few weeks, perhaps forever. But time no longer mattered. Not when I had the chance to be with him.

THE END

Before You Go...

HELP AN AUTHOR

write a review

THANK YOU!

Share your voice and help guide other readers to these wonderful books. Even if it's only a line or two your reviews help readers discover the author's books so they can continue creating stories that you'll love. Login to your favorite retailer and leave a review. Thank you.

ABOUT THE AUTHOR

After graduating from Cornell University with degrees in Biology and Education, Debbie Kump taught middle and high school science in Maui, Seattle, and the Twin Cities and worked as a marine naturalist aboard a whale watch and snorkel cruise. Debbie lives in Minnesota with her husband, two sons, and three Siberian huskies. She especially enjoys writing early each morning; teaching; coaching youth soccer, hockey, lacrosse, and baseball; and dogsledding her kids to school.

For more information, please visit her website: http://sites. google.com/site/debbiekumpbooks/

www.ingramcontent.com/pod-product-compliance
Lightning Source LLC
Chambersburg PA
CBHW030253200626
46816CB00002BA/623